THREE TIMES TO MAKE SURE

BOOK 3

VIRGINIA'DELE SMITH

Books are Ubiquitous

Published by Books are Ubiquitous, Inc.
Tulsa, Oklahoma in the United States of America
www.booksareubiquitous.com
contact@booksareubiquitous.com
Books are Ubiquitous is a federally registered trademark.

This book is a work of fiction.

Paperback ISBN: 978-1-957036-10-6

———

Titles by Virginia'dele Smith

Sadie & Sam: PART 1 - Introductory Short Story (FREE)

Book 0: My Manifesto - Short Story Memoir (FREE)

Book 1: Grocery Girl

Book 2: In the Trenches

Book 3: Three Times to Make Sure

Book 4: Take a Chance on Love (coming soon)

To: Me.

Three is my favorite number,
so I saved the character most like myself
for this story.

All M'Kenzee's worst traits come directly from me…
hard-headed, unyielding, impatient, bossy, critical,
irritable, and difficult to love.
I had only to look in the mirror to see her flaws.

What a blessing for us both that amazing people
believe we are worth the challenge.

1

I'll try anything once,
twice if I like it,
three times to make sure.
Mae West

Three months ago — Kansas City, Missouri

"Max, I—" M'Kenzee Davenport didn't get a chance to finish what she wanted to say as her big brother stormed through the room. He didn't look her way — or even hesitate to acknowledge her — before disappearing into the training room where doctors and trainers buzzed around their friend Janie Lyn after someone had brutally attacked her during Max's football game.

Ooooh! M'Kenzee stomped her foot at his dismissal. She needed to tell him something, and she would not be ignored.

"Ma'am, I'm sorry, but you're still not allowed in here," said the FBI agent seated like a guard dog just outside the door she needed to enter. He grated on M'Kenzee's last nerve. She'd tried reasoning with him multiple times. He refused to pay attention. On top of that, Max couldn't be bothered to acknowledge her. How ridiculous.

"I have to talk to someone about what happened," she said. Again.

"Officers will get around to your statement when they can. Until then, you need to stay out here." He brushed her off, not even glancing her way as he spoke.

"You just let my brother—"

"Ma'am, don't make me tell you again," he threatened, looking up at her. His eye contact lasted less than an instant before his gaze went back to his phone.

The little twerp didn't appear old enough to shave. M'Kenzee decided she could take him…even with his shiny FBI windbreaker, his fancy badge hanging on a lanyard around his neck, and the compact sidepiece strapped in the holster on his belt. If this guy represented the future of law enforcement in America, the country was in grave peril.

"If I could just—"

He scooted his chair sideways to ignore her.

She'd had enough.

M'Kenzee glimpsed over her shoulder. Her sister and friends huddled in the far corner, fine together. She inhaled to shore up her resolve and shoved the door open behind the agent.

In his scrambling alarm, she sidestepped the agent and entered the training room. Max sat beside Janie Lyn's physical therapy table. Her eyes were closed, her face and arms already turning black and blue. Dried blood crusted on her hair and clothes. Max held her hand. He leaned forward, his forehead resting on the cushion next to her arm. M'Kenzee stopped short.

If a picture spoke a thousand words, the image before her narrated an epic novel of despair.

Ohhh.

She'd had no idea. Their little sister, Maree, had hinted that she thought something might be going on between Janie Lyn and their big brother, Max, but Maree, a hopeless romantic, liked to imagine the entire world was falling in love at any given moment. M'Kenzee usually allowed Maree's ramblings to go in one ear and out the other without giving them too much credence. Perhaps she'd been on to something concerning Max and Janie Lyn.

Janie Lyn had spent the past few days in Kansas City. M'Kenzee assumed Janie Lyn needed to help Max with a few house projects he couldn't make time for during the football season. Clearly, there was more to it. Much more.

"Ma'am, you cannot be in here!"

The agent reached forward to grab M'Kenzee. The instinct to protect herself kicked in. In a defensive move, she turned, grabbing his wrist to twist the man's arm behind his back. At that precise moment, a strong, deep voice behind her took control of the room with a quiet, but commanding, statement.

"She's fine."

Oh.

M'Kenzee released the agent and lifted her hands placatingly. Agent Nadir snarled at her, likely embarrassed a civilian had bested him, and a girl, at that. She raised an eyebrow and pursed her lips, a silent challenge. His features twisted. She hoped he wouldn't spit on her…for his sake.

"That'll be all, Agent Nadir," the man across the room said, dismissing the weasel.

M'Kenzee closed her eyes, dreading what came next.

"Hello, M—" Brennigan Stewart's Scottish brogue had a distinctive, mocking tone.

M'Kenzee whirled to face him before he could finish the greeting. The look in her eyes threatened his death if he said the wrong thing.

"—Kenzee." He chose wisely. "Max is spending a moment

with Janie Lyn. The team doctor sutured a pretty nasty cut, and she's going to be terribly bruised. Otherwise, she's okay, all things considered."

A family outing to cheer on Max, who played tight end for the Kansas City Chiefs, had somehow turned into a crazy, chaotic afternoon.

Wanting to grab drinks and a pretzel before the second half started, M'Kenzee and Janie Lyn were working their way to the concession stand, fighting upstream through the crowd, when they'd been separated in the melee.

Next thing M'Kenzee knew, a fierce-looking man just a few steps ahead of her grabbed Janie Lyn, pulling her away by her hair while Janie Lyn kicked and screamed with all her might.

M'Kenzee pushed people out of her way, rushing to catch up, fighting to get closer to Janie Lyn and her abductor. Years of working around the world as a photojournalist had her grabbing the camera hanging around her neck. M'Kenzee aimed the lens toward the action and clicked photos on the run.

Just as M'Kenzee got close enough to lunge for Janie Lyn, the hulk noticed M'Kenzee. He shoved Janie Lyn into a tiled concrete column in the stadium's concourse. She cried out as her face cracked against the structure.

"Help us!" M'Kenzee bellowed as security officers ran toward them.

When they were mere steps away, the would-be abductor released Janie Lyn, giving her one last shove to the ground as he pushed people between them and ran.

M'Kenzee didn't wait to see which way he went; she dropped to Janie Lyn, who huddled in a heap on the floor.

Within seconds, the EMTs arrived. They put Janie Lyn on a fancy golf cart equipped for medical response and drove her down the ramp to the team facilities under the stadium. Since then, M'Kenzee had been desperate to figure out what had happened, get a detailed update on Janie Lyn, and find someone official to tell what little she knew. The entire ordeal felt surreal. Unbelievable!

To make matters worse — infinitely worse — she stood face-to-face with Bren.

Well over six feet tall, with disheveled auburn hair, a scruffy day-old beard, and startling green eyes, he looked exactly as M'Kenzee remembered. Perfect.

Every bit the confident FBI agent, he reeked of power and superiority.

"Why are you here?" she asked without preamble.

"I'm sure Max will fill you in when he can," he said instead of providing a real answer.

"I need to talk to someone. I was with Janie Lyn when that brute—"

"Are you okay?" he interrupted. His tone of voice didn't change, but the alertness in his eyes reached a new level.

"Yes, but I need to talk to someone. I saw him and tried to stop him. I scraped my nails down his disgusting face and arm. Maybe there's enough DNA to help find him. Also, I have to give this memory card to someone. They're not my best work, but I got photos of the attacker."

Bren stood there, frozen in place, just looking at her. His eyes darted over her features, down her body, and back up to her face. He studied her dark blond hair. She wondered what he thought of the pixie style, so different from the last time he'd seen her. His thoughts remained unreadable as his gaze lingered on her mouth. Tingles pricked her lips, although he remained several feet away.

The sensation made her uneasy, and when her hackles went up, her temper went with them. She lifted her chin, determined not to let her nerves show.

"I'm *verra* glad you're not hurt." His voice rasped, revealing his fiery heritage. He'd whispered the words for her ears only.

M'Kenzee's heart rate sped up. He walked forward until they stood so close she could smell the heady, spicy scent of his cologne. Still, she refused to back down.

"Who should I see about the DNA? And who wants the memory card?"

"I'll take the card," Bren said, holding out his hand, palm-up. M'Kenzee trembled when she removed the card from her camera and set it in his open hand. *Infuriating!*

Bren clasped her shaky hand with his other one, immediately running his thumb over the back of her knuckles. Was he trying to calm and soothe her? Or was he testing the softness of her skin for himself?

She tried to pull away, but he held on.

"We need to get that DNA," Bren murmured. He didn't release her hand, but he did call a forensic tech over to scrape her nails and collect a sample. Once the tech was done, Bren walked M'Kenzee to a sink, turned the faucet on, and lifted her hands under the stream of warm water.

"I can wash my own hands," she grumbled when Bren lathered soap and started massaging the suds into her fingers.

But she didn't stop him.

His touch felt too good.

Once he'd rinsed their hands, turned off the water, and pulled a few paper towels from the dispenser, she'd gathered her wits enough to yank them away.

"Always so prickly," Bren mused.

M'Kenzee finished drying her hands with jerky motions, wadded up the towels, and chucked them in the trash can.

Finished with that little encounter, she moved to leave. Bren reached out and grabbed her arm as she walked past him.

She felt the warmth of his firm yet gentle grasp all the way to the pit of her stomach. She kept her eyes glued to the floor.

"You're as gorgeous as ever," Bren said in a low, husky

voice, rolling his Rs and revealing his natural Scottish brogue, a sure sign he'd lifted the veil of his cool veneer.

"You shouldn't talk like that," M'Kenzee replied. She tried to sound indifferent, but her voice betrayed her.

"Why not?" Bren countered, pulling her arm toward him until she finally met his gaze.

His emerald eyes gleamed, glistening with flecks of white diamonds. She indulged in one last sniff of his scent, so masculine and clean. She even enjoyed their test of wills for a split second — until he spoke again.

"Can't a man compliment his wife?"

2

Love is patient, love is kind.
It does not envy, it does not boast,
it is not proud.
It does not dishonor others,
it is not self-seeking,
it is not easily angered,
it keeps no record of wrongs.
Love does not delight in evil
but rejoices with the truth.
It always protects, always trusts,
always hopes, always perseveres.
Love never fails.
1 Corinthians 13:4–8

Three weeks ago — Green Hills, Oklahoma

Standing in the middle of Miss Sadie's living room, so large that *parlor* better described it, Brennigan scanned the space. An oversized, overstuffed sofa faced the fireplace and encouraged curling up with a good book. Photos lined the mantel, a myriad of frames varying in shapes and sizes celebrating beloved friends and cherished memories; logs crackling in the firebox warmed occupants, both literally and emotionally. With an essence of home, the space filled one's soul.

He walked past the sofa and fireplace to stand in front of a tall window, taking in the impressive view of rolling hills and the dense groves of trees scattered across them. Staring out, Bren imagined — daydreamed, really. He thought about what life felt like for normal people. He'd lived the military life so long, he'd forgotten the deep pull of connection…to land, to neighbors, to a house and a home. To family.

Being in Green Hills, particularly with M'Kenzee there at the same time, brought back a longing for home.

How pathetic to love the same woman since elementary school.

He'd realized it on the playground during recess, the spring of 1999. He'd been nine years old, in the third grade. M'Kenzee, only six years old, was just a kindergartner. But no one dared tell her that. The sport never mattered…red rover, freeze tag, flag football, kickball, four square. She made her presence known in each and every one. M'Kenzee Davenport had been just as rough, tough, and athletic as any kid at that school, pre-K through third grade — a force to be reckoned with.

That day, the Friday before spring break began, the teachers had been strained past their point of patience, desperate to survive the final few hours before vacation. To save their own sanity, they'd declared the entire afternoon to be free time outdoors. The students interpreted that as a *free-for-all* and decided an afternoon of recess meant they had enough time for a full nine-inning baseball game.

After grabbing gloves from backpacks and cubbies, setting out the bases, and distributing bats and helmets, captains picked teams. Max, Bren's best friend even back then, and another third-grader appointed themselves leaders; the draft process began.

Max chose Bren first to guarantee they'd be together. Of course, Max planned to pick M'Kenzee, but assuming no one wanted kindergartners on their team, he figured he could save her for last. In hindsight, he shouldn't have waited.

Terk Douglas, the other captain, chose her first. His smirk said he'd done it to prove a point. He had no intention of employing M'Kenzee's pitching skill; tired of losing to Max over and over again, he'd simply wanted to have power over Maxwell Davenport, who tended to dominate every competition.

After three innings, down by seven runs, M'Kenzee'd had enough. When her team took the field for the top of the fourth, she walked right to the pitcher's mound. She began warming up, ignoring Terk when he joined M'Kenzee in the pitcher's circle. "Get outta my way, Davenport," he told her. "The babies can play later."

"Ah, brother," Max groaned in irritation. Guessing what was about to happen, he stood up from his seat in the dugout to forestall the inevitable altercation. Bren touched Max's arm to halt him.

"Give her a sec," Bren urged, spellbound by the small but mighty girl standing her ground.

Only half as tall as the wannabe bully, M'Kenzee glared up into the boy's sweaty, dirt-streaked face. Hands on hips, feet planted wide, she looked every inch the headstrong woman she'd grow to become. Hot-pink ribbons tied into bows at the bottom of long braids hinted at a softer side, but only those closest to M'Kenzee Davenport got to see that part of her personality.

When Terk lifted his hands to push M'Kenzee off the pitching mound, both Bren and Max started walking. They'd only made it halfway to where M'Kenzee and Terk faced-off when she darted an icy glare at Bren and Max, stopping them in their tracks.

The boys couldn't hear M'Kenzee's words, but her body language spoke volumes. Her right hand curled into a fist by her side, her left pointed at home plate. Braids whipped like blades on a helicopter as she made her point. In no uncertain terms, she ripped into Terk.

And the longer she ripped, the more he cowered.

Eventually, Terk barked something at her, which only made her grin victoriously as he huffed his way to their dugout.

Nine pitches later, she'd retired the side.

Bren had been on deck and would hit first in the fifth inning.

Beaming with confidence, she tossed the baseball in the air and caught it with her ungloved right hand. As though she knew he couldn't take his eyes off her, she looked directly at him as she dropped the ball to the pitcher's mound.

"You're next, Brennigan Stewart," she'd taunted with a sassy glint in her eyes.

That was the moment.

Watching M'Kenzee face down an ugly giant — with M'Kenzee knowing he was there if she needed him, but determined to do it herself — had done something to his heart.

It took years for him to realize, to fully comprehend, that the spell she'd cast over him that day was love. But he'd grown to understand.

Yes, since that day on the playground, he'd learned many valuable lessons about love.

Love brought joy to gloomy days, created hope when life appeared bleak. It also rained on parades, shattered perfectly good moods, and left him feeling bruised and hollow from time to time.

M'Kenzee would never know the number of times her image in his mind had served as his only tenuous thread to survival. Nights burrowed in a foxhole, listening to war erupt around him. Days rotting away in a putrid cell, awaiting rescue. Weeks, months, and seasons away from home. She'd gotten him through every moment.

Footsteps halted outside Miss Sadie's kitchen. Bren turned from the window to see who had come in through the front door.

There she was — his angel, his muse, and his tormentor, all in one heart-stopping package.

Intent on whatever she'd overheard from the kitchen, she hadn't noticed Bren in the front parlor. Without so much as a creak of the old wooden floorboards, he walked to stand behind her.

"It's rude to eavesdrop," he whispered in her ear.

Startled, she jumped and turned to face him, juggling the load of quilts she carried.

He steadied her arms by setting his hands on each of her elbows.

"Shhhh!" she rebuked him… Ah, it was a day ending in Y.

"Can I help?" He gathered the quilts into his arms and carried them to the long velvet sofa facing the fireplace.

"I think they know," she blurted. She didn't answer Bren, but she did follow him to where he'd lifted a quilt to fold. A trace of panic colored her voice.

"Would that be so bad?" He kept his eyes on the quilt, but every fiber of his being gauged her response. *Would that be so bad?* He assessed the question, testing it in his mind. Bren rather believed it might be wonderful.

"Yes, it would," she retorted. "It absolutely would."

Well, there he had it… It would *absolutely* be horrendously, terribly, inconceivably awful if people knew about them, if they knew he loved her, had married her, wanted to spend the rest of his life with her.

"Hmmm," he allowed. "And why do you think *they know* about us?"

"I was about to walk into the kitchen when I heard Maree, Miss Sadie, and Landry talking. They mentioned a secret ceremony in Las Vegas, said they were shocked. One commented it would take some getting used to. They must know." She ended with a cringe.

"You, *mo ghràidh*, are brutal on one's self-esteem. If I didn't know better, I'd take to heart how desperately you *don't* want to be associated with me. A fatal wound, that would be." Bren let his Scottish dialect shine through. That always got to her, heated her icy eyes into deep pools of cornflower blue. A childhood spent going back and forth between his family's native country in the United Kingdom and their home in the United States afforded Bren a unique command over his accent. He'd taught himself to turn it on and off to suit his needs, and he wasn't above using it to his advantage where M'Kenzee was concerned.

She pursed her lips and glared in return. Oh man, were those lips kissable.

He'd sampled them. Thrice, to be exact.

And each time had reaffirmed that she was meant to be his.

3

What happens in Vegas,
stays in Vegas.
Slogan and advertising campaign
for the city of Las Vegas, Nevada

Three years ago — Las Vegas, Nevada

"He won! And not just won, he was named MVP! I don't even know what to say. I'm just so happy for him," M'Kenzee screamed over the noise of the people celebrating postgame at the team hotel, which was one of the resort casinos on the strip. Her big brother: hero for the day.

Max was somewhere in the crush of bodies — players, families, and fans alike — filling the nightclub; she hadn't seen him, or their little sister, Maree, in a while.

Bren hadn't left M'Kenzee's side.

They'd danced with the throng, whooping and hollering, sipping champagne, and soaking up the thrill of victory. What a night for their family!

They'd been through so much…losing their parents to a

drunk driver just before M'Kenzee turned seven, fighting the system to stay together, and getting all three of them through the challenges of adolescence and into adulthood. It hadn't been easy, but they'd done it together.

And just look at us now.

After graduating from college, Maree had quickly begun making a name for herself as a talented artist and innovative fabric designer. Drafted in the first round to the Kansas City Chiefs, Max had wasted no time establishing his career, scoring touchdowns and earning MVP titles. Not nearly as famous as her siblings, M'Kenzee had still reached impressive heights in her own rights as a photojournalist. All three of them were doing what they loved, and they were doing it in a way they loved. Life was good.

Well, at least as good as it could be.

M'Kenzee had learned a hard lesson: love and happiness were fleeting, fragile.

She believed one could enjoy moments — like their postgame celebration — and *should* make the most of them because in the end, the ball would drop, the other shoe would fall. The source of one's love and happiness would always disappear.

Like Bren.

Brennigan Stewart had simultaneously been a constant in her life and a source of agony each time he left. And he always left.

When she was five years old, he'd circled back to help her with a kite when all the neighborhood kids ran ahead in the park. But as soon as they'd gotten the beautiful butterfly in the air, he'd taken off to join the others. Watching the stunning patterned wings flutter and the long colorful streamers wave in the wind through the watery haze of tears served as her earliest memory.

When she was six years old, Bren had winked at her on the

baseball field. It hadn't been flirtatious. He'd been issuing a challenge. She'd struck out every batter she'd faced that afternoon, and he'd intended to be the one to best her. Heart racing and nerves skittering, she'd battled him from the pitching mound. Bren hadn't gone easy on her, taking the count to three balls and two strikes.

Just as she'd wound up to zip the last pitch to the plate, the teachers had blown their whistles. Recess was over; spring break had officially begun.

M'Kenzee had looked back to home plate, to Bren, but he'd already gone. He and Max had run for their backpacks and dashed for the bus line. By the time she'd joined them, the only seat available was in the front by the driver. She'd sat alone while they laughed and cut up in the back row.

That evening, Bren and his parents had flown to Scotland to spend the school holiday visiting family. She'd spent the week snapping photos in her backyard, wondering what pictures people liked to take in the famous Scottish Highlands.

A few months later, M'Kenzee had married Bren. For the first time…

The PTA's annual back-to-school carnival rivaled the midway at the state fair. Games, fried foods, craft booths, a karaoke stage, and kids running like wild banshees set the tone for a fun semester ahead. That year, M'Kenzee's momma and Bren's mom were in charge of the wedding chapel, where, for five tickets, one could marry their true love.

She would've pummeled anyone who accused her of liking the booth. But secretly, M'Kenzee adored the Hitching Post, which was set up in a decorated horse trailer with streamers, balloons, and a billion fake flowers.

She'd been milling around their moms, taking a few pictures of the people, the games, and the food, but mostly just feeling out of place in the enormous crowd. Bren had come to the booth to beg Mrs. Stewart for more tickets.

"Hey, M'Kenzee," Bren said as he yanked one of her braids.

She punched his arm and frowned.

"Whatcha doing?" Unfazed by the punch, he bestowed all his attention on M'Kenzee. He always did that: talked to her in a way that made her palms sweat.

"Taking pictures," she replied.

His mom continued to ignore him as she finished performing a wedding ceremony for two junior high kids. He fidgeted trying to get her attention.

Great, he's stuck with me and can't wait to leave.

"Wanna get married?"

"What?" She must've heard him wrong.

"Come on, I need your help," Bren begged. "The only way my mom is going to give me more tickets is if I corner her in the trailer. And Max is waiting for me."

He grabbed her hand and started pulling her toward the end of the line, where several kids — and a few adults — rifled through bonnets, cowboy hats, gloves, and veils.

M'Kenzee dug in her heels.

"Go on, M'Kenzee. Marry Bren," her momma said with a gentle nudge and her stunning signature smile.

M'Kenzee relented, mostly so Bren would let go of her hand. But he didn't.

He slid a headband on top of her braids and fluffed the gauzy layers of tulle attached to it until the white veil framed her head and shoulders. Then he placed a bouquet of silk roses in her hand. They were fake, but gorgeous nonetheless through her child's eyes, with deep yellow petals that turned bright pink at the edges.

True to his Scottish roots, he stuck a page boy hat on his head and smiled down at her as though he were a king.

He kept holding her hand while they waited their turn.

He continued holding her hand while his mother married them.

He even held her hand while his dad filled out their 'marriage certificate' and passed it to Bren with a wink and a grin.

Then he gave her a satisfied nod — ten dollars' worth of tickets in hand from his parents — and said, "Here, you can keep it." Before she'd blinked twice, he dropped the hand he'd held, pushed the sheet of cardstock into her other hand, and sprinted toward the jousting pit, where Max impatiently waited.

He'd disappeared again.

As had her mom and dad.

That night, her parents had left her for good. The car wreck hadn't been their fault, but that didn't change the result. They were gone.

Because everyone left in the end.

*A*lthough he'd stayed by her side so far at the casino after Max's Super Bowl and throughout the victorious revelry, she had no doubts Bren would be gone again in a flash when it suited him.

"This is crazy!" M'Kenzee commented, gawking at the room teeming with partygoers.

"*Aye*, it's pretty wild in here," Bren said in response to her exclamation about Max's game and the party atmosphere.

"What?" The music blared, the people screamed, and M'Kenzee struggled to make out what Bren had said.

As he leaned down to repeat himself, the music changed to something rhythmic and sultry, like the air in the club.

A couple bumped into M'Kenzee, pushing her into Bren.

They stood so close that his chest touched her shoulder.

Then he wrapped an arm around her waist, laid a warm hand on her lower back.

"I said, *It's pretty wild in here.*" He breathed the words into her ear. The moist heat sent shivers down her arms.

Bren tugged her closer and lifted her hand over his shoulder. Of its own volition, her other arm mimicked the movement.

When he refused to look away from her eyes, M'Kenzee gulped. Loudly.

Bren smiled his ultra-sexy half-grin, the one that never failed to tie her stomach in knots. She couldn't stand it; she had to look away.

Then she felt, more than heard, him chuckle as he rose to stand at his full height, tucking her into his chest while they swayed to the music.

M'Kenzee lost track of time; they might've danced for hours, or it might've been mere minutes. M'Kenzee was never one to let down her guard, but something about the darkness of the club, the flickering of party lights, and the glittering of ladies' dresses lent a daring, mysterious ambiance to the room that made it okay to luxuriate in Bren's embrace.

As they danced, girls costumed in sequined leotards with feathered hairpieces and thick high heels continuously supplied drink after drink. Not much of a drinker — not one at all, to be honest, after what drunk driving had done to her family — M'Kenzee took only a sip here and there as she handed the drinks back to the next waitress she saw.

"Come on," Bren said, easing away from her. He lifted her chin until their eyes met. "There's somewhere I want to take you."

Her pulse skittered to an erratic beat.

When he led her to the wedding chapel just off the casino floor, she realized he must've imbibed the free drinks much more than she had.

"It's not a horse trailer, but the second time around might be more legal." He challenged her with that infuriating half-grin.

Is he serious? He can't be!

"May we help you?" An elderly man with bushy white eyebrows, thin wire-rimmed glasses, and a priest's collar emerged from a doorway. M'Kenzee presumed it led to the chapel, to a wedding, to a marriage. To Bren.

"Yes, we'd like to be married," Bren announced without an ounce of hesitation.

He's drunk. It's the only explanation. Oh Lord, what do I do?

As the prayer for guidance flitted through her brain, Bren turned his enigmatic, magnetic, charming smile upon her.

"And does the gentleman speak for you both?" A woman wearing a floral dress followed the man through the doorway. She'd twisted her white hair elegantly on her head in a snowy bun; her delicate voice sounded almost ethereal.

Could it be a magic portal? A chance at a dream she'd never dared voice, even to herself?

Can I do this?

"Yes," Bren said, answering the question she'd thought but not said aloud. "Say *yes*. Please, M'Kenzee?"

She looked down at the silver-and-white vintage flapper dress Maree had insisted she wear for the after-party. Fringe covered the dress from the sleeveless straps and V-neck to where the hem fell a few inches above her knees; the tassels sparkled in the romantic lights. Her mid-length dark blond hair, which normally looked tousled, had to be a wild mess after all the dancing. Did a shred of lipstick remain? That had never mattered a single day in her life, so why did it seem critical all of a sudden?

I must look like a raving lunatic.

She *was* a raving lunatic to be considering going through

with the wedding. Where had her infamous backbone and determination gone?

"You're gorgeous," Bren promised, reading her thoughts once again. "Come on, say yes," he encouraged.

M'Kenzee gulped.

"Yes," she croaked.

"Yes," Bren repeated, victorious. He turned his gaze to the kind woman. "Do you have a veil we can purchase?"

"Of course," she said with an indulgent smile. "Come with me, dear."

As though a puppet on a string — something M'Kenzee had never been in any sense of the word — she let the woman lead her through the door and into the unknown.

Thirty minutes later, with a veil on her head, fresh makeup on her cheeks and lips, and a gold band on her finger, M'Kenzee Davenport had officially become Mrs. Brennigan Stewart.

She'd allowed Bren to assume she, too, was inebriated, caught up in the silliness of Las Vegas, enraptured by the thrilling Super Bowl victory, or simply too far gone to make wise decisions. And although she'd floated through the ceremony on a cloud of wonder, the wedding had been crystal clear. She'd known exactly what she'd been doing, and she'd done it anyway.

Somewhere between dancing in his arms and saying *I do*, M'Kenzee convinced herself that Bren would wake up too hungover in the morning to remember what they'd done. She figured she'd file for a quick annulment before leaving town, and he'd be none the wiser.

Love didn't last; people didn't stick. Shouldn't she get to live — to love — for just one moment? Didn't M'Kenzee deserve to have and to hold him once, for one night, in a lifetime of craving his love?

Yes, I do.

4

**It is a truth universally acknowledged,
that a single man in possession
of a good fortune,
must be in want of a wife.
Pride and Prejudice by Jane Austen**

*S*he said, Yes. *She repeated* I do *when it was her turn. She's mine.*

Bren marveled as the thoughts cycled through his mind in a continuous loop.

And when the preacher said, "You may kiss your bride," Bren had finally touched his lips to hers, as he'd imagined doing a thousand — no, a million — times.

And what I plan on doing a billion more.

She probably wanted to believe he'd drunk too much, but he hadn't. Those free drinks in the club had been ninety percent ice, nine percent soda, and one percent alcohol. That was how he'd known M'Kenzee's mind hadn't been the least bit impaired, either.

He would let her believe what she needed to, for the time being.

Bren knew the truth: they were married — good and truly this time — because she loved him just as he loved her. They'd tiptoed around it for a long time. Finally, it was out there. Their relationship was real; *they* were real.

Max might grumble a little, but who better to honor and cherish a guy's sister than his best friend?

Maree would be elated. An eternal optimist and a hopeless romantic, she'd shower them with congratulations.

His parents would be delighted; the Davenport kids had taken up residence in their hearts even before they'd been called to act as parents from time to time after the three were orphaned. It might not even surprise them. Bren was pretty sure his mom had noticed his feelings for M'Kenzee ages ago.

He admired the gold band on his left ring finger. It looked good there; it looked right.

"I'm ready," M'Kenzee announced, a quilted bag in one hand and a nervous flutter in her tone. She'd stopped by her and Maree's hotel suite to grab a few things. She hadn't balked when he suggested they go by there on the way to his room, but her voice revealed obvious trepidations about their wedding night.

Bren could've put her mind to rest — he'd happily take all the time she needed to consummate their marriage — but he didn't say anything quite yet. No, he enjoyed the flush in her cheeks and the gleam in her eyes too much to see them dissipate so soon.

Bren took her tote, hooked it on his shoulder, and lifted her fingers to his lips. He kissed them softly and noticed the matching gold band on her hand. His chest inflated with pride. *Mine.* The thought refused to go away.

With a large group filling their elevator, the ride to his floor didn't allow for conversation. Instead, Bren stood behind her, hands on her toned shoulders, enjoying the silkiness of her exposed skin. When his lips itched to trail along the side of her neck to replace his hands, he forced himself to settle for a chaste kiss on the top of her head.

She looked up at him over her shoulder, oblivious of the passion in her eyes, laid bare for him to see. A lifetime wouldn't be enough with M'Kenzee.

Wound tightly even before they made it to his room, Bren needed a few minutes to catch his breath and steady his heart.

M'Kenzee followed him through the sitting room, the bedroom, and into the bathroom, where he set her bag on the vanity and opened the closet door.

"I know we're supposed to head home tomorrow, but you're welcome to unpack. There are plenty of drawers in the dresser, and I only used a few of the hangers in the closet. Besides, maybe we'll stay. What do you think? Start our honeymoon with a few more days in Vegas?"

Her eyes darted to his; clearly, she hadn't thought past tonight.

Bren had. He'd dreamed about this night, this week, this life with her, during many lonely days. That dream had kept him alive, kept him going when nothing else could.

He trailed a hand down her cheek, tucked a lock of hair behind her ear. "Give it some thought. We can hammer out the details tomorrow. Now, I'm going to call room service. We need a midnight — make that a 2 a.m. — snack. Bathroom's all yours. Take your time," he told her, closing the bathroom door on his way out.

As Bren lifted the phone to place their order, the shower water turned on. The sound of her moving around in the bathroom, the certainty of her presence, grounded him, pleased him.

You're a goner, Stewart.

He looked out the window, high above the frantic activity of the city below. Peace he'd never felt settled into his bones.

The creak of the bathroom door prompted him to turn from the bedroom window. A vision of innocence and strength stopped his heart, made his breath catch.

A pale peach nightgown hugged her body. The spaghetti straps called his attention to her shoulders, supple and toned. The silk didn't reveal a thing, instead leaving all of her to his imagination. All the while, he was certain her beauty would far exceed the vision in his mind. Trimmed in soft lace, the bottom of the negligee rested on her thigh, the femininity of the material highlighting rather than contrasting with the sculpted muscles below.

"Did *ye* already own this?" Desire took his brogue to a whole new level.

"Yes," M'Kenzee admitted, lifting her chin to display her trademark defiance, the first he'd witnessed of it in hours. "Fancy — sometimes expensive — lingerie is my guilty pleasure."

"And now mine, as well."

Bren's hands ached with the need to touch her, to hold her. His lips burned to kiss her. He didn't want to scare her, but he had to close the distance between them; she was unquestionably too far across the room.

He raised an arm, reaching toward her. She took a visible breath, and without taking her eyes off him, she walked to meet him in front of the window. When their hands touched, he pulled her the rest of the way into his arms.

His other hand lifted to brush the back of his knuckles from her temple to her cheek, down her neck to trace the line of her nightgown. His fingers brushed across her skin, testing its heat, but never delving below the fabric's natural drape.

He'd just lifted both hands to cradle her jaw, lowering to take her lips, when the doorbell chimed.

She jumped.

"Just room service," he whispered, placing a kiss on her forehead before walking away.

"They're gone," Bren announced from the sitting room.

M'Kenzee joined him, knitting her eyebrows when she saw how much he'd ordered.

"I didn't know what you'd be hungry for," he answered with chagrin. "And I don't want to leave this room for a very long time."

She swallowed slowly, but she didn't shy away.

Instead, she fixed a plate, piling toppings on a burger and pouring ketchup on a mound of fries. She added a heaping spoonful of coleslaw. Then M'Kenzee grabbed a bottle of water and settled on the couch, legs crossed with a blanket and pillow across her lap as a makeshift table.

"Well, then." Bren smiled. "Let's eat."

They talked while they ate; it came easily.

They relived the game, rehashing Max's best plays. They agreed that the small town of Green Hills where Maree was building her life was the perfect fit for her. They discussed remote lands and distant shores they'd both seen through work travels. They commented on how much their parents would've loved being at the game that night — Bren's watching on television in Scotland and hers watching from heaven.

Talking had never been their problem. No, talking *about their feelings* had been their issue.

Every time Bren had tried to show M'Kenzee how he felt, her armor had clicked into place. As if she'd expected him to disappoint her, she'd become irritable and impatient, prickly and sharp. A smart man, he'd always taken the hint and backed off, given her the space she seemed to need.

And yet, there had been glimpses, snatches of time, when she'd sheathed her claws…

After the state championship football game his senior year of high school, fans had rushed the field, and she'd run straight for his arms. Still wearing full shoulder pads and his jersey drenched in sweat, he'd lifted her into his embrace, swinging her in circles like an idiot, but too thrilled to put her down.

And he'd never forget her senior prom. Max had called him at the Naval Academy, asked if there was any way he could get to Tulsa for the weekend. Max's spring football game at the university and M'Kenzee's high school prom fell on the same night. Without Max or one of his teammates she knew as friends available to be her date, M'Kenzee had refused to go.

Bren had finagled to trade a pass for weekend leave and bartered with someone to cover his KP duty so he could fly to Tulsa Saturday morning, take M'Kenzee to her prom that night, and be back in Annapolis by 3:30 Sunday afternoon. The favors had cost Bren extra duties and a month of laundry service for each of his buddies, but the night with M'Kenzee had been well worth the added chores.

Max hadn't told M'Kenzee that Bren was on his way, working with Maree to ensure M'Kenzee had a dress to wear when Bren arrived on their doorstep. The way her face had lit up, the expression of shock, surprise, and radiance, in the time between her opening the door at his knock and her remembering to keep all traces of joy and happiness well-hidden from the world, had burned a vision in his brain he'd never forget.

"Going somewhere?" Bren asked, leaning casually against the apartment doorjamb, wearing a black tux, crisp white dress shirt, and plaid bow tie specifically chosen to coordinate with the deep raspberry pink of her evening gown.

For once, someone had struck her dumb. He loved it.

"Go," Bren told her as he opened the front door the rest of the way to brush past her, giving her a gentle turn and a push toward her room. "Get dressed."

Within minutes, she'd traded her cutoff denim shorts and football t-shirt for the floor-length sheath dress. She'd taken her ponytail down and shaken out her natural waves. With her springtime tan and the shade of that dress, the messy, wind-blown effect of blond, auburn, light brown, and golden strands created the perfect kaleidoscope. He'd forever been unable to put a name to the color, yet was often mystified by it.

"You don't have to do this," M'Kenzee said under her breath as he slid the corsage Maree had ordered for him onto M'Kenzee's wrist. "I'm sure you'd ra—"

Once the flower was in place, Bren put a finger to her lips.

"I want to," he insisted. "Now, let's go. I understand we have a fancy dinner reservation, and Max is paying." He winked as he said it.

Dinner was scrumptious; the prom was idyllic — as far as proms went, he figured.

The most gorgeous girl there walked in on his arm and danced in his embrace.

Best of all, she left her walls down for the night, relaxing, talking openly, and laughing with him.

"I can't believe Max called you," she said for the umpteenth time. "I'm so sorry."

"I'm not," he replied for the umpteenth time as well. "It's a good thing he did," Bren admitted.

M'Kenzee slowed their swaying bodies to look into his face. "What do you mean?"

"I don't like the thought of someone — anyone — else holding you this close." His voice was low, his words dripping with possessiveness. Only M'Kenzee could've heard him.

"Why?" Her question escaped on a faint breath.

"Don't you know?" He searched her eyes. "How can you *not* know?"

Then he lifted his hands to wrap around the back of her neck, fingers tangling in the mass of her hair. His thumbs stroked the velvet skin of her jawline.

"You have to know," he whispered as his lips lowered to hers.

What he'd intended to be a brief kiss, one to open her eyes, to make her acknowledge the attraction between them, turned out to be a sucker punch to his solar plexus.

It wasn't until someone tapped him on the shoulder — vigorously — that he reoriented himself to the present. The wormy, weaselly teacher might've been as tall as Bren's shoulder, but the little guy made a valiant effort to look commanding. Bren nodded his apology to their chaperone and wrapped M'Kenzee into his arms, her head nestled under his chin.

He resumed their dancing to give himself time to slow his heartbeat and clear his befuddled mind.

That had been one incredible kiss. With M'Kenzee. Two facts that guaranteed trouble.

He hadn't been wrong.

Upon his return to Maryland, he'd shifted into a different training schedule at the Academy. The new program prepared him for a particular area of service where his talents were needed, one where he'd be able to make a bigger impact, one that benefited the greater good. But it also meant being off the grid for long periods of time.

When he'd called M'Kenzee for the first time after her prom weekend — six full weeks *after* her prom weekend — she avoided him. When he'd finally gotten her on the phone, she sounded cool and aloof. And that was putting it mildly.

"I've been thinking about you, wishing I could call," Bren had told her.

"Don't, Bren. I'm not worth a second thought," she'd

replied. "You've got much more important things to think about. And above all, Bren, I— we," she corrected, "want you to be safe and sound, not distracted."

He'd let it go. Although, when they'd been back together a year later for Max's draft into the NFL, Bren had detected even sharper edges to M'Kenzee's usual bristle.

She'd made it a point to never be in a room alone with him. Meanwhile, he'd been desperate to find any place they could talk.

The one time he cornered her, they'd been in an elevator, just the two of them.

She'd made her wishes clear by standing rigid, arms straight at her sides as he stepped over to hug her. When he tried to caress her cheek, she shrugged away, and when he leaned down to kiss her lips, she turned her head in rejection.

Emotions roiling, Bren punched a button on the control panel to pause the elevator. Her surprised response provided the chink in her armor he'd needed to back her against the wall, hold her in place with a hand on either side of her face, and plant the kiss on her he'd been craving.

Her aloofness melted away. Her lips turned soft and pliant under his. Then she became the aggressor.

Her hands gripped the collar of his sport coat. She pulled him down to close the space between them.

Minutes later, reason surfaced in his muddled mind.

"You're mine," he repeated, hugging her to him, smoothing her thick blond waves down the back of her head.

He reengaged the elevator.

When a group of guests joined them, Bren had no choice but to loosen his hold on M'Kenzee.

By the time they found their friends in the hotel lobby, she'd been back to her usual, unyielding self.

. . .

erhaps now, as husband and wife, we can find smooth sailing.

At least the night in Vegas was showing promise.

After they'd eaten and put the perishables in the mini fridge, Bren offered the bathroom to M'Kenzee to use first. She took time to brush her teeth and comb her hair.

"All yours," she said with an attempt at a small smile. Her nerves had resurfaced; the blush had returned to her cheeks.

He wanted to wash off the smoke from the casino and nightclub, but he didn't want to be away from her too long. He compromised and flew through his shower as quickly as he could.

In the end, he'd had no reason to rush.

He opened the bathroom door to let out the steam. M'Kenzee lay sound asleep in the middle of the bed.

Bren sat on the edge of the mattress and studied her. He indulged in watching her sleep for a few minutes.

She wasn't nearly as feisty and dangerous asleep. In fact, she looked like an angel lying there, long tanned arms and legs, silky peach nightgown, and a halo of thick hair askew across the pillow.

Bren had just finished getting ready for bed, thinking through the events leading to that moment, praying it was real, when his cell phone rang.

"Stewart," he answered in a hushed tone, not wanting to wake M'Kenzee. He walked out of the bedroom and into the sitting area of his rooms.

It was real, all right.

His very real job had just burst their bubble.

Eight minutes after he hung up the phone, two light taps sounded on the door.

Dressed in slacks and a sweater over a silly t-shirt — half of a matching "Mr." and "Mrs." set they'd bought from the casino gift shop — Bren gifted himself a light kiss on M'Kenzee's warm lips. Then, carrying his suitcase, Bren walked out of his suite, leaving M'Kenzee behind.

"Take her to Maxwell Davenport when she wakes up," Bren barked at the agent he'd assigned to be her bodyguard in his absence. "And don't let her out of your sight until she's there."

5

***The reason it hurts so much to separate
is because our souls are connected.
The Notebook by Nicholas Sparks***

*Back in Miss Sadie's living room (3 weeks ago) — Green Hills,
Oklahoma*

Determined to stand her ground, M'Kenzee refused to acknowledge the thumping of her pulse, the thickness of the surrounding air. Bren had always had that effect on her.

Too bad she'd always been a joke to him.

"Tease all you like, Bren" — she spat the words at him — "but that *association* you speak of would break Max's heart. And while you might find it funny, I don't. I'm not willing to risk upsetting him when he's finally found happiness."

Her barb hit its mark.

Bren sobered. But then he stepped toward her. And kept getting closer.

Trying to keep the situation in perspective, and desperate

for the willpower required to resist him, M'Kenzee closed her eyes.

When his chest collided with her, her body moved of its own volition, lifting her lips and leaning into Bren's sturdy strength. M'Kenzee tried recalling every tear she'd cried for him, tried focusing on every night she'd dreamed of him, only to wake up alone.

"Then I guess it's lucky for both of us that the ladies in the kitchen aren't referring to you and me." His cool tone belied the hot intensity of his gaze, the rigid clench of his jaw.

M'Kenzee's eyes popped open and searched his. She admired their emerald depths, even while reminding herself she needed to despise him.

"How do you know?" She stepped back, needing space, air.

Again, Bren eased forward. He consumed all the oxygen. She couldn't breathe. In a last-ditch effort to regain control, M'Kenzee raised her hands to halt his progress. The instant she touched him, heat burned through the crisp cotton of his button-down shirt, scalding her hands.

She jerked them back, but his hands flew faster, covering hers and holding them in place against his chest.

Positive she was about to hyperventilate, M'Kenzee tugged harder at her hands, frantic to get away. "Tell me what you know," she begged as she attempted to twist away from him. "Just say what you have to say, and go away again."

As though she'd dowsed him in icy water, the look in Bren's eyes cooled. He released her.

"I believe the ladies are referring to the text message we received from Max a while ago, the one he sent from the airport in Las Vegas, where it seems he and Janie Lyn are catching a flight to Paris for an impromptu honeymoon weekend before Max has to be back at practice on Monday."

Bren's even tone sounded matter-of-fact, as if he were completely disinterested in her.

The passionate heat in his eyes said otherwise.

"What?" Flustered and confused, M'Kenzee glanced around the room, half expecting her phone to reveal itself out of thin air so she could check her messages. When had she last looked at it? How had she missed something so important?

She'd been shooting photos. That was how she'd missed the big news.

"Here, read mine; we're all in the same group chat."

Bren held his cell phone out to her. Their fingers brushed as she took it. A weight settled in her bones. Could she withstand another hairline crack forming in her already-shattered heart?

M'Kenzee skimmed through the long text message. Tears filled her eyes at Max's declaration of love, admiration, and desire for Janie Lyn.

- …I couldn't wait another day, not even another hour, to make her my wife. So we did it. We found the coolest couple running an awesome chapel in the resort casino where we stayed a few years ago. They were precious — been married sixty-two years. They claimed they could feel the connection between our souls long before we walked into the room. Who's to say if that's true? But I am sure Janie Lyn is my soulmate, the missing piece I needed to finish putting my life together. I'm sorry I didn't invite y'all. I didn't want to hurt your feelings, but we wanted this moment to be just for us. With her grandparents gone, Janie Lyn didn't want or need a big ceremony… We'll leave that for Maree and Rhys. And you, too, 'Kenz, when you holster your weapons and let someone love you.

Max had added a red heart emoji, which softened the blow of his words, before finishing his message:

- We only have a couple of days left during the team's off-week, so we're headed to France. Dinner under the Eiffel Tower, a boat ride along the Seine, and all the bread and pastries Janie Lyn can tolerate sound like a good way to kick off this marriage. MARRIAGE! Can y'all believe it? What would Momma and Dad say? Something wise, I'm sure. I love y'all, and we'll be home soon.

"What are the odds they'd find our chapel?" Bren's voice sounded low and haunted, his brogue thick.

His question sent chills down M'Kenzee's spine.

Our chapel.

M'Kenzee licked her lips to hide their quiver. When she continued to worry the bottom one, Bren lifted his hand to her chin. His thumb eased her lip from between her teeth; his eyes studied the movement.

Butterflies took flight in her stomach. A whimper escaped.

"I've dreamed of you, M'Kenzee." His mouth mere inches from hers, she had no choice but to relent. She couldn't fight the weight of her eyelids, nor the pull of his heat. "Of *this*," he whispered as his lips took hers.

Their first kiss at her senior prom had been sweet — a moment of discovery and bliss on the dance floor. It had held a promise and potential, prophesied of young romance ready to blossom into everlasting love. That kiss had left her head spinning and her heart full.

Their second kiss in the elevator during Max's draft party had been volatile, full of his pent-up longing and her incessant anger at wanting what she couldn't have: Brennigan Stewart. That kiss had left her lonely, sad, and done with love.

Their third kiss, the one after their Vegas wedding — ahh, their third kiss. It had been lovely. What a fool she'd been. Enraptured by the night, the lights, the chapel, the groom. M'Kenzee had been naive enough — stupid enough — to believe he loved her. She'd fallen for his act: hook, line, and sinker. Imagine, Bren seeing her as a real woman. He'd said, *Marry me*, and, gullible and clueless, she'd said *Yes.* Again she berated herself for trusting him, for trusting herself around him. But that kiss... That kiss had made M'Kenzee believe fairy tales really did come true.

Right up until the moment she'd awoken to find him gone. He'd slunk out in the middle of the night; actually, it had been the wee hours of the morning. Finding his side of the bed unwrinkled, she'd known he'd never intended to be with her, had never planned on sharing a wedding night together.

Remembering her innocence, the way she'd called his name and looked all throughout the suite for him, colored her cheeks with shame. She'd hunted everywhere, only to open the door to the hallway to find a young but burly FBI agent standing guard. He'd looked her up and down, guffawed at her silk lace negligee, and told her to get dressed so he could deliver her as ordered.

It had been a joke. She'd been a good chuckle, a crazy memory of a wild night.

And she hated him for it.

The irony of it all, the real kicker that made M'Kenzee hate herself even more than she despised Bren, was that despite it all, she also loved him. Still.

He didn't want her love, but she couldn't set aside her love for him. The harder she tried to forget him, the stronger his hold over her. Would she ever be free?

Not as long as you let him kiss you this way.

The voice in her head found purchase, and although tempted to ignore it, just to savor his kiss one last time, she heeded its warning. M'Kenzee mustered the self-control to extricate herself from Bren's embrace.

They both drew deep breaths. Bren raked a hand through his rich, dark auburn hair. "M'Ken—"

"That was a mistake. My fault. I'm sorry," she said over him.

"*Nae,* it wasn't."

"I won't let it happen again." M'Kenzee tried to gather up the quilts still strewn upon the sofa where Bren had admired them earlier.

He stopped her, firmly yet gently curling his fingers around her bicep and turning her to face him.

"M'Kenzee," he began, ducking until her eyes met his. "It — This— *That kiss* is as right as rain on the Highland moor. It's beautiful, strong, and burgeoning with life. *We* are meant to be. As Granda would say, natural as a babe's first breath. Destined—"

"Stop." She yanked her arm from his grasp. "I don't understand you, Bren," she said, walking away to pace in front of the window he'd been gazing through when she'd entered the room. She rubbed her forehead, attempting to assuage the headache forming there.

"What is there *not* to understand?" He sounded so shocked by her statement.

That halted her mid stride. Dropping her hand, she only stared at him in response, eyes squinting in consternation.

"M'Kenzee, why'd you marry me?"

She started to answer, then stopped, and swallowed the words on the tip of her tongue. To stall, she turned her back to him and looked out over the pasture, watching the cattle lumber from a shade tree to a watering hole.

When she remained quiet, Bren walked to stand behind her. He set his hands on her shoulders, then slid them down to her elbows and up again in a show of support and encouragement.

Finally, she turned around to meet his searching gaze.

"Because Momma told me to," she answered, proud of her even, certain tone.

6

*Holding on to anger
is like grasping a hot coal
with the intent of throwing it at someone else;
you are the one who gets burned.
the Buddha*

That made no sense.

Mrs. Davenport died years before that night after the Super Bowl, the night they'd married.

Bren proceeded with caution. "I'm not sure what you mean, but I'm sure glad she did."

Like a gift from on high, M'Kenzee let down her walls. Then, making his heart soar, she opened up to him, talked to him…not avoided him, not ignored him, and not spat hateful looks at him. She *talked* to him. With someone else, it might not be that big of a deal. With M'Kenzee, he'd take it. Gladly.

"Go on…marry Bren," she whispered. "It was the last thing Momma told me, the last words I heard her speak."

"That night after the carnival, that was the night of their accident," Bren stated.

She nodded, lips white and pressed together in a straight line. The color had drained from her beautiful face.

"After you ran off to wrestle, or whatever, with Max, I wandered the school grounds. I took photo after photo... pictures of messy bowls holding mounds of nachos, kids flushed with sweat and sloppy with sugary threads of cotton candy, parents drooping under the weight of heavy toddlers sleeping on their shoulders. I wanted to stay all night to take more — always fighting to take more pictures. When Dad said it was time to go home, I pitched a fit. Typical M'Kenzee, right?" She scoffed after the self-deprecating comment. "Angry I hadn't gotten my way — regardless of how silly it had been to believe they would leave me there — and bent on making everyone pay for my bad mood, I pouted all the way to the car, refused to talk as Dad drove us home. But Momma and Dad never made it home. Their last memory of me is of a first-rate brat. And my last happy memory of them is Momma saying, *Go on, M'Kenzee. Marry Bren.*"

Her words trailed off as she stared into vacant space.

"Do you still have them?"

"Hmm?" He'd lost her to a haze of memories.

"Do you still have them?" Bren asked again.

"Do I still have *what*?"

"The photos. From the carnival. I bet they're incredible. Even then, you had an unbelievable gift for bringing life to your photography. Our parents used to go on and on about it, about how talented you were— *are*. M'Kenzee, we're all very proud of you; we love *you*, just as you are: subtle and raw, prickly and sharp. Your parents did, too. It was written all over their faces every time they looked at you, plain as day for the world to see."

He wanted to dry the tears from her cheeks, but Bren sensed she wouldn't welcome his calling attention to them, so he stayed put, sliding his hands into his pockets to curb the desire to comfort her.

"Can I see them? The pictures from that day?"

"I've never looked at them," she confessed, her voice so low Bren strained to make out her words.

"Never?"

"No, never." Her chest lifted as her shoulders slid back. Her signature head tilt dared him to challenge her.

"I want to see them. I want to see what you saw that day. You'd just gotten a new camera, one that hooked up to a computer instead of using film. Where's the disk?"

M'Kenzee's hand curled around the chain on her neck.

Observant by nature and inquisitive by trade, Bren didn't miss her subconscious gesture.

He eased her hand away and pulled the necklace from its hiding place under her crew neck sweater and fitted white undershirt. Not a charm, but rather a small gold trinket — about two inches long and half an inch wide — like a locket, but more three-dimensional.

"What is this?"

"It's called a shadow box pendant." Her eyes stayed on him, gauging his response.

"I've never seen anything quite like it," he marveled, admiring the jewelry in the palm of his hand.

"I had it made, special." She took her time, pausing before stating her chosen adjective: *special.*

He stood close enough to inhale her floral perfume, to notice the warmth of her blush heating her cheeks. He wanted to get lost in those sensations, but this was too important to let pass. Yes, *special.* Exceptional… He found her extraordinary.

Bren studied the intricate clasp. He raised an eyebrow, requesting permission before opening the latch.

She swallowed slowly, but M'Kenzee didn't stop him.

A smile bloomed on his face when he opened the shadow

box. Inside lay her gold wedding band, the one he'd put on her ring finger three years earlier. Someday, he'd see it back there, where it belonged. Until then, he could find satisfaction in knowing it would be next to her heart.

The other item, a tiny computer chip, had to be the pictures.

"Do you have what we need to view these?"

"Yes, there's an adapter with my equipment. But they won't be any good, not worth seeing. I can't tell you why I keep them — proof of my selfish pettiness, I suppose." She tried to dismiss him, to go back to folding quilts on the sofa.

"I don't care what they are, or how they look. I want to share them with you. I want to share everything with you." Bren pushed the pile of quilts to the side and tugged M'Kenzee by the hand to sit beside him on the couch, hip to hip and knees touching.

He glanced down at their entwined hands. When he lifted his head to look into her eyes, he removed his usual stoic mask, the filters of everyday life, and any veil hiding his emotions. He did it on purpose, so she could see for herself how he truly felt.

"M'Kenzee, I—"

The vibration of Bren's cell phone against the coffee table interrupted him. On a sigh of irritation, he dropped one of M'Kenzee's hands to flip the screen so he could see the caller's name. Bren expelled the rest of his breath with an even deeper exhale of frustration.

"I'm sorry," he said, genuinely sad. "I have to take this."

"Imagine that; you're leaving," M'Kenzee taunted, wiping a tear from her eye before it could fully fall.

7

———

Every duty is a charge,
but the charge of oneself
is the root of all others.
Mencius

"What wonderful news," Miss Sadie proclaimed as she, Maree, and Landry joined M'Kenzee in the parlor. They'd passed Bren on his way out, phone to his ear, intent on whatever he heard from the other end of the line.

Miss Sadie, the Davenports' adopted grandmother — not by law, but by choice — possessed a knack for simplifying things in a way that put everything into perspective. She owned and operated a bed-and-breakfast in the home her dad built by hand in the late 1930s. M'Kenzee loved being there, meandering through the gardens, running her fingers along the intricate woodwork highlighting every room, soaking up the essence of drama and love and loss the walls had witnessed over decades and generations of life. Rich with history, Marshall Mansion reflected it all. What a magnificent place.

From an early age, M'Kenzee'd heard a call to preserve, to

weave together the past and the present. But instead of a home brimming with people and stories and laughter, her medium was photography, a camera her tool. M'Kenzee's life was much lonelier. The stories were present — visible in every picture she took — but rarely the people, and almost never the laughter.

Even in that room, amidst joy over Max and Janie Lyn's news, M'Kenzee sensed a distance, like she was on the outside, watching the world through a lens. Would God ever give her a place to belong, or had He taken that opportunity away, along with her parents?

"We have to plan a party!" Fun, flirty, and often the brightest bulb in the room, Landry Stark jumped up and down, squealing at her amazing idea. Officially, Landry boarded at Marshall Mansion while working through her medical school residency. In reality, Miss Sadie had adopted her, too.

Over the past couple of years, they'd formed a family, one M'Kenzee loved. She didn't have Landry's exuberance or Maree's capacity to love so grandly, but M'Kenzee adored each member of their crew. Standing back and guarding her heart didn't make M'Kenzee any less a member of the family. No, those were simply methods of preservation — self-preservation — so M'Kenzee could withstand the pain when loved ones inevitably left.

"Let's do it," Maree exclaimed, joining in Landry's excitement and increasing the room's level of glee another octave. "A surprise reception when they return! Rhys can barbecue, and I'll do the rest of the cooking. Landry, you're in charge of the music, and M'Kenzee, will you do the decorations?"

Maree extended one hand toward M'Kenzee and the other toward Landry.

Powerless against Maree's beaming smile, M'Kenzee's defenses failed her. Holding hands with the two girls, M'Kenzee allowed them to pull her into their dance. She forced herself to focus on their hopping and skipping and side-shuffling around Miss Sadie and the sofa and the lamp tables. She plastered a grin on her face and even sang along with Maree, belting out the Dixie Cups' classic "Chapel of Love."

M'Kenzee did *not* think about her vision for a reception… the vision she'd dreamed a thousand nights. In her dreams, twinkling lights illuminated an open area, strung from rafters or trees to cast a soft glow over a makeshift dance floor below. A couple swayed to a cheerful tune, the woman's long blond hair arranged in a loosely braided updo; wildflowers fastened here and there added a touch of innocence, while copper high-lights reflected throughout the mahogany strands of his clean, military style. The bride gazed into her groom's face with adoration; the groom beamed like the luckiest man on earth. They couldn't get enough of one another, but they relished the thought of trying throughout a lifetime together.

M'Kenzee feigned fatigue and bowed out of their celebra-tion. She lifted a hand to the back of her neck, feeling for long waves no longer there. She'd sheared them off in a fit of rage when she'd returned home a wife with no husband.

Aghast with indignation, her hairstylist had cried as he chopped off what little she'd left intact. He'd said there was no other way to salvage the damage than to crop it into a very short pixie cut. What had been no more than an inch in length at that time had since grown into a style M'Kenzee owned: undercut at her nape, with the sides and back just long enough to hint at her natural waves, yet short enough to taper. She liked to keep the top longer, shaggy and messy.

M'Kenzee loved how she could simply wash and go when on assignment. In fact, she loved the look altogether. But it would never fit her dream image of a bride with a braided crown of wildflowers. That girl was gone.

Shrugging off her gloom, she turned to Miss Sadie. "May we use the barn? For the reception?"

She'd gift her vision to Max and Janie Lyn — two people

who'd know what to do with it. She'd make it the most beautiful night of their lives.

Renting tables and chairs, making a run to Tulsa for supplies, and setting up the barn provided perfect excuses for avoiding Bren.

"Can I help you with that?" he asked a dozen times a day.

"No thanks. I've got it," she replied each time, also avoiding his eyes, which bored into her wherever she went.

"We need to talk, M'Kenzee," he also said on repeat.

"I can't now." She'd shrug and fake an apologetic expression.

Bren must've seen through her ploy; by Saturday, his normal warm, welcoming demeanor had disappeared, and his stoic secret agent glare had returned. When she tried to dismiss him that afternoon, he'd cornered her in the kitchen.

"Whatever you're doing can wait," he said.

"Really, I—" She moved to sashay past him, but he gripped her arm, stopping M'Kenzee in her tracks. Neither menacing nor cruel, his touch heated her skin on contact.

"M'Kenzee, I have to tell you something." Bren paused to make his point. He wanted her undivided attention.

"Fine. I'm listening," she whispered, unable to speak any louder when he made it impossible to take a full breath. *Why does he do this to me?*

"I have a location on Janie Lyn's uncle, Axel Lyndale. He's resurfaced in Athens, hiding, but our intel is solid. He's there."

A flashback of Janie Lyn being attacked and dragged through the concourse at Max's football game turned M'Kenzee's stomach. Contemplating that Janie Lyn's uncles had forced her into hiding, tried to steal her inheritance, and were responsible for her grandfather's death sobered M'Kenzee's wild imagination. What might've happened — what could've happened — did not bear thinking.

"Hey." Bren lifted his hand from her arm to her cheek, which also burned under his touch. He nudged her to look up from the ground, into his arrestingly turbulent and vivid green eyes. "It's okay now, *ye ken*."

Safe and sound, Janie Lyn was far from the danger and havoc her uncle could wreak.

Thanks to Bren. When Max had called Bren to share Janie Lyn's story and her fears, Bren had pulled together an FBI task force to protect Janie Lyn, uncover her uncles and their criminal activities, and put her attacker in jail. Brennigan Stewart was the epitome of honor. When duty called, Bren answered.

With a Herculean effort, M'Kenzee resisted the urge to deflate with disappointment. Of course someone needed Bren. Something more important than M'Kenzee always presented itself to take him away.

With Janie Lyn's other uncle, Stanton, already in custody, catching Axel Lyndale would close the case. Bren would see to it.

"When do you leave?"

8

____

The backbone of surprise
is fusing speed with secrecy.
Carl von Clausewitz

"We have a problem," Maree announced as she entered the kitchen, completely unaware of the strained tension between the room's two occupants. She effectively halted Bren's intention to tell M'Kenzee how he felt, how he wasn't leaving *her*, how he had to do his job. And to convince her that he would always be back.

He had no choice. M'Kenzee was as vital to his life as the air he breathed. Bren would *always* return home to her.

"We're not finished," Bren murmured. He kept M'Kenzee in his peripheral vision as he stepped away to face Maree. M'Kenzee's face had paled, her eyes had gone cold when he'd mentioned they had a lead on Axel. She'd never in a million years admit she feared Axel and the thugs he ran with, but after what she'd been through, she'd be crazy not to be wary. He wouldn't let anyone hurt her; surely she knew that.

And while she'd tried valiantly to maintain an air of indifference, the hurt he'd caused them both became evident by the slump of M'Kenzee's shoulders the moment she realized Bren had to go back to work so soon.

"What's up?" he asked Maree once Miss Sadie and Landry joined them, sitting at the breakfast table.

"Janie Lyn just called from France. They found a flight directly to Kansas City, so instead of flying back through Dallas to get Max's truck at the airport, he's hiring a service to drive it to his townhouse in KC. They'll bypass Green Hills completely on their way home. Our narrow window of opportunity for Sunday night's party just slammed shut."

Maree looked dejected, Miss Sadie looked sad, and Landry looked bewildered.

M'Kenzee looked stoic. She'd done her best to hide her emotions, clammed up to mask her true thoughts and feelings. Her hopes and fears remained an unflinching mystery.

"I'll take care of it," Bren offered. "You ladies keep getting ready for the reception. I'll have them here as planned, Sunday night at seven o'clock."

Maree jumped up to give him a huge hug, delight lighting up her face. If only her big sister would be so easy to please.

Bren cast a glance at M'Kenzee before he left the room; her eyes remained locked on the tea towel she twisted between her hands. She didn't so much as spare him a glance.

Their tug-of-war continued.

"*B*ren?" Max answered with worry in his voice.

"Maxwell," Bren teased in answer, drawing out Max's full name as only his new bride was allowed to do. "How's married life?"

"The best…" Bren's greeting eased the concern in Max's voice, and Max flew into an animated ramble. When he began describing the wedding chapel in Vegas, Bren had to stop him.

"*Ye* know, I've actually seen it before."

"The one in the team hotel we used for the '17 Super Bowl? Really?"

"Yeah, I'll tell you all about it someday. Someday soon," he pledged. "Listen, I'm sorry to interrupt your last day in Paris, but I have some news. I can't get into it over the phone, but we've located Axel Lyndale."

"Where are you?" All business at the flip of a switch, Max had gone on high alert. "What about the girls?"

"I'm with them, here in Green Hills. I had a little vacation time the bureau was nagging me to take, so I thought I'd hang out here — with you — only to discover when I arrived that you'd eloped. Miss Sadie's still hosting a houseful, so Maree lent me the key to your house. I want to fill you in. We can meet as soon as you get back to the States, but I don't feel good leaving them alone out here, not just yet."

"And M'Kenzee's still there? She hasn't taken off for a photography assignment?"

"Still here. She and Maree are working on some book project; each day they gather another set of quilts and drag them to the garden, the lake, the park, or the pasture, with furniture, props, and lighting — more mess than you can imagine, just to take a few pictures. Miss Sadie's been spoiling us with dinner each evening since the girls have stayed so busy during the day."

"Good," Max said. "That's good. I'm glad you've been with them. Of course, Maree has Rhys, but there's something going on with M'Kenzee."

"Like what?" Bren tiptoed on thin ice.

"She's angry all the time, upset with the world. That's nothing new, but it's worse. Maree and I can't put our finger on it, but we're both worried. M'Kenzee's never been bubbly and jubilant like Maree, but she used to be happy. I haven't seen her happy in a long time."

"How long?" Bren waited with bated breath for Max's answer.

"What?"

"How long since you saw M'Kenzee happy?" Bren asked a second time, his words more clipped than the first.

"Man, I'm not sure," Max sighed. "You know, it started with our parents' wreck. Then she changed, spent the summer after high school on cloud nine; I thought she was eager and excited to go to college. But by the time I was drafted at the end of her freshman year, she was grumpy and irritable all the time. I'm embarrassed to say that those next few years, I probably didn't pay enough attention. She finished up her degree and immediately went to work as a photojournalist. The news magazines had her flying all over the world, remote places where it was difficult to stay in touch. I was juggling a new career in the NFL, and Maree was working her way through the University of Tulsa. We didn't see M'Kenzee much during that time.

"When Maree landed in Green Hills, M'Kenzee started spending more time there as well. I wouldn't have described her as giddy or anything, but she seemed content. She'd stay at the Lodge at Daisy Lake a lot and seemed to enjoy puttering around Marshall Mansion, taking landscape shots and helping Miss Sadie with the boarding house. I prayed she was feeling better, discovering a sense of home.

"Then, when we got back from Las Vegas, from the Green Bay Super Bowl we were talking about earlier, M'Kenzee just split," Max explained. "We didn't get to tell her goodbye. She left a note saying she'd gotten a call from work that required she catch up with her travel team immediately. She stayed in touch throughout that entire time, but from a distance. We didn't see her for months — almost a full year, I'm afraid.

"And when she showed up, she'd cut off her hair, had a different demeanor. She'd put up barriers that must've resulted from things she'd seen on rough assignments," he continued. "Poor Rhys. He took the brunt of it. No matter what he did or what he said, she flat out refused to believe he was worthy of Maree. M'Kenzee didn't trust that he would be there for Maree when she needed him. Luckily, M'Kenzee's come around — begrudgingly, for sure — but she agrees Maree found her soulmate."

Max paused and let out a deep exhale. "And now I've found mine," he admitted, a sloppy, smitten grin present in his tone, one so crystal clear Bren detected it all the way across the Atlantic Ocean and half of North America.

Bren's thoughts whirled, snippets of memories and time-lines ricocheted around in his mind like the metal balls in a pinball machine. So much to think about. Everything Max had told Bren rattled around in his heart as well as his head. Pretty positive he could match each of M'Kenzee's bad moods with their own interactions, Bren conceded that her unhappiness rested squarely on his shoulders.

"You there, buddy?"

"*Ye*, I'm here; the line just cut out for a second. So, when will I see you? To bring you up to date on the situation with Janie Lyn's uncle."

Wait for it… 3, 2, 1…

"I'll fix our flights. Stay in Green Hills, and I'll meet you there tomorrow afternoon, early evening at the latest," Max instructed.

Voilá! Party saved.

Now, if only he could salvage his heart and marriage, as easily.

9

***The greatness of a community
is most accurately measured
by the compassionate
actions of its members.
Coretta Scott King***

To say that Sunday resembled a whirlwind would've been quite an understatement.

With task lists in hand, M'Kenzee, Rhys, Maree, Miss Sadie, Landry, and half of Green Hills scrambled through the day like ants on a mission. When they'd called around town to invite a few friends and gather party supplies, word had spread like wildfire, and everyone asked to help. With so many hands on deck, M'Kenzee had added layer after layer to the reception. Originally intended to be an intimate family celebration, the reception had bloomed into an all-out bash.

The outpouring surprised M'Kenzee.

Of course, Max was very well-known. Who *didn't* want to attend the wedding party of a famous sports figure?

Although… M'Kenzee had noticed when the townsfolk

spoke of Max, it wasn't with the tone of a celebrity crush. No, the people of Green Hills had taken time to get to know him, to have genuine conversations with him, and apparently to love on his dog, Hank, when they saw them out on walks or playing fetch at the park.

That part did not shock M'Kenzee. Her entire life, everyone had adored Maree and swarmed around Max.

No one could resist Maree's open, honest, sweet nature. She was a beacon of light, bestowing her brilliant smile on loved ones and strangers alike. Simply being around Maree lifted moods and brightened spirits.

Max was just the same: a magnet. Whether at school, church, the playground, or a sandlot, people flocked to his side. *His* team had always been where kids wanted to be; teachers had requested him for their homeroom, coaches had jumped in line to recruit him, and girls had begged for his attention. Although quiet and wise in his own way, Max listened intently and made the people crammed around him feel as though they were special, as though each one had his undivided attention.

M'Kenzee offered a quick prayer of thanksgiving for the way this community had adopted her siblings. She gave praise that both Max and Maree had a place to belong, a place to call home. Not as effusive or demonstrative with her faith as her brother and sister, M'Kenzee nonetheless believed in the Lord's guidance. She couldn't understand the *why* behind what happened in the world, but she did find peace in knowing she wasn't alone on her journey. For some reason, her parents had not survived one car accident, but Maree had walked away from three: the one that killed their parents, the one during Maree's senior year of college that led her to Green Hills, and the one a year earlier, when someone ran a stop sign in Green Hills. There was no explaining that — through no lack of trying on M'Kenzee's part — so she'd finally accepted that having faith presented the only viable way forward.

While genuinely grateful for the town's response and envelopment of Max and Maree, it was the way the residents of Green Hills spoke of Janie Lyn that stopped M'Kenzee in her tracks. What they said, and how they said it, had M'Kenzee considering how belonging somewhere might feel. This town cherished Janie Lyn. In a relatively brief span of time, Janie Lyn had impacted many people in profound ways. And all the while, she'd desperately tried to fade into the background, hoping to go unnoticed because she'd been escaping her family. M'Kenzee could only describe the entire chain of events as utterly incredible.

Now the people of Green Hills had shown up to make Max and Janie Lyn's wedding celebration a dream come true.

The ladies from Janie Lyn and Maree's Mah Jongg group had asked to be in charge of the desserts. M'Kenzee had gladly agreed; then they blew her away with what they'd accomplished. A stunning three-tiered wedding cake with edible pearls and fresh roses acted as the centerpiece on an oversized wooden worktable they'd found in the barn's storeroom. They'd draped it in gauzy white fabric and added white, cream, silver, and gold candles in varying shapes and heights. The candlelight cast a soft glow over large white platters of homemade cookies, brownies, and lemon bars, which surrounded the gorgeous cake. The smell of sugar and heaven wafted throughout the barn.

Meanwhile, the savory aroma of barbecue floated in from where Rhys's friends and coworkers from the Green Hills Fire Department had parked an industrial-sized smoker. They gathered around it, talking, teasing, and teaching while perfecting their masterpieces of brisket, ribs, turkey, and sausage. The reality that Rhys was a pretty great guy sank into M'Kenzee's consciousness. She'd resisted liking him as hard as she could, but it looked like he was going to win her favor in the end. She would sooner go mute than admit as much to Rhys. Nope, she'd never let him off the hook. She fully intended to make him earn the right to spend a lifetime with her baby sister.

Once they'd gotten the smoker doing its job, the firefighters had also helped a group of kids set up yard games, reminding M'Kenzee of a tailgating celebration at a sporting event, with cornhole boards, washers, Frisbees, bubble wands, badminton, and jumbo Connect Four. The "older" kids — the retired set — had stacked dominoes and cards on folding tables along with scorecards and pens. Where in the world had all that come from? Not one of those items had been on any of her multiple planning lists. She loved it.

Audrie Boucher, owner of the yoga studio at Daisy Lake that Maree liked to drag everyone to on a weekly basis, had offered to coordinate the nondessert, nonmeat items. She'd sent out a text to their Saturday morning classmates, and the masses had answered her call. Broccoli salad, potato salad, green salad, relish trays, fruit trays, cheese trays, baskets of crackers and crisps, and dishes of vegetable sides created a twenty-foot buffet. Again, a staggering response to support her family.

They had enough food to feed an army. A football team. Both!

Scotty Philips, the head football coach of the Green Hills High School Wolf Pack and a good friend of Max's, had teamed up with Landry to build a small sound stage for a deejay. He'd gone one step further and brought along someone to handle the playlists, one of his players who hoped to launch his own music business after college. They'd strategically placed speakers around the barn. Tunes played everywhere. Music floated in the air, yet magically, the sound didn't overpower the space.

Members of The Book Belles — Miss Sadie's book club — and the Busy Bees Quilt Guild had joined forces to arrange bouquets of fresh greenery and winter flowers. Their artistry sat all around the room. Small pots of lavender cyclamen added pops of color. Medium containers of ornamental cabbage and kale added shades of pink, purple, cream, and red with their fancy, frilly leaves, all complemented by the soft lighting. Fat barrels of winter heath exploding with magenta blossoms stood watch from the corners. Dozens of tiny ceramic planters, finished in a marble swirl of glittery white glaze, each holding a single viola plant, sat in clusters on every surface, waiting to go home with guests at the end of the night.

Between the mouthwatering foods and the sweet desserts, a lovely, heady scent permeated the barn.

Clucking instructions in her no-nonsense manner, Miss Sadie supervised the teenagers milling about as they hauled in hay bales and positioned them to create sitting areas. Then she unfurled huge quilts in all shapes, sizes, patterns, and colors to cover the itchy straw. They layered quilts two and three at a time, overlapping one another, so appliqués, prints, designs, and motifs peeked out in disarray. The menagerie created an exquisite effect.

M'Kenzee turned in a slow circle, taking in the barn with amazement and awe before snatching her camera to snap photos of the decorations, tables, arrangements, and displays.

With the doors open and light streaming in, the sun provided a natural filter that turned the air into a brilliant sheen of mystical proportions. M'Kenzee could not have recreated that lighting with an entire team of professionals. She'd already filled one memory card and expected she'd go through a few more by the end of the night.

"It's stunning," Maree acknowledged, putting an arm around her big sister. "You should do this full time. Truly, however you pulled this together in just a couple of days is incredible."

"I was happy to do it," M'Kenzee replied. "Who knows,

maybe in another lifetime I was a party planner. I sure have fun throwing events together."

"And you have an eye for it!"

"You might be biased." M'Kenzee turned a sardonic but loving glance on Maree. "And I can't take the credit for this," she said, tilting her head toward the impressive display around them. "I would never have imagined so many people coming together to make this happen. And they did it for Max and Janie Lyn, who've only been around Green Hills a few years. It's mind-boggling."

"They're great people. Like I keep telling you, Green Hills is a wonderful place to be," Maree said with the pride of someone who'd staked her claim and put down roots. "You should give it a try," she finished with a sly smile.

"Well, they've certainly proven themselves in a very big way today," M'Kenzee conceded before moving on to chat with the deejay, photograph the game zone and barbecue station outside, and double-check everything one more time.

10

———

So the darkness shall be the light,
and the stillness the dancing.
T. S. Eliot

*U*nlike the multitude of Green Hills' residents in attendance, Bren had been missing in action for most of the day, somehow completing his assignments for the party, yet secluded on work calls hour after hour.

Determined not to notice his absence, M'Kenzee scolded herself each time she caught her eyes searching for him. *He's leaving,* she reminded herself. *You'll never be worth staying for. You've never been enough to hold him.*

If only her heart would listen.

By seven o'clock, the grounds around the barn at Marshall Mansion were hopping.

Again, the sheer numbers of people, kids, dogs, and plates piled high with food overwhelmed M'Kenzee. It was lively and lovely and beautiful. She hated feeling a slight stab of pain. Plain old envy, if she was being honest. She loved this — this wonderful sense of community and camaraderie. But she'd never experienced it. She didn't expect she ever would. She couldn't envision a future that included a community of friends, a love to celebrate, and a life to look forward to living with *her* one person. What a sad realization amidst such joy and happiness.

Barely audible over the din of activity, the crunch of Max's truck coming up the drive alerted M'Kenzee and diverted her thoughts. They'd arrived.

M'Kenzee stepped into the barn and made eye contact with Frankie Boucher, Audrie's son and the football player from the high school who was working as their deejay. She gave a slight nod in the boy's direction, letting him know their guests of honor were mere minutes away.

With a huge grin on his face, Frankie faded out the music, which turned all eyes his way. Then he spoke into the microphone, anticipation and joy clear in his voice. "The newlyweds are almost here. Let's all slide into the barn and be ready to yell *Congratulations!* when they walk in."

M'Kenzee's heart raced. She looked over to smile at Maree and take her hand, but Maree had walked to Rhys, who was chatting with Davis, Landry, and Coach Philips. Maree stood in front of Rhys; his arms draped around her, he'd nestled her into the powerful frame of his chest. He leaned down to whisper something in her ear. Maree's face lit up, her smile turning into a gleeful laugh. M'Kenzee lifted her camera just in time to capture the moment.

Letting her camera fall to hang around her neck, she indulged in a heartbeat of self-pity. Then M'Kenzee cleared her head and set her loneliness to the side. She'd allow herself to feel only happiness for her baby sister. And her big brother. She loved them immensely and wanted only the best life had to offer for them both.

As the resolution percolated through her mind, muscular

hands took hold of her shoulders. The warmth of a solid body behind her heated her flesh.

Bren.

"*Braw*," he said, not bothering to hide his brogue. He lowered his mouth toward her ear to speak only to her, much the same as Rhys had done when speaking to Maree. "That means it's amazing, M'Kenzee. Beyond lovely."

His warm breath sent chills from her neck to her belly.

Good Lord, his effect on her. *Ridiculous is what is.*

And yet, she didn't budge, instead remaining in place to absorb his nearness and bask in his compliment.

As the sliding barn doors opened, Frankie hit play on the music. Beyoncé and Jay-Z began belting out "Crazy in Love" as Max and Janie Lyn slowly — cautiously — stepped in from the evening dusk.

"What—?" Max asked as M'Kenzee clicked the shutter in continuous mode to ensure she preserved their looks of disbelief.

"Family and friends," Frankie said, his voice booming over the microphone, "may I present to you, Mr. and Mrs." — he drew out the words with animation — "Max and Janie Lyn Davenport!"

The crowd erupted.

With enormous eyes and beaming smiles, Max and Janie Lyn held tight to each other and scanned the room in wonder.

Janie Lyn found Maree, and her hands flew to her face as Maree walked their way, holding out her arms.

At the same moment, Max found M'Kenzee. She lowered the camera from in front of her face. He lifted an eyebrow. She shrugged in a guilty reply.

Max shook his head in amazement at M'Kenzee, love glowing in his expression. He, too, reached out an arm, gesturing for M'Kenzee to join him.

Photographs were priceless, but M'Kenzee wished that, in addition to the pictures she took, she could bottle this moment, this jubilation. Then she could pull it out to experience again and again, like Dumbledore and his pensieve, when life felt too heavy.

Frankie played another song, allowing time for greetings, hugs, and more congratulations. Then he called Max and Janie Lyn to the center of the room for their first official dance as husband and wife.

Max twirled Janie Lyn into his embrace as Etta James crooned "At Last."

With joyful tears threatening to overflow, every eye in the room watched the two move as one, each completely absorbed in the other. They were a three-dimensional portrait of true love.

Frankie transitioned to an upbeat tune that encouraged the rest of the crowd to rush the dance floor.

Max and Janie Lyn remained rooted to the center, staring at each other with smitten bliss until Max's teammate Daran Campbell and his wife, Gloria, entered the barn with Hank in tow. The moment Max and Hank saw one another, Hank busted free of Daran's hold on his leash, and Max dropped to his knees. Man and dog embraced as though they hadn't seen one another in years, as opposed to just the past few days.

Earlier that fall, Hank had been away at training school for three full months. After that, Max had sworn they'd never spend more than a night or two apart. He'd missed the stout cane corso worse than he'd ever imagined possible. By the time the training program ended, Max had been desperate to get his buddy back home. The impromptu wedding and honeymoon had again tested the limits of how long those two could be away from one another.

When it appeared Max's arms would be full of fur for the foreseeable future, Bren stepped in to dance with Janie Lyn. M'Kenzee's heart skittered with another brief stab of jealousy at the sight of someone else in his arms. She dreamed of it being her.

But those thoughts were a path to chronic pain, so instead of watching them float around the barn, she meandered from table to table, picking up discarded drinks, tidying dessert trays, stirring sides and salads to keep everything looking fresh and appetizing. Every couple of steps, she stopped to click another photo. She'd long ago acquiesced to the role of party-doer rather than party-goer.

In a large group setting, she struggled to find topics to talk about with people she barely knew. She simply wasn't good at small talk and mundane conversations. She'd found herself much more comfortable working, viewing the world from behind her camera, staying focused on tasks rather than people, sheltering her heart rather than sharing it. Life felt safer that way.

She admitted, however, that together, all the people in the room had thrown a really grand party — a reception for the record books.

It went without saying that the barbecue, sides, and sweets were beyond fabulous.

The decorations were beautiful.

Frankie, essentially one with the music and impressively efficient with his sound equipment, energized the vibe and kept the fun flowing with a perfect balance of slow love songs for snuggling couples, fast club mixes for all the singles in the house, country and western ballads for two-stepping, line dances for the youngsters, and golden oldies for everyone to enjoy.

Seeing everyone have such fun filled M'Kenzee with a sense of accomplishment and reward. She really loved this medium of design — building venues for others' enjoyment with themes, colors, decorations, food, and music. Photography fulfilled her essential needs; event planning served as icing on the cake, a sweet indulgence that brought her great satisfaction. What did she need love for?

M'Kenzee glanced around for Bren. Par for the course, he'd disappeared shortly after his dance with Janie Lyn and was still nowhere in sight.

Determined not to care where he was, M'Kenzee lifted the woven strap from her shoulder and set her camera on a table at the back of the barn, safely out of the way. With two free hands, she resumed her rounds of housekeeping.

Gathering a stack of used paper plates, napkins, and plastic cups, M'Kenzee made her way to the trash bin in the back corner. She focused solely on balancing the stack to prevent it from toppling early and jumped in surprise when she bumped into someone else.

Her gaze flicked up.

Bren.

He, too, dumped a handful of rubbish in the can as she tossed what she'd been carrying. Without pause, he took her now empty hand and led her to the edge of the dance floor.

"I Can't Help Falling in Love with You" began as Bren wrapped an arm around her waist. He folded her hand in his and pressed them against his heart. She'd always been a sucker for the authentic, aching emotion in Elvis Presley's voice.

"Bre—" M'Kenzee tried to pull away from the heat emanating from his body and enveloping her in a foggy haze of rapture.

"Shh," he breathed into her hair, locking his arms to hold her in place. "Just let me hold you," he begged.

They swayed slowly on the outskirts of the crowd. M'Kenzee tried to be content with the moment, to take what she could get and be happy with it. Why must she feel cheated if she couldn't have it all?

As the song progressed, the brace of Bren's arms tightened

more and more. The closer he secured her, the more panic set into her nerves.

By the time the last notes sounded, M'Kenzee's hands trembled. A heavy weight in her chest made breathing a challenge. She stood frozen, afraid to look up into his eyes, afraid to move.

The hand engulfing hers released its hold, allowing Bren to caress the side of her neck. Then he turned her cheek and held it to exact spot where his heart beat rapidly. He rested his chin on the top of her head as he inhaled a deep breath, hugging her even harder. His lips kissed her hair.

Then Bren shifted his hold to cradle her face with both hands and look deep into her eyes, straight to her soul.

Tilting her head back, he kissed her.

Right there in the barn, in front of everyone…where Max, Maree, anyone could see.

He kept right on kissing her.

Bren planted an absolute earth-shattering kiss on her. One that stole her breath, her senses, and her heart.

M'Kenzee didn't care who saw. She knew what was coming, and she couldn't deny the indulgence of the moment — the kiss.

When he lifted his lips from M'Kenzee's, Bren tried to smile at her. The effort came off hauntingly sad. On a faint sigh, he swiped a tear from her cheek. She closed her eyes to prevent a stream of them.

She reopened them and looked at him through her lashes. He stroked a thumb over her bottom lip. Then Bren turned and walked away.

Let us have faith that right makes might;
and in that faith, let us, to the end,
dare to do our duty as we understand it.
Abraham Lincoln

Brennigan Stewart didn't get emotional. He loved deeply, but he didn't let it show.

He always chose duty, had made a name for being steadfast and reliable, and he never lost control.

But he'd unleashed his emotions and lost all control during that kiss.

M'Kenzee.

His angel.

She perceived his leaving for work as leaving her, but nothing could've been further from the truth.

He held her close at all times. When he closed his eyes, he saw her. He spoke to her when he needed an anchor, and Bren heard her voice in his mind when he needed a raft.

She'd kept him alive again and again during deployments

and assignments. His imagination could conjure her in a heartbeat. M'Kenzee was home.

And unfortunately, Bren was on the road.

On the road…on the hunt… It all meant the same thing.

Pursuing bad guys had proven to be Bren's gift. He'd get Axel Lyndale, too.

And then he'd get home to M'Kenzee, once and for all.

Atlanta, Georgia

*E*ven dumber than Bren had predicted him to be, Axel Lyndale walked himself directly into the FBI's possession within a week of the task force's arrival in Athens.

Sloppy and desperate, Janie Lyn's uncle had jumped on a chance to connect with her.

Bren's team had left a note for Axel at a trashy bar he was known to frequent. The note said Janie Lyn wanted to check on him, was worried about him since his older brother, Stanton, would be in jail for a very long time. It claimed she needed to tell him something important about Pops and Gram's estate. The note instructed Axel to take her call at a pay phone booth just around the corner at ten o'clock in the morning in three days' time. The note had closed with, *I know you didn't mean to hurt me. Love, Lizzy*, and a heart scrawled after her name.

Axel had answered on the first ring, eager to let someone else sort through the heap of trouble he'd found himself in. Special Agent Jia Liú mimicked Janie Lyn's Southern accent to a tee, and Axel had confessed every lousy thing he'd done, incriminating and condemning his older brother and their corrupt partners.

Agent Liú, enjoying the undercover role-play, had maintained the phone conversation long enough to hear the sirens and his arrest.

Wanting to see Axel behind bars with his own eyes, Bren had accompanied the police escort to Atlanta, stayed for the arraignment, and booked a flight that night for Dallas. He hoped to be back in Green Hills — with M'Kenzee — by midnight, December 11.

They had a lot to talk about…a lot to decide.

After four years at the Naval Academy, four years of active duty deployments, and over three years in the field as an FBI agent, Brennigan Stewart had accepted a desk job.

Maybe not a desk job in the strictest sense of the word, but essentially the same thing.

In his new role, he'd travel to branch offices and Quantico to teach classes, train new recruits, and consult locally. As an agent placed in the Office of Partner Engagement, he'd still be on the move, but no more war zones, no more classified ops that required agents to disavow their identity in case of capture, and no more being out of contact for extended periods of time.

The type of work trips he'd be taking in the future allowed for a plus-one; a wife could accompany him across the country…particularly ideal for a wife who liked to take pictures everywhere she went.

They'd have a home base in Green Hills, close to her family and friends. Bren already had the ball rolling on that, prayed she would be pleased when she found out. He'd intended to tell her last week, when they'd been there at the same time. He'd sensed she was softening a tiny bit, sharing the story of their first wedding at the school carnival and promising to show him the pictures she'd taken that day but had never seen herself. She'd been wearing his ring — albeit hidden in a charm box, hanging on a chain, instead of on her finger where it belonged.

But duty had cut their conversations short, ended their time together.

No, not *ended*. Paused. Their time together had simply been put on hold.

"Hey, Stew?" Michael Vela, the assistant special agent-in-charge of the Atlanta field office and a friend from their time in Annapolis, called out to Bren from across the bullpen of desks and activity. "Do you have a few minutes before you leave for the airport?"

Bren glanced at his phone, checked the time, and cringed. He should've already called Max to update everyone about Axel Lyndale before the press found out they had caught him. Janie Lyn's family drama had been quite public, a news piece often sensationalized throughout the past two years. Bren didn't want her finding out about her uncle via gossip shows or soundbites. He'd call as soon as he finished talking to Mikey.

"Sure," Bren answered, setting down his pen and closing the notebook in front of him. "What's up?"

Thirty-six hours later, Bren was on a flight headed to Africa.

He'd managed a quick text to Max:

- *It's done. Can't call right now, but Janie Lyn can rest easy. Everything's taken care of. Hope to be back for Christmas.*

And one to M'Kenzee:

- *I'm sorry. I'll be back as soon as I can, mo ghràidh. And then we'll talk. About us.*

Other than the thirty seconds it had taken to type those messages, Bren had remained behind closed doors with a roomful of agents and officers from every branch of national security and ranging from the CIA to Naval Special Warfare, better known as SEALs. Meeting both in-person and via video-conferencing, they'd spent the last day and a half strategizing a covert joint-agency operation in Eritrea, a country on the coast of northeast Africa.

A group of American citizens on a holiday mission trip had disappeared in Ethiopia. Their itinerary showed they'd planned to visit a series of refugee camps along the Tigray region before spending ten days with churches and communities around the capital city, Addis Ababa.

They'd arrived in Ethiopia, checked into their hotel for the night, and had been seen eating dinner in a restaurant nearby. Camera footage showed them in the van they'd rented, with the driver they'd hired, leaving the city per their set schedule. Then their trail ended.

Concerned with the proximity to Eritrea — the world's worst hotbed for human trafficking and forced slavery — and considering the high risk of kidnappings in the Horn of Africa, the United States government prioritized moving quickly to locate and extract the group. Every person in that briefing had spent time in Africa; each one of them understood time was of the essence.

Bren had deployed to the Horn of Africa multiple times during his four years of active duty for the Navy, including operations in Somalia and Uganda, as well as stays in Libya and Pakistan. They had also sent him into the Middle East: Afghanistan, Yemen, and Iraq. In his four-year tour, Bren had logged a lot of time and miles in the most unstable parts of the globe.

He'd done his job well. His service had garnered him a reputation for being a skilled and successful soldier. His knowledge of the people and the land could tip the scale in their favor.

And what if one of his loved ones had been with a group that went missing?

M'Kenzee traveled the globe for work as a photojournalist. What if she ever needed help in a rough part of the world? He'd want the best, most determined operatives getting her out.

Bren saw it as his duty, plain and simple. He'd had no choice but to help with the rescue mission.

On the other hand, a tight timeline and extenuating circumstances made this operation anything but plain and simple. Bren would've said they'd lost their minds to even try the op, which teetered on treacherous and suicidal. But there were no other options. They'd thought through every alternative, and this plan provided their best odds of returning home…every one of them: missionaries, agents, soldiers, and all.

And he *would* get home. To M'Kenzee.

12

Three things cannot be long hidden:
the sun, the moon, and the truth.
the Buddha

December 22 - Kansas City, Missouri

M'Kenzee smiled at Hank, who waited for Max by the back door. The sweet dog always jumped to attention when the garage door opened and Max's truck rumbled into the space.

"Hey, buddy! You keeping the girls in line for me?" Max greeted the dog and kneeled to hug, pet, and scratch his faithful companion.

"Wow — something smells good in here," he exclaimed, rising and nudging Hank forward. Max entered the house, where the women scuttled around in a blur of activity. "And looks good," he added. An enormous Christmas tree stood in front of picture windows overlooking the Kansas City skyline. A massive wreath hung over the fireplace. Boughs of greenery draped over the mantel, the banister, and even the curtain rods, adding a rich pine scent.

"It sounds good, too, " he said with a dramatic nod toward his sound system, where the needle of the record player slid gracefully from Gene Autry's "Here Comes Santa Claus" to Eartha Kitt's sultry plea for presents in "Santa Baby."

After setting his keys in a dish and his backpack on a barstool, Max walked straight to Janie Lyn, who was prepping sugar cookie dough on the countertop. Without waiting for her to set down the rolling pin, he cozied up close behind her, moved the long braids she'd crafted to hold back her hair to one shoulder, and bent to kiss her neck.

"Hello, Mrs. Davenport," he murmured past playful nibbles and kisses.

M'Kenzee tried to ignore them.

She forced herself to focus on placing ribbon and bows in the copious amounts of greenery the girls had purchased at the tree farm earlier that morning. Meanwhile, Maree dashed around the living room, choosing the perfect ornaments for the perfect spots on the tree.

"Mmm, hello, Mr. Davenport," Janie Lyn whispered back to Max before closing her eyes and shifting her weight to nestle into the frame of his arms and chest. A look of blissful peace settled across Janie Lyn's stunning features.

"Yuck," M'Kenzee grumbled to Maree when they were shoulder to shoulder working on their decorations.

"Aww, I think they're cute," Maree said, turning woeful puppy dog eyes on M'Kenzee. "Makes me miss Rhys," she sighed, with a dramatic whine and a pouty look back at the lovebirds in the kitchen.

The sisters had driven from Green Hills to Kansas City the day before to spend the week with Janie Lyn and Max. He had a game at home against the Seattle Seahawks on Christmas

Day, so it made the most sense for them to convene at his house in the city for the holiday.

Maree's fiancé, Rhys, would drive up on Christmas morning in time for the game's two o'clock kickoff. Then they'd open presents, eat dinner, and attend the church's candlelight ceremony.

"Double yuck," M'Kenzee announced, feigning dislike for the man her baby sister had chosen to marry. What began as M'Kenzee's tumultuous distrust of Rhys, had evolved into genuine respect and sibling-type love. M'Kenzee figured the best way to display her affection for Rhys was to continue razzing him at every turn.

But even M'Kenzee was feeling the uplifting spirit of Christmas.

It had been three weeks since Bren left Green Hills, twenty-one lonely days. The past eleven had been the worst, as they'd had no contact with him at all since the terse texts Max and M'Kenzee had received from him the day they'd caught Axel Lyndale.

Where are you, Bren?

His text had said he hoped to be home for Christmas. Just two more days — surely she could survive that long.

What will happen when you get back? What will happen to us after that kiss we shared right before you left? What did you mean by "we'll talk…about us" in your text?

The questions whirled around in her mind as she fluffed the bows, added ornaments, wired antique trinkets and treasures to the branches, and tucked in floral picks to make the greenery come alive with color and embellishments.

As usual, her one-sided "discussion" with Bren did little to ease the ache his absence left in her soul.

This time, when he returned, they'd have a heart-to-heart. She agreed with his text on that point: it was past time to talk. But was there an *us* to discuss?

Tired of living in fear of his rejection, she needed to face the fact that he might not want a life with her. Knowing that painful truth would be better than putting her life on hold, hoping he'd love her someday.

Right?

Grrr — she hated the doubts that crept in every time she resolved to either move forward with Bren or end it for good.

M'Kenzee kept primping the decorations, lost in her own diatribe.

"Hey, 'Kenz?" Max called, shaking her out of her thoughts.

"Hmm?" she asked in reply, finally hearing Max. He stood at the open front door, where a visitor looked past Max, directly at M'Kenzee.

"This man says he needs to speak with you." Unspoken questions weighed heavily in Max's voice, but M'Kenzee didn't have any answers; she'd never set eyes on the guy before.

Setting down the Christmas baubles in her hands, she made her way to the entryway and held out her hand in introduction.

"I'm M'Kenzee Davenport. May I help you?"

The man was above average height, but not nearly as tall as her six-foot, four-inch brother. He had close-cropped hair the rich ebony of dark burnished wood. His eyes, equally dark and rich, emanated an apologetic sympathy.

M'Kenzee gulped. Her heart fluttered.

This man carried Bren's calm, serious, always-in-control demeanor like a second suit.

"Yes, ma'am," he began. "Perhaps I could come inside to talk?" He tilted his head toward the living room, which overflowed with joyful Christmas objects strewn about that belied his tone and body language.

A flush of fear ran down M'Kenzee's neck and arms.

"Yes, of course," she replied, lifting her chin, determined to face the man eye to eye, no matter what he had to say. "Please, come in."

Maree had joined Janie Lyn in the kitchen. They huddled close to one another, hushed with concern.

Max closed the door and followed the man, who followed M'Kenzee into the sitting area.

Both men waited until M'Kenzee had settled on the sofa. Max sat next to her; the man took the chair next to M'Kenzee's end of the couch.

"Ma'am, I'm Special Agent Michael Vela." Her heart stopped completely. "I'm a friend and coworker of Brennigan Stewart's," he explained. "You're listed as his next of kin."

M'Kenzee's hand involuntarily flew to her throat. *Oh, Lord. No.*

"That can't be right," Max argued. "Bren's parents are in Scotland. I'm his emergency contact here in the States."

"I'm sorry, sir. Agent Stewart updated his personnel records effective February 6, 2017, to designate *Mrs. M'Kenzee LeighAnn Davenport Stewart, DOB 11/03/1992,* his beneficiary and next of kin. That *is* you, correct?" He and Max both turned to look at M'Kenzee.

"Yes," she whispered at the same moment Max erupted.

"This is wrong! Someone made a mistake," he stammered, arms flailing and feet stomping. "Get Bren on the phone. He'll straighten this out. Something's not ri—"

"Max," M'Kenzee interrupted with an icy chill. "Sit down."

Too dumbfounded to disobey, Max sat. Within seconds, Janie Lyn perched on the edge of the cushion next to him, resting one hand on his forearm in solidarity, the other on his knee in reassurance. Maree had also joined them, sitting in the armchair closest to Janie Lyn.

M'Kenzee looked each of her loved ones in the eye. She

captured the worried expression and unconditional support on their faces, stored the images in her mind and in her heart in case they hated her very soon.

Then she gave their visitor her undivided attention.

"Mr. Vela, where is my husband?"

13

———

Bad news is bad news because
it drops your willingness to carry on.
Meir Ezra

"*Y*our *what?*" Max roared.

"Maxwell, sit down," Janie Lyn said in a soft, yet commanding tone. Likely the only person who'd ever get through to him in such a state, her touch worked; Max ran his hand through his hair and plopped back on the couch for a third time in a matter of minutes.

M'Kenzee read the questions in Max's mind as if he'd screamed them at her…

How could Bren and M'Kenzee be married?

His best friend! And his little sister!

"Would you rather speak in private?" The special agent asked M'Kenzee, and she imagined if it weren't for Janie Lyn's gentle but restraining hand on his leg, Max would've come unglued. Again.

"No, of course not. This is my family — Bren's family. Where is he?"

"We're not sure," Michael Vela admitted to M'Kenzee. "I'm not at liberty to share confidential information about Agent Stew—"

"Bren," M'Kenzee interjected. "You said you are his friend; please call him Bren."

He dipped his chin in an affirmative gesture. "As I was saying, there's very little I can tell you about the operation Bren was on when we lost his location." M'Kenzee nodded her understanding. "On Friday, December 13, Bren landed in northeast Africa as part of a rescue mission. We were tasked with finding a group of United States citizens who'd traveled to that area on a two-week faith-based mission trip over the holidays. Intel showed they arrived safely, but they never made it to their first organized destination to minister to refugees. Our mission was to locate and extract the group members as quickly as possible. Bren's knowledge of the area, the people, and the languages spoken where they'd gone missing were deemed crucial to the success of our forces."

"And did you get them out? Safely?" M'Kenzee asked.

"Yes, ma'am. Most of them," Vela added with resignation.

"But something happened to Bren?" She could barely voice the words.

"He's presumed missing in action—"

"MIA. Not dead?" M'Kenzee grasped on to that technical difference like a life preserver.

"No, ma'am. We do not believe that Agent— Bren— What I mean is that we believe Bren is alive." Vela's voice strengthened, which somehow reassured M'Kenzee. "He's a high-ranking, decorated operative with extensive survival training. If he'd been taken, his captors would most likely have already contacted the US government with demands. If he's wandering the terrain, he knows what to avoid and how to stay safe. He will find us; I feel that in my gut."

"When?" Max barked.

"I wish I could say—" Vela began.

"When did he go missing?" Max's question came out as a demand. "You said he arrived in Africa on the thirteenth. Today's the twenty-second. How long has he been missing?"

"The rescue extraction occurred December 15. It's been a full week since Bren made contact."

M'Kenzee's stomach dropped.

A week wandering the desert, the Nile, or the Atlas Mountains. Was he injured? Had he found food? Shelter? Help?

Oh, God — please be with him.

"And you were there?" Maree inquired in her typically thoughtful, empathetic manner. "On the mission?"

"Yes, ma'am." Vela's answer spoke volumes, although he'd barely whispered the words.

"And how do you know Bren, Agent Vela?" Maree asked.

Michael Vela smiled, his first one since he'd arrived at the town house.

"We attended the Naval Academy together," he said, his posture relaxing a fraction from the ramrod tension he'd displayed so far. "Stew's top-notch, both as a soldier and a man…always best of the class, vying for the highest ranking, but without fail, the first to lend a hand and offer support. We were fierce competitors, but also fast friends. Trying to beat Bren forced me to work my tail off, much more than I'd expected going in. I'm certain our camaraderie forged us both into better warriors than we'd have been without the other." Fondness and reverence colored his description.

"And you both chose the FBI after service?" Maree asked.

M'Kenzee appreciated Maree's ability to keep Michael talking. Having the agent share bits and pieces of Bren made him feel closer than where he actually was — where he'd gone missing — eight thousand miles away.

"Yes, but not together. After graduation at Annapolis, Stew — Bren, I mean, he was hand-picked for a CJTF; that's a

Combined Joint Task Force. Considered force multipliers, these special operation groups can deploy quickly and focus on one specific mission or threat to national security and world peace. It's a great commendation to be selected to serve on one, but the tour isn't easy," Michael ended on a sobering note.

"I'd imagine no tour of military service is easy," Janie Lyn offered in her sweet Southern drawl.

"No, ma'am, but the CJTF combatants see the worst of the worst, region by region, and task by task. They're deployed to diffuse situations when normal channels of security and warfare aren't working. By definition, they're the best, the top soldiers from multiple branches of service from multiple countries. They get the job done."

"And Bren did that for his entire tour, for four years?" M'Kenzee wondered out loud.

"Still does," Michael confirmed. M'Kenzee's brow furrowed in confusion, and he expounded. "After— Well, when Stew's tour was up, he stepped away. But within a few months, we were both at Quantico, training for the FBI. I hadn't seen Stew since our college graduation, but we immediately fell in together again, like no time had passed. The FBI Academy lasts twenty weeks; after that time, I took a job with CID, the Criminal Investigation Division. Somehow, Stew ended up back on a CJTF, this time representing the FBI rather than the United States Navy, but the call of duty was still the same. Day in and day out for almost eight years; I don't know how he's done it this long. He mentioned he requested a transfer to OPE. I'm glad. He deserves it."

For a man who'd appeared reluctant to speak when he'd first arrived, Special Agent Michael Vela rolled once he got started.

And he'd given M'Kenzee plenty to think about. Even more to pray about.

"Mr. Vela?" she asked as he stood to leave. "What is the OPE?"

"It's the Office of Partner Engagement."

"And what does that division do?"

"We like to tease that they sit behind a desk…grading papers and planning lessons. They're the face of the FBI in local communities — the educators and the agents who no longer need to watch their six so closely," he said with a jovial smile.

When no one else in the room moved to escort Michael Vela out, M'Kenzee walked him to the door.

"Oh, I need to give you this," he said, taking a metal lockbox from the entry table where he'd set it earlier. He placed it in M'Kenzee's hands.

"What is it?" M'Kenzee's voice trembled; she feared what it meant that the FBI would release Bren's belongings. Did they not expect him to be found alive?

"His love box, ma'am," he said gently before nodding and turning to leave.

M'Kenzee stopped him before he could close the door behind himself on the way out.

"Mr. Vela?" She'd bolstered her strength, all hints of fear and frailty removed from her tone. "Shouldn't this go to his mom and dad instead?"

"No, ma'am. His direct orders were to hand it to you. *Only* to you."

With that, he tipped his head goodbye.

14

To love means loving the unlovable.
To forgive means pardoning the unpardonable.
Faith means believing the unbelievable.
Hope means hoping when everything
seems hopeless.
Gilbert K. Chesterton

*L*ater that night, Max paced the floor of their master suite. "Bren better be alive," Max growled. "So I can kill him when he gets back."

"Maxwell, really?" Janie Lyn removed the fancy pillow shams and turned back the sheets on their bed. "You love Bren. You certainly love M'Kenzee. Why shouldn't you love them together?"

For the first time, Max hated Janie Lyn's level-headed reasoning.

That wasn't true. He loved everything about his new wife. *Everything.*

But how could Bren have married his little sister? Almost three years ago? After the biggest game of Max's career? At least it had been at that time. And shouldn't his best friend in the entire world have spent that night by his side to celebrate? *Yeah!*

"What were they thinking?" Max asked, turning a petulant scowl on Janie Lyn. "Why wasn't he with me that night?"

"Why didn't you notice him missing?"

Max answered her counter question with an even more sullen, incredulous frown.

"I don't remember," Max said succinctly.

"Maxwell, have you ever noticed how M'Kenzee often leaves the room when Bren comes up in conversation? Or how her eyes are usually puffy and red-rimmed when she returns?"

"No," he replied with his most kindergartner-like pout.

"Hmmm…"

She walked into their enormous closet. Max heard the drawer of her lingerie dresser open and close. Then she walked back into the bedroom, wearing a vintage silk nightgown. *How does a piece of fabric that covers her from shoulders to ankles look so sexy?*

"You're trying to distract me," he grumped. "But it won't work."

"Okay," she agreed, going into the bathroom to brush her teeth. When she returned a few minutes later, he caught a whiff of her uniquely hypnotic nighttime scent: a perfect blend of perfume, face cream, body lotion, and lip balm.

Janie Lyn ran a graceful hand across his chest as she passed him on her way to the far side of the bed.

God, she's beautiful.

But I'm mad. At Bren. And M'Kenzee. And…

"Perhaps you should listen to M'Kenzee tomorrow. Hear what she has to say. Then be there for her — for one another — while we wait for word that they've found Bren, healthy and safe."

She said it so patiently that Max had to consider it sage advice.

And Janie Lyn did look incredible in that silk gown, the way it clung to her muscles and curves.

As she lay beside him, the heat from her body drifted right through the fine fabric.

She'd taken out her braids and brushed her hair, so it floated freely across the pillows, beckoning him to feel the strands, especially the tendrils framing her face.

When she turned toward him and cradled his jaw in her hand to hold his lips in place for her kiss, Max knew he was a goner.

Thank you for this woman in my life, Lord. And please, please bring Bren home.

Max switched off the lamp and rolled back to Janie Lyn, scooping her into his embrace, and continuing where her kiss had left off.

"You okay?" Maree asked softly as she carried two cups of hot chocolate to the couch, where M'Kenzee sat staring at the still unopened box in her lap.

Accustomed to seeing M'Kenzee stalwart and strong, Maree didn't know what to make of this silent, almost frail version of her big sister.

"I'm sorry," M'Kenzee replied after a long moment. "I'm sorry I never told you. I'm sorry I hid our silly wedding ceremony. I'm sorry I lied, and pretended not to love him, and pushed him away again and again." Her litany ended on a broken sob.

"Oh, honey, no." Maree sat next to her, wrapping both arms around her to absorb the emotion shuddering through M'Kenzee. "It was your story to tell whenever you and Bren were ready. Please don't apologize."

"I've been so hard on Bren, believing he was abandoning

me every time he went away. Did you hear Agent Vela, hear what Bren has been through? I was juvenile and selfish," M'Kenzee cried without restraint; tears streamed down her face. "He was facing down the very worst examples of humanity, serving as a hero to so many, and I was holding it against him. I should have been there for him, to encourage him, to build him up when the places he went and the things he saw got too horrific. I agreed to marry Bren, and then I refused to be married. I was useless to him. I ignored him, stayed away anytime I thought he might be around. I even cut off my hair to make Bren mad." M'Kenzee listed her self-proclaimed crimes with vitriol. "Why am I so difficult? Why am I so hard to love?"

Maree rocked M'Kenzee back and forth, letting her say all the things she needed to get off her chest.

When the crying jag and body-wracking shakes subsided, Maree handed M'Kenzee a handful of tissues and waited while M'Kenzee wiped her face and eyes. Tears escaped, but they were manageable.

Maree scooted back on the cushion just enough to tuck one leg beneath her and face M'Kenzee. She took both of M'Kenzee's hands in her own and forced her sister to look into her eyes.

"You are amazing," Maree began.

"No." M'Kenzee shook her head, trying to pull her hands away from Maree's. Fresh tears filled her eyes.

"Listen to me," Maree continued, holding fast to M'Kenzee's icy fingers. "You are honest and bold; you speak the truth and do what is right, even when it's hard. You see the world for how it really is, past the fluff, the fake, and the phony. You're capable and confident and strong. If you've chosen to love Brennigan Stewart, it's because he's worthy of your love. He's up to the task of loving someone fearless and unflinching. And if he's ridiculously hot and incredibly brave, well...

That's just icing on the cake." Maree ended with a wink and a shrug.

M'Kenzee rewarded her with a small grin. "He is rather gorgeous, isn't he?" M'Kenzee asked with a sly smile.

"And that accent." Maree moaned the words in exaggeration. "He hides it so well, but when he lets it loose? Watch out, ladies!"

They giggled together, and Maree handed M'Kenzee her mug of cocoa, which had cooled off just enough to be drinkable.

"I've loved him since I was five years old," M'Kenzee confessed. "I thought surely I'd grow out of it, my stupid infatuation with my big brother's best friend. But my schoolgirl crush just grew and grew until I thought my heart would burst." She paused, taking a second to sip her hot chocolate. "And it did. Every time we were around one another, my love deepened, only to be dashed when he walked away. Whether it was to get to class, to catch up with friends, or to go fight wars, he always left. Again and again, my heart shattering each time. He's not mine, but I can't seem to let him go." Longing and deep sadness resounded in M'Kenzee's voice.

"I think he is," Maree countered.

"He is *what?*"

"I think he is definitely yours," Maree stated. "I wasn't in love with him, so I probably didn't pay as much attention when we were growing up, but I'm not blind. Brennigan Stewart is a catch. I'm positive he could've had all the dates, girlfriends, and wives he wanted over the years, but I don't remember a single one.

"The day of their junior prom, the boys had a playoff baseball game in the afternoon. It was out of town, so they didn't take dates to the dance. In fact, if I recall correctly, they wore their dusty, dirty jerseys over their tuxedo shirts to celebrate winning the game."

"And their caps," M'Kenzee filled in. "Mrs. Stewart was not happy, said she could smell them from outside the high school gym, but she really never got onto the boys one bit."

"For their senior prom," Maree reminisced, "Max convinced Bren to take the twin sister of Max's date. Again, they chose sports over prom, attending the spring football game at the University of Tulsa before picking up the girls. I think all four of them knew they'd be going as friends; both Max and Bren had already shifted their sights to college.

"M'Kenzee," Maree continued pointedly, "I've never seen Bren take a girl out on a date — besides you. Not once throughout my entire lifetime." She lifted an eyebrow at M'Kenzee and tilted her head, challenging her sister to deny the facts as they'd been presented. "Brennigan Stewart loves you. And he always has."

*H*ours later, M'Kenzee stared at the ceiling fan above her bed, replaying Maree's words of wisdom in her head.

Could he love her? Could anyone?

Maree had sugarcoated M'Kenzee's personality traits. She knew herself to be unyielding, critical, and impatient. Maree had chosen kinder words — *bold* when she meant *outspoken*, *confident* when she meant *a know-it-all*, and *fearless* when she meant *headstrong*. But really, they all meant the same thing.

M'Kenzee couldn't change her nature. She *was* all those things.

She also had a big heart, loved deeply, remained fiercely loyal once her trust had been earned, and possessed an innate gift for compassion. She enjoyed a good debate, had fun picking apart the opponent's rebuttal, and didn't mind arguing just for the sake of playing devil's advocate.

More than once, M'Kenzee had tried being more like

Maree, more like their momma. She'd attempted to be soft-spoken, but everyone around her had continually asked her to repeat herself with *Huh?* and *What'd you say?* She'd gone to dance lessons to learn grace and poise, but after two months, the teacher had told their parents that elegant activities might not be the best fit for M'Kenzee. Who flunked out of ballet at the ripe old age of four?

One week in the fifth grade, she'd refused to speak at school, pledging to be a quiet student and a good listener after she'd heard a teacher praising Maree for those exact qualities. By Thursday, the teacher had sent her to the principal's office for belligerence and refusing to answer when spoken to.

She'd even tried wearing the flowery blouses and pleated skirts that looked so nice on her classmates. The girls on the playground didn't know what to make of her, and the boys had laughed. Laughed at her!

M'Kenzee Davenport approached the world with raw edges and spiny bristles because she'd never found a nicer, softer, smoother way to survive.

Had self-preservation turned her into an unlovable creature?

Or did Maree have a valid point?

What if Bren *had* seen through her tough exterior, looked beyond her defensive maneuvers as Maree suggested? Had he discovered someone he wanted to spend a lifetime with? Had he recognized her redeeming qualities? If so, were they enough? Enough to deem her worth the challenge of loving?

Would she and Bren get another chance for him to try?

Please, give us a chance to try. And above all else, Lord, please keep Bren safe.

15

There is no love like the love for a brother.
There is no love like the love from a brother.
Astrid Alauda

"Good morning, M'Kenzee." Janie Lyn greeted her while setting plates on the breakfast table, which was laden with platters of pancakes and bacon, bowls of scrambled eggs, a tray of fruit, and glasses of orange juice, beside empty mugs awaiting coffee and hot tea.

Max joined them from where he'd been feeding Hank in the laundry room.

He and M'Kenzee eyed one another.

"Good morning," he said, his voice coarse, either from sleepiness and the early morning or from frustration with M'Kenzee; she wasn't sure which.

Then he opened his arms, and she rushed into his hug.

"I'm sorry," she wept, apologizing through tears. She'd cried more in the past eight hours than in the past eight years put together.

"I know," he soothed. "But you shouldn't be. As Janie Lyn

wisely pointed out, there's no one I'd trust more with my loved ones than Bren. And M'Kenzee..." He paused, forcing her to look up at him. "I just want you to be happy — to feel cared for, content, and complete. If Bren is the person who does that for you, I'd be the last person to stand in your way. I find no fault in your loving one another."

M'Kenzee wiped her eyes...for the millionth time. She squeezed him tight for one more hug and then released him to move toward the table.

"Thank you." She smiled at both Max and Janie Lyn. Then she ducked her head, unsure what else to say, as she pulled out her chair.

When she lifted her head and took in the enormous amount of food on the table, a giggle escaped her.

When Max and Janie Lyn looked at her in confusion, M'Kenzee couldn't stop herself...

"No wonder you're putting on weight," M'Kenzee teased.

Max started to protest, but he shrugged instead.

"It's a rough problem to have," he admitted with chagrin.

Max, M'Kenzee, and Janie Lyn were laughing aloud when Maree made her way down the stairs.

"What's so funny?" she asked. "Good heavens, this is a lot of food," she exclaimed, sending the others into absolute fits of laughter.

Their powerful response didn't match the comedic level of the moment, but it proved to be exactly what they'd needed to relieve the tension and worry all four of them were experiencing over Bren. He was out there somewhere, and while they each refused to acknowledge any possibility of the worst-case scenario, it hung heavy in the air.

"I have one question, 'Kenz," Max said when their giggles had subsided and they had piled their plates high with breakfast.

"Okay," she allowed. "That's fair."

"Why did you keep your wedding a secret? Did you feel you couldn't trust us with the truth?"

His words revealed how deeply she'd hurt him, which caused M'Kenzee pain.

In all honesty, avoiding pain — Max's pain, her own pain, *any* pain — had been her initial motivation for pretending the wedding had never taken place.

"That night, Bren and I sat up talking and eating food from room service for hours and hours. I guess I fell asleep while he was showering. When I woke up the next morning, he had disappeared in the middle of the night. Obviously, Bren had to have been inebriated to marry me. I couldn't think of a single reason to stir up trouble when it had just been a big mistake, and one that could be annulled and erased with ease."

"Annulled? Is that what you wanted? Was that even possible? I thought once a marriage was— you know. Consumma—"

M'Kenzee cut him off to cease his awkward stumbling. ""No reason to worry. Our entire relationship comprises five kisses, spread out over the past ten years."

"Ten years?" Max questioned. "You were still in high school ten years ago!"

"You sent him to me, for my senior prom. Remember?"

"That backstab—"

"Maxwell," Janie Lyn interrupted, sweetly patting his arm and then clasping his hand. "Let's listen to M'Kenzee." Then Janie Lyn smiled at M'Kenzee, encouraging her to continue.

"Maree knew — not about the kiss, but she'd been aiding and abetting behind the scenes. After he arrived, heart-stompingly handsome in his tuxedo, I dashed to change into an old formal. But when I got to my room, *someone* had draped the perfect dress across my bed, selected shoes from my closet, and chosen a fabulous necklace from Momma's collection of costume jewelry."

"That was a magnificent dress," Maree reminisced. "A luscious, deep magenta with sequins embellishing the entire bodice and scattering across the satin skirt, which hugged your hips just right before cascading out to flow fully at the hem. More sequins trailed down the center of the back side of the skirt, and it was sleeveless with thick spaghetti straps. I remember thinking the satin ribbon used to lace up the deep V in the back was the perfect touch. The entire dress turned out to be utterly *you*: such a bold color, structured and strong, athletic even, as it showed off your toned shoulders and incredible arms. There was nothing dainty or frail about it. But at the same time, the dress reflected a soft, subtle femininity, a desire to be held, cherished, and loved. It screamed, *Yeah, I'm drop-dead gorgeous, and I can still kick your—*"

"Sounds like some dress," Janie Lyn interrupted, ever the timely voice of reason.

"It was," Maree confirmed. "Oddly enough, I found it at the thrift shop down by the university... Paid twelve dollars for it."

"What?" M'Kenzee and Max asked in unison.

"Only twelve dollars?" M'Kenzee marveled. "I think I sold it to a friend in college for one fifty. I should've kept it."

"And I gave you two hundred to buy it," Max said to Maree. "Where's my change?"

Janie Lyn elbowed him. Maree waved off his mock outrage. "Let's get back to the story of the kiss," she said. "I want all the details."

"One should never kiss and tell," M'Kenzee teased. "But it was wonderful — a wonderful dinner, wonderful dancing, and a wonderful first kiss, in the middle of the high school gym. It felt like we were the only two people who existed — when, in reality, the entire junior and senior classes surrounded us. It felt as though time had suspended just for us, under the hanging fairy lights. Completely *wonderful*."

"Wow," Maree commented, stars glistening in her eyes, her hopelessly romantic heart full to the brim with giddy delight. "What happened next?"

"He left." M'Kenzee sobered. "He flew back to school the next morning, and I didn't hear from him for six weeks."

"But he did call," Janie Lyn prompted.

"Yes," M'Kenzee answered with a conceding whisper. "Eventually."

"He always comes back, M'Kenzee. To *you*," Janie Lyn added.

M'Kenzee offered a half smile to Janie Lyn, grateful for Janie Lyn's unflinching resolve and support.

Then M'Kenzee tried to eat some breakfast. Janie Lyn had outdone herself making it; the least M'Kenzee could do was try to do it justice.

In the end, she'd barely pushed her pancakes around the plate, making swirls in the syrup.

Would Bren come back this time?

She'd never wanted anything as desperately. As much as she'd begged God to bring her parents back after a drunk driver killed them, she wanted — *needed* — Bren to come home even more.

"You need to open the box," Max prodded.

His flat tone broke through her reverie, and she looked up to meet his eyes — so solid, so steady. Her heartbeat skidded before fluttering back in rhythm. A wave of distress must've flashed through her eyes.

"You can do this," he promised. "And we're right here if you need us."

*M*ax had more confidence in M'Kenzee than she had mustered for herself.

She'd taken the box onto Max's back patio. A conduit for

the crisp winter air, the cold metal of the safe-style container sent chills up M'Kenzee's arms. She wrapped a quilt around her back and over her shoulders, hovered over the chaise lounge she straddled and stared at the "love box," as Michael Vela had called it, which she'd placed before her on the outdoor cushion.

Her hands trembled as she slid the key in the lock. Since when had she become a woman whose fingers shook with nerves?

Since the man you love but refused to acknowledge went missing in a deadly, war-torn desert, her conscience answered.

Max was right — she could do this. She didn't cower; she didn't retreat. The version of her that Bren knew, the version of herself that he might even love, didn't shy away from challenges.

I can do this.

With her resolve firmly in place, she turned the key and lifted the lid.

His scent — the woodsy, leathery cologne he'd worn since high school, a hint of spearmint from his favorite gum, and a trace of his spicy yet subtle aftershave — assaulted her senses, causing her eyes to close of their own volition. As the aroma-tinged air filled her lungs, warmth spread through her body, beginning in her chest before expanding to heat her skin with electrifying tingles.

Half-ecstatic to have any piece of him in her hands and half-terrified that whatever she found in the box might be all she would ever have of Bren, M'Kenzee forced herself onward, opening her eyes, and exhaling the breath — filled with his essence — that she'd been holding.

An envelope — a plain white one that came in a package of fifty or one hundred, the kind people used every day for the most mundane of purposes — lay on top. Across the face of it, Bren had written her name in his strong, precise script. His grip had been so firm on the pen, an indention marked each stroke of ink. Reading it sent a tremor through her arm as she reached out to smooth a finger over the letters.

Gathering her gumption, she flipped the envelope over, eased the adhesive free, and slid out a single sheet of notebook paper.

> Thursday, December 12, 2019
>
> Dear M'Kenzee,
>
> I've rewritten this letter dozens of times. Replaced the envelope and prayed you'd never have to see it.
>
> But I have a bad feeling about this mission, so I think it's vital that I update it one last time.
>
> You might've heard of a love drawer, a place in a family's home where important stuff is kept... documents, passwords, birth certificates, passports.
>
> Because of the transient lifestyle of the military, soldiers put those items in a lockbox so their beneficiaries have a road map through the landmine they find themselves in when one is called home, asked to pay the ultimate sacrifice.

M'Kenzee heard a smothered caterwaul of pain before it registered that she'd made the horrible noise, audible through the fist she pushed fiercely against her lips.

> You are my greatest love, so there's no one else I'd want to have it. I'm sorry.

Again, a strangled cry slipped from her throat.

Inside, you'll find my will and last wishes, the deed to a house I bought in Green Hills (in hopes we'd make it a home together some day), and a bunch of journals. It's not much, but it's mine. And as I've always been yours, my few belongings are yours now, too.

As you'll see if you look through the journals, you've had my heart for a very long time. You've been a magnet I am pulled toward and a light so colorful and bright, you have the power to both blind my sight and illuminate my way.

I've wished a million times that I'd followed my da's footsteps into a nice quiet career in finance or banking or anything that would've put me behind a desk in a stable, albeit staid, office somewhere safe and predictable.

But that's not what the Lord called me to do, and you don't do boring... If I'd followed that path, you'd likely never have paid me a moment's notice. I don't regret the career I've had or the life I've lived; I only regret we didn't have enough time to turn the page of our next chapter. Together. We were almost there — I could feel it; we were on the brink of something. Something perfect.

'Kenzee stopped reading and let her hand holding the letter fall to her lap. Suddenly, it seemed too heavy, the weight of it all too much. She needed a moment to process. She paused to take it all in.

He'd written this to her in case he died. Written that last part in past tense.

It was to be given to her when he was dead, but he wasn't. He couldn't be. She'd have known. Surely, after loving him throughout her entire life, she'd have felt his absence, no matter how far away he'd been when it had happened. A piece of her heart would've stopped beating with his. Bren was still alive; M'Kenzee would have it no other way.

She looked down at the letter. The words blurred on the page, but not because of tears this time. No, the air had a strange quality about it, a mystical haze that fused Bren's voice in the past, his absence in the present, and the future, so uncertain, yet so clearly defined, that M'Kenzee visualized every detail.

We were on the brink of something.

She'd felt it too. She'd grown tired and weary of pushing Bren away so he could find a better woman, someone easier to love, someone who deserved him. Too direct, too bossy, and too jaded, she'd never be an easy person, but if she loved Bren more than anyone else ever could, didn't that mean she would love him best?

She could also admit her disproportionate fear of his leaving had begun to mature into a more normal level of concern for someone whose job was dangerous. If only she hadn't been so stubborn, hadn't turned her back on her feelings so he couldn't be the one to leave, they could have stayed in touch when he was gone on missions and ops. Bren had communicated with Max with some regularity; if she'd not hidden their marriage, she would have enjoyed that direct contact, rather than desperately hoping Max would think to mention that he'd heard from Bren and share his updates. She hadn't done a great job of staying in touch with Max and Maree over the past few years, either — which neither deserved. But, too afraid to vocalize her fear of abandonment, staying in control of the leaving, being the one to leave before she could be left by someone else, had been the only survival mechanism M'Kenzee had known to employ.

Realization clicked into place; she'd grown out of that mindset. She'd felt the change occurring over the past year, when she'd been with her family more often because of Maree's car accident, subsequent knee surgery, and the months of recovery and rehab. As she sat on Max's patio in that moment, exhaustion set in at the mere thought of another photography assignment in a nether region of the world. The idea of sleeping on hard dirt in a tent or a hut had lost its appeal and made her yearn for her soft mattress and fluffy pillows, the smell of freshly laundered sheets and the vibrant colors of her favorite quilt. After a decade of trying to escape the risks associated with settling down in a place that could disappoint her, or being near people she loved so much they could hurt her, M'Kenzee Davenport wanted a home. A real one. With Bren.

She smiled faintly, refocusing on the letter as she lifted it — not nearly so heavy now — and continued reading.

So, yeah, I bought us a house.

M'Kenzee let out a nervous laugh. A house!

It's the three-story white Victorian on Main Street, the one that's been abandoned as long as

we've all been going to Green Hills. It caught my
attention the very first time I drove through town
on my way to meet you, Maree, and Max out at
Daisy Lake. Do you remember? That was a
great day!

She remembered. It had been a rare occurrence when she'd agreed to be where Bren was and even let down her guard, allowed herself to simply enjoy being. They'd played on the water, been lazy all afternoon, and then cooked out using the campfire stations and picnic tables at the lodge. The smell of their burgers and hot dogs had attracted other families and random strangers. Within a few minutes, an informal potluck had resulted as other visitors to the lakeside rental property began adding their own dinner dishes. When someone brought out a guitar, other instruments had appeared. One woman even had a fiddle in her RV. A teenage boy had pulled taped and aged wooden drumsticks from his backpack and flipped a plastic five-gallon bucket upside down to tap out a rhythm. M'Kenzee and Maree had sung while the musicians played. She recalled Bren commenting that he'd known Maree had an amazing voice, but he hadn't known M'Kenzee did too. Whereas Maree sang a crystal clear soprano, M'Kenzee had inherited their momma's rich, earthy contralto timbre. He'd said her voice was as unique and as rare as she herself…that he'd like to discover everything about her, including all her secrets. He'd said it in his own low, husky, very Scottish way, which had curled her toes.

But family had surrounded them all throughout the day, and then a horde of new friends all evening, so that brief conversation was as intimate as the day had grown. Perhaps that was why she'd felt safe in dropping her defenses? In the end, it hadn't mattered. As they'd been cleaning up the grill and putting away the leftovers, Bren had received a call from work that had him leaving without so much as a goodbye.

"Where's Bren going?" M'Kenzee had asked, trying to sound casual.

"He couldn't say," Max had answered. "But he did say to tell you he had fun today and that he hopes to be back before you head out on assignment. He said he'd be hearing you sing in his mind for a good long while," Max said with a laugh. "It's always fun to watch people's reactions when they hear you and Maree sing together!"

Then Max had followed Maree up to his cabin, Maree carrying a tray of dirty dishes and Max carrying a load of life jackets, beach towels, and a cooler. Neither had given M'Kenzee a second thought; no one had paid attention or noticed that, again, she'd been left alone.

But it had been a good day, one Bren had obviously held on to fondly. M'Kenzee determined she could do the same, and with a quick cleansing breath, she found her place on the page once more.

The next time I drove into Green Hills, I noticed a For Sale by Owner sign in the window, not the front yard like you normally see. I think the seller wasn't quite sold on the idea of letting it go, so they'd only halfway advertised it was available. I called the number on the sign right then and left a message. The next morning, on my way out of town, the sign was down and the window was empty. I feared I'd scared them into keeping it.

But a few months ago, when I took Janie Lyn home after accompanying her to Georgia, there was another For Sale sign, this time with a brokerage logo and an agent's name and number on it. I signed a contract that day. Now it's ours. Yours.

I won't lie to you: it needs a lot of TLC. There's a fellow who owns the hardware store and lumberyard just outside Green Hills who can help you. His name is Jinx Malone; ask for him. We've talked, and he seems like a nice guy; he'll be a good friend and guide. With your eye for space, I can only imagine what you'll create there. I'm so sorry I'll not be there to transform it with you. I'd give anything to have been there for you.

M'Kenzee, my love, I don't remember a time when you weren't on my mind.

She heard his lilting brogue in her head. The way he rolled the *M* and *K* together to emphasize the *N*. She loved the way he said her name, so different from all the others who made her name sound brusque and choppy. Only Bren made her — and her name — feel smooth and beautiful.

I couldn't have explained it in elementary school, that feeling of needing to watch out for you like Max did, but with more urgency than a big brother. I'm embarrassed to tell you the thoughts and feelings I had about you in high school — yikes...

adolescence! By the time I finished college, I knew there'd be no one else for me but you.

Along the way of my days, that childhood friendship, adolescent crush, and teenage infatuation grew into love — a love so strong I rarely know what to make of it. A love so overwhelming I was scared to frighten you with it. My mistake was forgetting how incredibly strong you are. M'Kenzee, you can handle anything.

You'll handle this. And you'll love again. Do that — for me. Open your heart to someone and let them love you every day for the rest of your life, just the way you are.

There's an old Celtic blessing that says, "May God be with you and bless you. May you see your children's children. May you be poor in misfortune, rich in blessings. May you know nothing but happiness, from this day forward."

That is my prayer for you, mo ghràidh.
My love,
B.

16

There is no surprise more magical
than the surprise of being loved.
It is God's finger on man's shoulder.
Charles Morgan

"M'Kenzee," Max called out from the patio door. She remained stooped over the paper in her hand. "M'Kenzee. 'Kenz!" The demand in his last attempt finally turned her attention Max's way.

His heart cracked at the desolate pain on her face when she looked up at him, as if she'd gotten lost and still didn't have her bearings. Max had never seen her so forlorn. She liked to be in charge, in control. The moment revealed a foreign side of his strong, dominant sister, not good or bad…just different.

"It's snowing."

"What?" M'Kenzee still seemed to claw at the surface of her sorrow, trying to break through.

She'd been out there for hours, hadn't even noticed when Maree wrapped another blanket around her. Nor had she touched the thermos of hot tea Janie Lyn placed on the small table next to the chaise lounge where M'Kenzee sat.

"Come inside," Max said. "Before you get everything wet with snow."

M'Kenzee looked up at the snow flurries. Then she closed her eyes and let her face catch and absorb the light flakes.

For heaven's sake.

Max trudged out in the weather to retrieve M'Kenzee and *whatever* had kept her so engrossed all day. He gathered the box, closing the lid and tucking everything under his arm. He pulled M'Kenzee to her feet, huddled her under his free arm, and nudged her toward the house.

"I didn't know. It's snowing," she marveled.

"Yes, it is," he muttered. "And the temperature dropped about twenty degrees in the last half hour. Janie Lyn and Maree cooked dinner. It's almost finished. Come warm up by the fireplace so you can eat."

The spicy aroma of Mexican Cheese Soup — one of Max's favorites — and the crackle of wood popping in the fire greeted them.

"Looks like we might have a white Christmas," he announced, shaking his head to scatter the droplets of snowflakes that had fallen on him. Without releasing his hold on M'Kenzee, Max set the metal box on the coffee table and moved a wingback chair closer to the hearth. Then he deposited M'Kenzee in the chair, quilts still wrapped around her, and fingers still clinched tight on the paper she held and would not relinquish when he'd tried to put it in the box before he closed it up.

Maree brought M'Kenzee a new mug of hot tea. She had more luck retrieving the letter than he'd had and swapped the paper for the warm ceramic, wrapping M'Kenzee's hands around the cup before adjusting the quilts.

"You must be frozen solid," Maree clucked as she fussed over M'Kenzee.

"He bought us a house," M'Kenzee whispered.

Max dashed a questioning look at Maree, who simply shrugged.

He must've heard her wrong.

Maybe she's delusional. Or she's in shock. Or both.

Assured Maree had the mothering tasks under control, he retreated to the kitchen.

"I'm worried about her," he told Janie Lyn as she ladled soup into large bowls.

"She's doing great," Janie Lyn said, adding a dollop of sour cream, grated cheese, and diced avocado to each one before setting the bowls on large saucers. Max took just a second to appreciate how homey and nice Janie Lyn made everything in their life. Before she came along, Max would've opened a can of store-bought soup, mixed it with water per the instructions, and zapped it in the microwave. Then he'd have eaten with a plastic spoon while sitting on the sofa. If he'd gone to the trouble to add crackers to the meal, he'd have set the sleeve of them on the table and eaten directly from the packaging. Now they used real plates, bowls, and silverware. They almost always ate at a table, one she'd set with cloth napkins and real glasses to drink from. She added class to his life while simultaneously making it more personal — more rewarding and enjoyable.

"I don't know. I'm afraid she's losing it," he said, sharing his thoughts aloud.

"She isn't losing it." Janie Lyn shooed away his theory. Then she continued proving him wrong as she frosted a large pan of cornbread with butter. "And while she may very well be in a little bit of shock, I'd say she's handling everything beautifully." Without pausing, Janie Lyn sliced the corn bread into thick squares and tucked two pieces next to the soup bowl on each plate. "She's going through a lot of emotions right now: publicly admitting her feelings for Bren, confessing they've secretly been married — for almost three years, no less — and dealing with the terrifying fact that no one has heard from him in a week. Indeed, I'd say she's doing absolutely incredible." The longer she spoke, the more passionate she became. The more passionate she became, the deeper her Southern drawl. Without fail, that accent did a number on him. "Now" — which came out *nay-ow* — "add a couple of those taquitos to the plates while I get the TV trays out of the hall closet."

"You get the taquitos, and I'll get the trays. Are we eating in the living room?"

"Yes, close to the fire. I think M'Kenzee can use the creature comforts of home. We all can."

He set two wooden stands in front of the couch, one in front of the empty recliner, and one in front of M'Kenzee, who perched on the edge of her overstuffed chair, staring into the dancing, crackling flames.

"You okay?" He kneeled to the side of her chair, looking into her eyes.

She only nodded in response.

"Will you try to eat? At least a little to make Janie Lyn and Maree happy? For me?"

"Yes," she said softly. "And while we eat, I'll read you the letter Bren wrote to me."

"So you don't mind?" Max asked M'Kenzee after she'd read Bren's words to them. "About the house?"

"I probably would have if he'd just walked up to me and said, *I bought us a house, so you should move to Green Hills and fix it up for me.* But right now, I don't."

"And it's the big gingerbread house on Main Street?" Maree's eyes grew large as she asked, the wheels obviously turning in her head. Both his sisters had a knack for envisioning potential. They'd not yet stepped foot on the property, but he'd wager they both would have a ton of fun with it once they got their hands on the old structure.

"Yes, it's whimsical and charming. Or at least, it could be," M'Kenzee said. "It *will* be," she stated, correcting her word choice.

"Is that what you want? To live in Green Hills full time?" Janie Lyn asked with gentle wisdom.

"I think so," M'Kenzee admitted. "I've been struggling with the motivation to work abroad for a while. In fact, I turned down the last three offers I received. I just couldn't muster the energy and excitement it takes to live like that for months at a time. The last assignment would've meant being in Alaska for three months. Five years ago, I would've jumped at the chance to go, but lately I haven't felt the draw. Honestly, I've enjoyed being where y'all were this fall. So, yeah, this is what I want."

Contentment washed over M'Kenzee's face; Max liked the way it softened her sharp edges.

"You can stay at our house in Green Hills for as long as you like, to be sure of everything," he offered, not wanting her to rush into anything. She'd worked very hard to make a prestigious name for herself as a world-renowned photographer. He didn't want to see her throw that out on a decision made during such a stressful time.

"Thank you, but I'm going to stay at my house. Our house. The one Bren bought."

Max and Maree exchanged glances, questioning if this was a good idea. If the mission to find Bren switched from rescue to recovery, M'Kenzee living in a house he'd never return to might not be wise.

"Are you sure? If—"

"That sounds lovely," Janie Lyn interrupted him with a

pointed look. "It'll be quite an adventure. Now, if you get there and it's not quite habitable, or the contractors say they'd prefer you not live in an ongoing construction project, promise us you'll use the house in Foxtail?"

"Of course," M'Kenzee promised.

Perhaps his words had been on a path paved with good intentions, yet not actually all that helpful.

The strength of a good man is a wise woman. Amen to that!

Max watched Janie Lyn as she continued talking with M'Kenzee, asking questions that kept M'Kenzee talking, so she couldn't withdraw from them. So she wouldn't feel alone.

Janie Lyn must've felt his stare. She looked up at him, a questioning tilt to her chin and a focused wrinkle between her eyes. *I love you*, he mouthed.

He was rewarded with her immediate blush, a flush of peach and pink tinting her cheeks, while light gleamed in her pale green eyes. Warmth flooded his chest. He was truly a lucky man.

"What else is in the box?" Maree asked.

"I'm not sure," M'Kenzee answered. "I didn't make it past the letter on top. I just read it again and again, trying to memorize the words."

"Would you like company while you look?" Maree offered with kind compassion.

"Yes," M'Kenzee whispered, "I think I would. I can't imagine what we'll find."

"I'll clear these dishes. It won't take but a minute," Janie Lyn said, sliding from behind her TV tray and rising to gather plates and silverware. "Max, can you add more wood to the fire?"

"I can help you, Janie Lyn," Maree volunteered, also standing to collect her dinnerware.

"Me, too," M'Kenzee said.

A surge of pride flooded through Max. Bren wasn't wrong:

M'Kenzee was incredibly strong, and she could handle this, no matter what news they received.

*L*ess than thirty minutes later, the four of them sat around the coffee table, Bren's love box placed on it in front of M'Kenzee. Just as earlier that afternoon, she took a deep breath to summon strength and then opened the lid to be greeted again by Bren's scent.

Expecting it that time, the moment didn't overwhelm her senses. Instead, she relished it.

M'Kenzee folded the letter she'd read to her family and slid it back into its envelope. She set it on the table, facedown beside the box to begin a stack that would keep the box's contents in their original order.

She picked up a manila folder; a neat computer-printed label on the extended tab read 401 E. Main Street. M'Kenzee opened the file folder; brads held documents on both sides. The closing documents for their house, a copy of the deed the title company had filed with the county, and a recent survey of the property took up the left side. On the right lay a printout for each utility account Bren had opened — trash pickup and water from the City of Green Hills, electricity, gas, and even a quote and signed agreement for yard maintenance. Behind those was a loose envelope, one from the local bank, which contained a signature card, checkbook register, and a debit card in her name. *M'Kenzee Stewart.* She ran her fingers over the raised letters, marveling that he'd thought of everything.

"While I've been sullen and pouting these past few months, angry that I couldn't have the life I wanted because Bren always walked away from me, he was establishing a foundation for just that life. And I had no clue."

She continued to stare down at the plastic card.

"He loves you very much," Janie Lyn pointed out.

. . .

"Is that one of our second-grade spelling books?" Max reached for the next item in the box. They'd all used that same style of composition book throughout school — the kind with a thick marbled camouflage cover and lined pages inside — but Max recognized the unique construction paper label taped to the front of that one: *Brennigan Stewart, Ms. La Mare - 18*. With a last name starting with D, Max still remembered he'd been number seven on the class roster. Both boys had suffered a bit of a crush on their kind and welcoming homeroom teacher. She'd been so nice and pretty, and she'd made school lots of fun — hands down, their favorite year of elementary school. Max also remembered hearing Momma talk about Ms. La Mare to one of the other moms at a PTA meeting. She'd said that Ms. La Mare took the time to ensure every child she taught bloomed, that Ms. La Mare encouraged her students to love learning. He hadn't understood it completely, but looking back, Momma had been right: he and Bren and all their friends had blossomed into gifted learners that year.

Holding the notebook brought back wonderful memories: the books they'd enjoyed that year, like *Hank the Cowdog* and all of Matt Christopher's sports stories, he and Bren being partners for their science experiments — in particular the time they'd made Kool-Aid rock candy and when they'd incubated eggs to hatch baby chicks — and Career Fridays when grownups came to read a short story to the class before sharing what they did and letting the kids ask all kinds of random questions about their jobs. Those guest speakers had been inspiring and life-changing for Max; listening to college and professional athletes and coaches that year had opened Max's eyes to the possibility of becoming one himself. Max hoped Ms. La Mare knew what a tremendous impact she'd had on her students over the years.

"It is," Max exclaimed, flipping the first few pages to see Bren's youthful script in crayon and pencil, where he'd written word lists, then practiced them in sentences, drilled them three times each, and on a clean sheet, taken his weekly spelling test. "This is awesome." A nostalgic fondness made him smile.

"Can I see?" M'Kenzee asked, holding out a hand toward the book.

"It's really neat," Maree said. "But why'd Bren put it in the box?"

Max wondered the same thing.

M'Kenzee didn't answer, just continued turning the pages, scanning Bren's second-grade progress.

Several pages in, she found a yellow sticky note. Mrs. Stewart had placed it on the page so it extended above the edge just a tiny bit.

Brennigan, I think you'll want to have this someday ♥ *Mom*

M'Kenzee pressed her fingertips against her lips.

"Oh," she whispered.

17

"A Dream Is a Wish Your Heart Makes"
Song written and composed by
Mack David, Al Hoffman, and Jerry Livingston
for the Walt Disney film Cinderella (1950)

Wednesday, November 26, 1997

dinner dinner dinner
turkey turkey turkey
stuffing stuffing stuffing
sweet potatoes
sweet potatoes
sweet potatoes
pumpkin pie
pumpkin pie
pumpkin pie
football football football
family family family

friends friends friends
happy happy happy
Thanksgiving
Thanksgiving
Thanksgiving

   1. Tomorrow is Thanksgiving.
   2. Mom is making turkey and stuffing.
   3. I like pumpkin pie.
   4. After we eat I can play football with Max.
   5. I am happy M'Kenzee will be there.

"If that's Bren and Max with the football, then that's you with the long yellow hair and the pretty dress. That makes me the crying baby he drew to the side." Maree mocked outrage as she hugged M'Kenzee with one arm. M'Kenzee hadn't noticed her sister looking over her shoulder.

"Well, if the shoe fits," Max insinuated.

"I was not a crybaby!" Maree had a flair for the dramatic when the situation called for it. M'Kenzee couldn't help laughing at her, which felt good, and she figured that had been Maree's goal.

"Are there more?" Janie Lyn asked.

M'Kenzee flipped the pages, scanning the spelling words, skimming the sentences, and smiling at the childlike drawings.

"Not until Christmas, his letter to Santa..." Her voice trailed off as tears sprang to her eyes.

Would they never stop coming?

Friday, December 19, 1997

Dear Santa,

I think you are Mom or Da, but Ms. La Mare says we still need to write a letter.

She said it's important to share our wishes and hopes and dreams with other people. She made us watch Cinderella, too, so we could hear the song about dreaming. I didn't mind, though. M'KenZee loves Cinderella.

I took the picture of her dressed up like Cinderella at Disney World off the refrigerator. I used a painting from art class to cover up where Mom had it under the Mickey Mouse magnet that Mrs. Davenport brought home for Mom after their vacation.

I hope that doesn't put me on the naughty list. I just wanted to keep the photo. M'KenZee looked pretty dressed up like a princess. She always looks pretty.

Max says his sisters bug him, but he only says that because he gets to be around them all the time. He really loves them. And I think they are okay. Especially M'KenZee. Max is lucky to have them. It's boring being an only child.

That's what I want for Christmas — a baby brother or sister. Surely if Mom or Da are Santa, they can get us another kid.

I already have everything else I need, so a baby will be great.

Merry Christmas,

Bren

PS: In case you aren't my parents, if you're God or someone, thank you for my family and my friends. They are the best!

She looked up and shared a gracious smile with her family.

They are *the best.*

M'Kenzee had exhausted her emotional bandwidth. She closed the book and hugged it to her chest as she stood.

"That feels like a good stopping place for tonight; I'll save the rest, maybe for tomorrow."

"That's a good idea," Max agreed, flipping through the rest of the items in the box. "There are quite a few notebooks and spirals. That's a lot to read through."

"But no rush to get through them," Janie Lyn pointed out sweetly. "What a treat to take your time enjoying Bren's thoughts."

M'Kenzee swallowed a lump of nerves and nodded.

"I think I'll head to bed," she announced. She hugged each of them good night, but she didn't release the book, clutching it close to her heart.

"Tomorrow is Christmas Eve," Maree reminded them. "Movie night!"

"Sounds good." M'Kenzee tried to sound normal, even excited about their family tradition of watching *White Christmas* together, but her tone came out more hopeful than eager.

That was okay, though. Hope was good. She wouldn't lose hope.

. . .

*A*fter a fitful night of not much sleeping, M'Kenzee made her way to the kitchen. She looked a fright and needed a shower, but the smell of breakfast wafting to her bedroom had been a beacon of light in her groggy, sleep-deprived state.

"Do I smell cinnamon rolls?"

"That you do," Janie Lyn answered with a big grin. "*Not* the breakfast of champions, but it's become Max's favorite... I'm certain the team nutritionist wouldn't be too happy." She placed a huge pastry on a plate and set the plate on the bar for M'Kenzee. "But he's really hard to say no to," Janie Lyn added with a stage whisper. "Just don't tell him I said so. Pretty please?"

"Your secret is safe with me," M'Kenzee promised. "Although you might not be fooling anyone. It's pretty obvious you like him." M'Kenzee shared a commiserating shrug with her beautiful sister-in-law, so very grateful Max had found this incredible partner to share life with. She and Bren had received that gift, but in hiding their love from one another, they had denied the blessing and wasted their time. M'Kenzee would do just about anything to have that opportunity back.

"Breakfast looks delicious. Thank you," M'Kenzee said, pouring herself a glass of orange juice to go with the sweet roll and settling onto a barstool to eat where she could easily chat with Janie Lyn, who was chopping onions and green chilis on a large cutting board. "Where is he? Has Max already left for the football facility?"

"Yes, he had film and meetings this morning. They have a walkthrough practice this afternoon. And Maree is shop-hopping her favorite fabric stores around town. Should we wager on which of them will make it home first?"

"Max at football and Maree at quilt shops? It's a toss-up if either will *ever* return." She said it jokingly, but immediately sobered when her own words hit home. Janie Lyn immediately looked up, a strangled expression on her face. A stab of pain in M'Kenzee's chest forced her to place the fork in her hand back down on the plate.

"Oh, honey," Janie Lyn said, setting down the veggies and knife. She stepped around the workspace of the island to engulf M'Kenzee in a hug. "He's coming home; I just know it."

She held M'Kenzee tight, which helped to keep her upright. She might've crumpled to the floor without the staunch support.

"I know," she whispered before lifting her forehead from Janie Lyn's shoulder and straightening from Janie Lyn's kind embrace. She swiped her cheeks and tried to resettle her nerves. "I believe that, too."

Janie Lyn squeezed her hands in reassurance before returning to her task.

"What are you making?" M'Kenzee asked.

"Mmmm, layered beef enchiladas. Another of Max's favorites."

"Did you think it was weird when he told you we always have Mexican food for Christmas, rather than ham and turkey with all the traditional sides?"

"No, not too weird. Pops was just the same, could only do Thanksgiving foods once a year, so he liked to have steaks for Christmas dinner. He'd fix them on the grill while Gram and I prepared a feast of salads and sides. Of course, with the bakery, we had every dessert imaginable on hand. It's difficult to fathom the amount of baking we did leading up to the holidays."

"Yes, the famous Lyndale Christmas Cakes. What's happening with those this year?"

"Well, as you know, I closed down operations at the bakery

when Bren took me to Georgia for my Uncle Stanton's hearing in October. It was sad, but it was the right thing to do. Since then, a young couple purchased the building and is running a modern twist on a traditional tearoom out of it. I've heard they have a steady business of breakfast and lunch patrons and a frozen food menu for customers to purchase dinner casseroles that only need to be heated when they get home. It's brilliant, and I pray it will be as prosperous a business for them as the bakery was for Gram and Pops all those years.

"The restaurants, grocery stores, and gift shops that contract to receive our Christmas cakes each December weren't thrilled that they'd not be receiving any product this holiday season, but I sweetened the deal for next year. Sadly, the entire world seems to know about my family's drama. But that also made them more understanding…as long as I promised that they'd have Lyndale Christmas Cakes again in the future."

"And will they? Are you going to reopen the bakery?"

"Well, yes, but it's going to be quite different than it was," Janie Lyn hedged.

M'Kenzee raised an eyebrow, giving her an inquisitive look.

"I have a plan — with Mary Beth," Janie Lyn confessed. "We're buying an old warehouse less than five minutes outside Green Hills. It sits about a hundred yards off the road, so you've likely seen it a hundred times and driven right by. It's been sitting empty for a long time, and recently it was damaged in a fire, so we're in the beginning phases of applying for permits to repair and rebuild it. We'll make the warehouse a commercial bakery and kitchen, and we have plans to build a restaurant and a barn for retail space on the property, right between the warehouse and the highway. We're going to call it The Christmas Collection." Janie Lyn glowed with excitement.

"So, you — Max's brilliant, gorgeous, and fierce new wife — are going into business with Mary Beth Carmichael —

Max's brilliant, gorgeous, and fierce ex-girlfriend? That's quite a strategy… Keep your friends close and your enemies closer, huh?"

"Oh, no. It's nothing like that," Janie Lyn laughed, waving off the notion that Mary Beth could ever be an enemy. "Maxwell never felt that way about Mary Beth — they really didn't date for more than a week or so. She's been such a wonderful friend to us both. I just adore her!"

"So, Lyndale Christmas Cakes will be back with a vengeance next year? What else will The Christmas Collection consist of?"

M'Kenzee enjoyed listening to Janie Lyn go on about their plans. Janie Lyn had a knack for storytelling; M'Kenzee easily envisioned the kitchen with its bakery counter and soda-shop-style interior, the restaurant with its inviting atmosphere and savory comfort foods, and the gift shop stuffed full of Christmas decor, artificial trees and baskets of ornaments, barrels of ribbons and holiday picks, and the upstairs section of quilts and holiday fabrics that Maree had agreed to help curate and maintain. It would be fabulous, and it would bring a healthy caravan of shoppers to Green Hills just in time to help the local economy surge through the winter.

"Have you thought of planting a tree farm?" M'Kenzee blinked rapidly; her question surprised them both.

"Well, no. But it's a fantastic idea," Janie Lyn pondered. "Perhaps with a clearing for picnic tables where we could serve wassail and hot chocolate?"

"What about setting up a food truck? And music… Christmas carols and holiday jingles all year long? We could line walking trails with pine needles to connect the buildings and the tree farm, then people could come out for walks and to take pictures. Talk about the perfect backdrop for holiday card photos. I could help you with props to create a new setting each year." M'Kenzee's photographer's imagination and party-planning skills kicked into high gear. "Oooh, a vintage rolled-arm sofa upholstered in red velvet, positioned in front of evergreen trees." Her eyes, larger than saucers, met Janie Lyn's, which were full of joyful anticipation.

"And a quilt," they added in unison, which made them giggle.

"Yes, Maree will demand there be a stunning quilt in each photo," M'Kenzee conceded.

"Oh, M'Kenzee, you simply have to sign on to join us," Janie Lyn begged. "Can you imagine it?" Rapture filled her voice. "Of course, you can. You have such a gifted eye for beauty and the talent to create it. You'll be a tremendous asset, and we would love to have you on board."

"It sounds lovely, Janie Lyn," M'Kenzee said. "I would be honored to be part of it, if you'll have me."

"Of cour—"

"And before you say yes, you need to know I'm awful to work with. I'm controlling and bossy, and I like to have things my own way. I'm a terrible leader because I steamroll through things, forgetting to stop and have fun along the way. And I'm a terrible worker because I think I know it all and just like to do it all myself. Ask Max and Maree, and now Miss Sadie and Landry, after we put your reception together in less than two days. They'll all tell you: I'm truly *the worst*."

"I refuse to believe it," Janie Lyn countered. "And we will all be very intentional about boundaries within projects and duties and roles. I'm certainly not caving on my vision and ideas for the bakery. I'm sure Mary Beth feels exactly the same about the restaurant, and Maree will have her way with the fabric area and quilt displays. You will have total control of the farm and the event center."

"Event center?" M'Kenzee asked; she'd missed that in Janie Lyn's description.

"It just came to me…a stable. We'll need an indoor area

for parties and showers and gatherings. I think a stable might be just what the space needs."

"Yes, with carriage horses and a sleigh for rides across the grounds." M'Kenzee could see it, too.

"I think I need to call our real estate agent to see about purchasing more of the land around the warehouse," Janie Lyn stated. "I wanted to wish her a merry Christmas anyway. I think I'll ring her now. This is going to be phenomenal," Janie Lyn announced as she rinsed and dried her hands before reaching for her cell phone on the counter.

"While you do that, I think I'll grab a shower. Then I'm going to read through Bren's notebooks. I'll just camp out in the theater room, out of the way. But please, holler if I can help you do anything."

"I will, M'Kenzee," Janie Lyn promised, "as long as you will do the same. Take your time. Let his words bring you comfort." Then she set her phone back down to give M'Kenzee one more hug.

How do people survive moments like this without the love and encouragement of family?

M'Kenzee prayed she'd never have to find out.

18

I find as I grow older
that I love those most whom I loved first.
Thomas Jefferson

Curled up in an oversized leather chair, M'Kenzee lifted another childhood journal to her nose. The waxy odor of old crayons took her back to their elementary school. They'd been the Cubs — purple and white — and she clearly remembered wearing her khaki jumper over her white three-button polo with tall socks, adorable saddle oxfords, and two wide purple ribbons tied at the end of her French braids on the first day of kindergarten.

She'd been a nervous wreck, but after Momma had dropped them off, Max and Bren had walked her all the way to her homeroom class, helped her put her backpack in her cubby, and showed her where to leave her lunch box on the table by the door.

"Max, Bren, it's great to see you," M'Kenzee's teacher, Mrs. Tara, had gushed over the boys, whom she'd had in class three years earlier.

"Hi, Mrs. T," Max said with gusto. "This is my little sister, M'Kenzee; she's in your class."

"Well, hello, M'Kenzee. I'm excited to have you in my homeroom this year. We're going to have a lot of fun in kindergarten," she said with a wink and a conspiratorial smile.

M'Kenzee had nodded solemnly, then added, "Yes, ma'am. I'll behave; I already promised Momma."

"I know you will," Mrs. Tara said with a level of certainty M'Kenzee didn't share.

"You good?" Max had asked, ever the protective big brother.

"Yes, I'm going to talk less and listen more, just like Daddy said."

"Mrs. T's the best," Bren chimed in. "You're going to do great." His encouraging smile had fortified her confidence.

Everyone survives kindergarten, right?

Friday, March 6, 1999

Dear M'Kenzee,

I'm bored on the flight to Scotland to visit my grandparents, and I forgot to take my school journal out of my backpack, so I thought I could write you a letter.

I'm sorry Max didn't pick you first at recess today. If one of us had to be on Terk-the-Jerk's team, I wish it would've been me instead of you. Everyone calls him that for a reason. I'd sure like to put him in his place someday.

When I get home, I want to know what you told him. His cheeks were redder than a tomato when he walked away from the mound. Whatever you said, it was great.

I wish y'all were coming with us to Braemar. It's really cool there. My grandparents have a lot of land, and there are tons of places to explore. I think you'd have fun taking pictures.

It's gonna be boring without you there. And Max, too.

I thought y'all were coming. But then Mom and Da started acting kinda strange. And when I asked why y'all couldn't come anymore, they told me to "go on." I hate it when they say that. What kind of an answer is "go on" anyway?

While I stay at Granda and Nan's, they're going to London for some big meeting. That sounds even more boring, so I'm glad I get to hang out with Granda and Nan.

You'd love them.

I guess I'll see you next week.

Have a fun Spring Break, M'KenZee.

B.

———

Saturday, August 21, 1999

Dear M'KenZee,

Thank you for marrying me today.

I really needed those tickets, and you're the only girl I would ever marry.

The whole carnival was so fun! I beat Max on the pillow fight balance beam and threw faster at the pitching booth, but he scored better than me at putt-putt and the basketball toss. Your dad said it was because we are two peas in a pod — whatever that means.

I hope you kept our marriage certificate and our photo. You looked real pretty in it.

B.

———

Sunday, August 22, 1999

Dear M'KenZee,

I don't know what to say. I wish we could go back to yesterday at the carnival.

I just woke up and went to the kitchen to get a bowl of cereal. Mom was crying so much, and Da had been, too. It scared me to ask what was wrong. Now I wish I hadn't. I wish we could just go back.

I'm so sorry. I can't imagine what I'd do if my mom and da died. Who will take care of you and Max and Maree? I don't understand.

Da says you are okay, but you're still in the hospital for another day because your head hit the window so hard in the crash. He said Max and Maree are fine, too. But not your mom and dad. They're gone. Just gone. I hate that.

Mom just said we're leaving for the hospital. I'll see you soon.

B.

———

Tuesday, August 24, 1999

I'm so glad y'all are moving in with us. I stink at drawing, but I made this for you. To cheer you up a little. I hope it makes you smile.

———

Thursday, November 25, 1999

Dear M'KenZee,

I know you were sad today. It must have been hard to be without your parents on Thanksgiving.

You were so brave. You are always brave. Sometimes I worry, even get scared I can't fix something or take good enough care of someone. But you never do. You're the most courageous person I know.

We were awesome playing football — Max was so mad when we won!

He's asleep now. He always falls asleep first in our room. I like that, though. It gives me time to think. And to write.

It was a great day.

Mom's turkey and dressing were so good. I almost made myself sick on the candied sweet potatoes and buttermilk chess pie.

I had fun playing Monopoly when it started raining.

And I had fun looking at your pictures.

I always have fun with you.

I hope you know that,

B.

———

Friday, December 10, 1999

Dear M'KenZee,

I think everything is falling apart, and I don't know what to do.

When we got home from school, I saw Mom crying in her bedroom. I think she's been crying a lot lately. Her eyes are puffy and red all the time. I've been asking for weeks, but she and Da say there's nothing for me to worry about.

That means there's something for them to worry about, so something is wrong.

After dinner tonight, when we were supposed to be taking turns getting baths, I heard Mom and Da arguing with someone on the phone, saying that this is your home. Yours and Max's and Maree's. Mom was so mad. Not at Da, but at the person on the phone. She yelled, "You can't take them. We are their family!"

I don't understand what's going on, but I'm scared. I don't want you to leave. I love having you and Max and Maree here. It's not lonely or boring anymore.

You belong here. With me.

I'm praying,

B.

Wednesday, December 22, 1999

Dear M'Kenzee,

The day your parents died was the worst day of my life.

This is the second worst day.

We're flying to Scotland for Christmas break. Mom and Da have more meetings in London, and I'm going to be by myself at Granda and Nan's. I don't even want to go.

Not after they came today to take your things.

I tried to tell the lady to be careful with your camera, but the policeman with her pushed me out of the guest room that is yours and Maree's. Mom sat on the ottoman in the front den and pulled me onto her knees. I felt her crying with her forehead against the middle of my shoulders. I wanted to make her feel better, but I'm really mad at her, too.

Why would Mom and Da let people take you away? How can they do that?

I know y'all want to stay with us. I don't understand why the judge said "No." I don't understand any of this.

Da says we're fighting it. I don't know what "it" is, but I want you back home.

He promised that y'all will still be at school when we get back in January. He also said that Max refused to let you and Maree go with different families. Max must've argued a lot because Da said that one of the foster families finally agreed to take all three of you together.

I'm glad that if you can't be with us, at least you are together.

Try to have a good Christmas.

I miss you,

B.

19

———

Absence is a house so vast
that inside you will pass through its walls
and hang pictures on the air.
Pablo Neruda

Those days felt like yesterday, the good and the bad, both vivid in her mind.

Reading Bren's journal entries — his letters to her interspersed amidst math problems, more spelling lists, and writing assignments — created heavy tidal waves of memories that washed over her with a pounding rhythm, refreshing and overwhelming. Despite their losses and hardships, the Davenport kids had been loved and watched over. They'd had good times, exceptional moments, and rich blessings. They'd all three succeeded…graduated high school with honors, earned degrees from college, and found careers that provided all they needed and kept them close together.

If Max had raised a ruckus of epic proportions each time the system tried to separate them, so what? That hardheaded fortitude had also served them well, developed them into strong, capable people, a family not easy to walk over.

They'd made it through the hard parts. They'd found love. Now if only they could all three grab hold of their happily ever after.

"Ready for a late lunch?" Janie Lyn ducked her head into the upstairs theater room M'Kenzee had been inhabiting for hours.

"Sure, I'll be right down."

"No need — I brought it up." Janie Lyn came through the doorway with a large tray in her arms. Glasses of sweet tea, dessert napkins with a large homemade chocolate chip cookie on top of each, two cloth napkins, two forks, and two plates piled with grilled cheese sandwiches, chips, and fruit salad took up every inch of the tray.

"My goodness," M'Kenzee exclaimed, hopping up and setting Bren's notebook aside so she could help with the heavy load. "That's more than lunch; it's a feast."

"Well, I expect it'll be a while before Maxwell gets home from work, so dinner might be late."

"You've adjusted quickly to the football lifestyle," M'Kenzee commented. "It's a lot. A lot of hours, a lot of stress, and a lot of, well, *everything*."

"I honestly had not known." Janie Lyn shook her head, but in agreement with M'Kenzee's assessment. "The world sees a ballgame on Saturday, Sunday, or Monday night and doesn't think of the time and devotion it took to play in it. Professional sports are glamorous and pay ridiculous salaries, but there is so much more to it than what spectators realize."

"That's true," M'Kenzee said, picking up half her sandwich. "And in today's world — with digital videography and instant retrieval — there is no end to the amount of prep work the players and coaches can do. And are expected to do. They could literally spend every second between the end of one game and the kickoff of the next studying opponents, breaking down tendencies, and picking out strengths and weaknesses. That's not even counting time for their own game planning, installation, practice, weightlifting, conditioning, and recovery exercises. I remember Max saying one time that they are behind on the next game before they kick off the current one."

"It can feel like a vicious cycle — maybe even a wobbly hamster wheel. That's for sure," Janie Lyn said with her Southern twang. "But I'm glad Maxwell loves what he does. We both know he'd work those hours and give that much of himself regardless of what job he did; how lucky that he loves every minute. Like Bren." She picked up a potato chip and slipped it into her mouth, obviously finished talking.

My turn, I suppose.

"You're a much better supporter of Max than I've been of Bren," M'Kenzee allowed. "I was so afraid of losing him that I never let myself — either of us — develop what was between us. I didn't feel jealous of his job so much as I was terrified of loving him, of what it would mean to lose him. And here I am, in the exact spot I was so scared to find myself."

"They're very honorable men, Maxwell and Brennigan," Janie Lyn said between bites of fruit. "Honorable men aren't always the easiest to love."

"I don't know," M'Kenzee countered with a shrug. "Loving Bren came pretty easy. In fact, it just happened naturally. I always enjoyed having him around, wanted to go wherever he and Max went, wanted to be close to Bren. Then I couldn't help but notice how cute he'd become in junior high and high school. I might've experienced several moments of infuriating anger when girls at school threw themselves at him or flirted without a modicum of self-respect. By the time he left for college, I knew I loved him. Bren is the only man my heart has tolerated — the only man I've ever wanted in my life. Except for Max, of course, but brothers don't count." M'Kenzee grinned at Janie Lyn. It felt good to share the load of feelings and fears and emotions she'd carried solo for so long.

"How're the books?" Janie Lyn looked toward the box. M'Kenzee had only made it through one more composition notebook.

"Slow, I guess. Hard to read," she said. "But also wonderful."

"Do you need a break?" Janie Lyn asked.

"Only if you need me."

"Not at all. I've been falling down the rabbit hole of researching printing companies for menus, graphic designers for branding, and builders for the construction and remodeling. I could happily stay burrowed in this part of the project for days…more likely, weeks!"

"Well, let me help you clean this up, and we can both jump back in." M'Kenzee slid her cookie napkin off the tray and set it on the coffee table beside her tea glass. "For when I need a little sugary sustenance," she said with a smile.

"Here, take mine so you'll have two," Janie Lyn offered. "I've got a huge Christmas tin full of them downstairs."

"Thanks, Janie Lyn. For lunch, for the cookies, for being here, and for being you."

"There's nowhere else I'd rather be." Janie Lyn said it emphatically, and M'Kenzee believed her.

Friday, January 7, 2000

Dear M'Kenzee,

This stinks!

There's nothing to do without you and Max and Maree here.

Mom's sick. She's hardly gotten out of bed or

come out of her room since we got back home last weekend. Just like before, Da keeps saying for me not to worry, that everything's going to be okay. But it's not.

Max was too quiet in class this week. His eyes look sad. He said he's afraid to let you and Maree out of his sight in the foster home, said some of the older kids are creepy and keep saying things to you they shouldn't. He's afraid to get in a fight with them — afraid they'll split y'all into different cottages or send you to separate families. But he can't let those guys get away with messing with you or Maree. He's so tired, and there's nothing I can do to help.

I'm sure not everyone there is bad. But it sounds like there aren't enough adults to handle all the kids, especially some of the guys that are in junior high but still fall in the age group with elementary school kids. It's just messed up. And Da said the judge won't let him and Mom come to the courthouse anymore. If they keep trying, the judge threatened to put my Da in jail for "contempt," but I don't even know what that is. Maybe I'll be a lawyer when I grow up so I can fix this broken system. Someone needs to!

Sorry I wrote so much. I'm just really, really mad.

B.

———

Saturday, March 18, 2000

Dear M'Kenzee,

I know why they took you away.

My mom is sick. Cancer. Da says it's in her "girl parts" like I'm a baby.

I'm not stupid. I know what the doctors are talking about when they said, "stage 4 cervical cancer...metastasized...experimental treatment as a last resort."

That's why the judge wouldn't let y'all live with us anymore. Mom was too sick to attend one of the court hearings, and when he found out, he said that having three extra kids was too much for her at this time.

But he's wrong. Having you and Max and Maree at home gave her strength. Y'all made her feel close to your mom — her best friend in the whole world — and that helped her. I wrote him a letter, but Da says it probably won't matter.

I'm tired of not being able to do anything to make the world better for the people I love.

And I miss you. And Maree. I never see you anymore.

Max said the foster family you're with right now might let him play baseball this summer. But that won't matter, either, because I think Da and

I will be in London all summer. Mom stayed there when we came back from Spring Break. She's in the hospital. My da's a mess. I think it was really hard for him to leave her there.

We only came back to Oklahoma so I can finish the school year. As soon as the semester ends, we are flying to Scotland, and Da is going straight on to England.

I asked Da why Mom can't be in the hospital here, but he said the treatment she needs isn't covered by insurance in the United States. He said it's a blessing that she qualifies to receive the medicine in the UK since we were all born there.

We've lived in America for a few years now, but Da says that doesn't change the fact that we're still Scottish citizens. Well, I guess I'm both: Scottish and American. It's called dual citizenship, and it means I can be in the United States military when I grow up. That might not be too bad. At least then I could make a difference. I just want to fix things so bad.

I will, M'Kenzee. I promise I will fix this.

B.

At the time, no one told M'Kenzee and Maree about Mrs. Stewart.

Bren's dad had talked to Max, explaining what was going

on. Then they'd decided together that the fear of losing another motherly figure would be too much for the girls. So M'Kenzee had lived with unwarranted and undeserved anger toward Bren's family, whom she believed had chosen to run off to Scotland instead of staying in Oklahoma, where she and her siblings would've had a place to live and be fully loved.

When she'd learned the truth several years later — when miraculously Mrs. Stewart had beaten cancer and gone into remission — M'Kenzee'd hated herself. How selfish could a person be? Spending all that time thinking the worst of someone who'd always, if at all possible, been there for her.

In embarrassment at her thoughts and behavior, M'Kenzee had vowed she didn't deserve their love. Nor had she had the courage to admit how she'd felt. Not knowing how to process such deep-seated, negative emotions, M'Kenzee had done the only thing that made sense to her: she'd invoked a self-inflicted sentence of denying herself the comfort and security of accepting love.

By the time her seventh-grade teacher took the time to read beyond the surface of her English papers and journal entries, M'Kenzee had matured enough to understand her reasoning was faulty. She comprehended that no one blamed a child for being angry at the world, a flawed world that had stolen her parents and then taken away the only other home she'd ever known.

But she'd already erected walls and armored herself with a sharp wit and a hard shell. Over time, those defenses had become part of her core self. She'd grown into an often-challenging, sometimes harsh person. She'd deemed herself unworthy of affection, and then she'd developed into a person no one could — or would want to — love. Her standards held unattainably high, everyone fell short of her expectations. M'Kenzee was slow to trust and even slower to love.

Throughout that first year of junior high, that teacher —

Coach Pendras — had spent an inordinate amount of time with M'Kenzee, mentoring her, getting to know her, even sitting with her in the cafeteria when no one invited her to their table for lunch. She'd encouraged M'Kenzee to take her photography to new levels by researching techniques, entering prints into contests. She'd even driven M'Kenzee to and from a weeklong summer photography camp in Oklahoma City that M'Kenzee had won a scholarship to attend.

Coach Pendras never explicitly told M'Kenzee that she'd done nothing wrong; that would have belittled M'Kenzee's self-perspective. Instead, the encouraging mentor had listened to M'Kenzee, validated her feelings, and acknowledged the root of those truths. Then she'd asked guiding questions that allowed M'Kenzee to see another side of the events that had occurred.

Their time together meant the world to M'Kenzee. When Coach Pendras called her the week before eighth grade began, M'Kenzee had answered, eager to talk about plans for the year ahead.

The conversation had taken a turn for the worst when Coach Pendras told M'Kenzee she'd be moving back to Texas to take care of her mom, who was suffering from heart troubles leading to vascular dementia, so she could no longer live alone. The local high school there had offered Coach Pendras a job teaching, and since caregiving would require so much of her time, she'd be giving up coaching.

M'Kenzee's heart had broken. Another loved one leaving. She'd understood, but it had stung.

Coach Pendras had promised to stay in touch — and she had. Their friendship had withstood the test of time *and* the test of M'Kenzee's doubts. Fifteen years later, they still spoke several times a year.

M'Kenzee might've maintained her theory that Coach

Pendras was the exception, not the rule, but either way, she had proven to M'Kenzee that some people stay.

Bren had stayed. He'd never given up on her. As awful as she'd been, he'd apparently loved her through every petty cold shoulder, every snide thought and comment, and every effort to keep him at arm's length. He'd never stopped loving her, returning to her over and over again.

Please, Lord, return him to me one more time.

20

You don't choose your family.
They are God's gift to you,
as you are to them.
Desmond Tutu

"Janie Lyn, you cooked, so I'll clean," Maree announced. "Go sit with Max and relax."

"I'll help; I sat all day. Standing for a bit sounds good," M'Kenzee said.

"I'll wash. You dry," Maree instructed.

"Oh no, little sister. I'll wash, and *you* dry."

"Hmm, Rhys never argues when I tell him to dry."

"That's because your fireman is putty in your hands." M'Kenzee bumped Maree's shoulder to emphasize her point.

"Maybe a little," Maree conceded with a shy shrug.

"When will Rhys be here?"

"He's leaving Green Hills around six in the morning to be here by lunch. I can't wait to see him. And wrap my arms around him," she said with hearts in her eyes. And then her eyes widened in alarm. "Oh, M'Kenzee, I'm so sorry." She set down the silverware she'd been drying and turned to her big sister. "I wasn't thinking. Please forgive me."

"Maree, you did nothing wrong," M'Kenzee promised her. "I'm glad you're excited to see your fiancé — you're supposed to be. And when Bren gets here, I intend to do the same. I might wrap my arms around him and never let go. I'm done pushing him away. My efforts to prevent us from hurting one another have done nothing but cause the pain I thought we could avoid.

"All I've accomplished is wasting time when we could've been building a life together. If he'll still have me, I'll gladly take whatever time he can spend at home. And when he leaves for work, I'll send him off with my love and support, encouraging and enticing him to be careful, so he can come back again safe and sound.

"I know you understand," M'Kenzee went on. "Rhys walking into burning buildings and crisis situations can't be any easier than Bren taking off for secret missions — especially with everything the fire department faces with this crazy arsonist in Green Hills."

"I can't believe that's been going on for so long…over a year and a half now," Maree commented, shaking her head and reaching for another plate to dry. "They're fairly certain who's responsible, and it's the saddest story. He's a war veteran who went off the grid when he accidentally injured a local teenager during an episode of PTSD. The boy was fine, just startled and bruised from Mr. Armstrong taking him down in a full-body tackle. That was back in 1994, twenty-five years ago."

"I remember Rhys and Davis talking about how things continue to escalate." M'Kenzee replied. "It was that night we were together for dinner at Rhys's place. You remember…the night Rhys proposed." M'Kenzee enjoyed teasing her. Maree grinned from ear to ear and ducked her head, so M'Kenzee gave her sister another gentle bump, hip to hip and shoulder against shoulder. They needed to enjoy the good bits, even — no, *especially* — amidst the crippling fear of the unknown they were up against.

Bren might be M'Kenzee's soulmate, the only man she'd ever opened her heart to, and her husband, but her siblings loved Bren, too. He'd become family long before he and M'Kenzee had gotten married — even that first time at the school carnival, all those years ago.

"Have you set a date for the wedding? Started making plans?" M'Kenzee would love to help, but she didn't want to overstep.

"Yes, I think so, but we haven't set anything in stone. If you're up for it, I was hoping you'd be my maid of honor *and* my wedding planner." She looked at M'Kenzee with a hopeful expression.

"Yes, of course! I'm honored to do both," M'Kenzee replied. "You're going to be the most beautiful bride."

"I can't wait," Maree confided. "I'm so ready to be Mrs. Rhys Larsen."

"Are y'all done yet?" Max hollered from the living room. "I've got the movie ready, and you're just standing in there talking."

"We're making the popcorn; we'll be right there," Maree called out to appease him.

Three minutes later, all four of them were snuggled under quilts on the couch, resembling sardines wedged into a tin.

"I swear we used to fit better," Maree pointed out, trying to shimmy her rear into a comfier spot.

"Maybe it's me." Janie Lyn squirmed her way to the edge of the cushion and stood. "I'll just sit over there."

"Oh no you don't," Max said as he wrapped an arm

around her waist and pulled her down. She landed halfway on his lap and half-stuffed in the couch's corner. "This movie is not about comfort; it's about tradition — family tradition. And you, Mrs. Davenport, are part of the family. You're stuck with us now."

"Foooor-evvvvv-er," all three Davenport kids said at the same time, in the same singsong way, before erupting with laughter.

"Wow," Janie Lyn said, quite entertained and happily accepting her fate. "I guess I'll stay right here, then." Janie Lyn smiled at Max with adoration.

"Does everyone have popcorn?" Maree asked, passing paper napkins down the sofa.

"Let's do this," M'Kenzee answered, pulling her knees to her chest and pulling a quilt to her chin.

Max hit play on the remote, and the opening message greeted them as it always had…consistent, never changing, just the same as when Momma and Dad were watching with them: *Paramount proudly presents the first picture in…*

"Vista Vision," the three siblings belted out with exuberance. As before, their singsong dramatics reverberated in perfect unison.

"Oh dear," Janie Lyn whispered, which made Maree giggle. And maybe made tears come to her eyes — not sad tears, but love tears, formed from a bond so deep there were no words to describe how much her family meant to her. Maree smiled a little larger and settled into the movie.

When Bob and Betty, and Phil and Judy, along with all the singers, dancers, and children, took the stage for the final number, when the sweet ballerina girl rose *en pointe*, and when "White Christmas" began, Max, M'Kenzee, and Maree reached for one another's hands and sang along.

When Janie Lyn didn't join in, Maree glanced over to

check on her sister-in-law. Janie Lyn hadn't made it through her first Christmas Eve showing. Snuggled against Max's chest, she'd fallen fast asleep.

When the couples on-screen snuck behind the Christmas tree to steal a kiss, Max placed one on the top of Janie Lyn's head, too.

And when *The End* appeared on the screen, Maree believed. It wasn't a fairy tale. Love would win, Bren would find a way home, and Momma and Dad would watch from heaven as their three children found peace on earth. *Thank you, Lord.*

"I better carry her up," Max said, shifting Janie Lyn into his arms as he stood from the sofa.

"Janie Lyn's been working too hard," M'Kenzee said. "Cooking three times a day for us, working on plans for the warehouse, and researching everything that will go into that big of a project— She's worn out."

"Something — or *someone*…a tiny someone, actually — might be adding to her fatigue," Max whispered with a sloppy grin plastered on his face.

"Wait—" Maree gasped.

"What?" M'Kenzee yelped.

"Shhh." Max tried to shush them. "If so, she's only a few weeks along, and she's afraid to tell anyone until she sees the doctor, but yeah… You two better get ready to be the Dynamic Aunt Duo."

"Oh, Max," Maree gushed, her hands clasped at her heart. "A honeymoon baby," she cooed. "I'm starting a crib quilt right away!"

"That news is the best Christmas present I've ever had, Max. Thank you," M'Kenzee said, her voice husky with emotion. "Thank you," she repeated.

He nodded once, told them he loved them, and carted his beautiful bride — now mother-to-be — up the stairs.

"Aunts," Maree marveled, wrapping her arms around M'Kenzee for a hug.

"I fully intend to spoil that kid rotten," M'Kenzee announced.

"Oh, yes! Absolutely," Maree agreed. "I can't wait."

It's the repetition of affirmations
that leads to belief.
And once that belief becomes a conviction,
things begin to happen.
Muhammad Ali

*H*e's alive. He's alive. He's alive, M'Kenzee repeated in her mind, staring out the large bay window in her bedroom at the night sky. *Bren's out there. Somewhere. We're under the same moon, the same twinkling stars. He's fine. He's safe. Soon he will be home.*

If she never stopped saying it, she'd never stop believing it, and eventually, her wishes would come true. Surely.

*T*he litany must've put her to sleep in the wee hours of the morning, because her alarm going off at 8 a.m. startled her into consciousness.

It took a second to put all the pieces of the day together…
It's Christmas — happy birthday, big guy.

We're going to Max's football game this afternoon.
Max and Janie Lyn are expecting a baby.
Maree is engaged; Rhys should be here in a few hours.
Bren is missing.
Nope, not going there. If ever there's a day for faith, this is the day…
I will be glad, and rejoice in it.

M'Kenzee glanced out the window to discover they were indeed having a white Christmas.

She tossed back the heavy covers and crawled out of the warm cocoon she'd formed around herself. Shivering in response to the chilly air, M'Kenzee made a beeline for the bathroom.

After another night of restlessness, a hot shower did wonders to clear the itchy redness from her eyes and the fog from her brain. She emerged from her room an hour later, feeling much better.

"Good morning," she said, greeting Maree and Janie Lyn as she walked into the kitchen. "Merry Christmas."

"Merry Christmas." Maree hopped up from the breakfast table to give M'Kenzee a hug.

Maree looked adorable in plaid flannel pajamas featuring a Christmas moose wearing a Santa hat and saddled with gift bags appliquéd across the front. Battery-operated twinkling Christmas tree earrings dangled to her shoulders, and she'd tied her hair into a messy bun with a gingerbread-printed scarf. Looking at the glow in her cheeks and the gleam in her eyes, one would never guess at the tragedy and trauma Maree had overcome in her twenty-six years.

"You're already dressed and ready, too," Maree said with a faux pout.

"What do you mean by *too*?"

"Max already left for the game," Janie Lyn filled in. "They

had to report at eleven, but you know Max… He has his game-day routine, and he's pretty particular about following it." She moved to fill a mug with steaming hot water for M'Kenzee and slid a tea caddy toward her. Then she grabbed a butter dish and a bowl of fruit from the refrigerator. "Will you grab the blueberry muffins for me?" She nodded toward the basket covered with a tea towel, from which came the heavenly scent of tart blueberries and cake-like muffins.

"You're doing too much," Maree objected, albeit helping herself to homemade muffins that promised to be quite scrumptious while voicing it.

"She's right," M'Kenzee piped up. "You don't have to cook and clean for us… Maree can do it."

"Ohhh!" Maree pretended outrage and threw her napkin at M'Kenzee.

"I'm just teasing," M'Kenzee laughed. "We're all capable of pitching in. You shouldn't exhaust yourself just because Max's game means we're spending Christmas week under your feet."

"Y'all are always welcome, and never underfoot," Janie Lyn said. "Max said he told you about the baby." Her voice took on a wistful reverence when she said *the baby*. "Oh, girls — I'm elated and excited and scared to death, all at once."

"You and Max will be the best parents," Maree vowed.

"I can see it now… a little mini-me with your thick dark hair and Max's sky blue eyes, waddling around the yard, chasing balls with Max and Hank, and following your every step in the kitchen," M'Kenzee predicted. "Yep, you two are going to have some ridiculously gorgeous children."

"I just pray they are happy, healthy, and successful, all throughout their lives," Janie Lyn wished aloud.

"Well," Maree interjected, "we are here for you and Max and those precious babies, every step of the way."

M'Kenzee nodded her confirmation and spread a healthy

pat of butter on each half of the two muffins she'd just sliced open.

"Have you heard from Rhys? What time do you think he'll be here, and what time do we need to leave for the stadium?" M'Kenzee asked around bites of her breakfast.

"He's on the road," Maree answered. "If the snow isn't too thick and the roads are okay, I think he'll be here around 10:30 or 11:00. He got a really early start. What time should we leave for the game, Janie Lyn?"

"Kickoff is at 3:05. Pregame starts ninety minutes before that. Let's plan on lunch at noon, and we can drive over when we've finished eating."

"Only if you promise not to cook. There are tons of leftovers in the fridge," M'Kenzee said as she finished her hot tea and scooted her chair back.

"Agreed," Maree said. "Are you going somewhere?" She looked M'Kenzee up and down, taking in her winter boots, tall hunting socks, and flannel shirt over a thick long-sleeved waffle tee. Then Maree looked over at the couch where M'Kenzee had tossed a heavy coat, wool headband, and her camera. Finally, she looked back at M'Kenzee, an eyebrow lifted with questioning interest.

"I figured we wouldn't open gifts until tonight, after the game and the candlelight service at church, so I thought I might go wander Kansas City a little, see what a white Christmas looks like here. Maybe even get some pictures." M'Kenzee shrugged at the end of her explanation.

"That's great," Maree exclaimed, obviously relieved that M'Kenzee felt like going out. On the other hand, Maree could've been equally happy to hear M'Kenzee wasn't taking off indefinitely this time. She didn't blame her little sister; she'd had a bad habit of doing that in the spur of the moment over the past few years, particularly when she'd been told they expected Bren to arrive.

God, I was a fool. Why'd You let me ruin both our lives?

"Have fun," Janie Lyn chimed in. "It's a great city, and this area — called the Brookside neighborhood — has an eclectic mix of new and old, wild and conservative, quiet and loud. You'll love it!"

"Sounds great! Where's Hank? I can take him with me."

"Bless you! He'll love that. He's pouting in our room since Max left him here this morning. I'll go get him and his leash." With that, Janie Lyn dashed up the stairs.

"I'm glad you're going to take your camera out; I can't wait to see what you shoot," Maree said, confirming M'Kenzee's suspicions with a shy smile, which was out of character for the boisterous and vibrant young woman. "I'm glad to see you getting out, period. I was worried you'd never set down those books from Bren. At least until he's home."

"I've only read through the notes and letters he wrote to me through junior high. They're sprinkled in school journals and spiral notebooks, amongst endless spelling and vocabulary lists, class notes, football plays, and about a million games of tic-tac-toe. There are maybe ten or twelve composition books and several spirals in there, with loose sheets of scrap paper, postcards, and thick letters tucked between them. Quickly skimming until I noticed my name on a page, I made it to the end of the second composition book yesterday. I have a long way to go to finish them all. Besides, Christmas is a day for being present, not stuck in the pages of a book or staring at a screen. I'll go back to reading the rest of Bren's letters when I get home tomorrow."

"Tomorrow?" Janie Lyn asked, coming down the stairs, Hank leading the way on his leash with a definite spring in his step.

"Yes, I'm headed to Green Hills tomorrow morning. I need to be there — in our house — when Bren arrives."

A concerned look passed between Janie Lyn and Maree.

"Does Max know you plan on leaving so soon?" Janie Lyn asked as she handed Hank over to M'Kenzee.

"I didn't mention it yet, but I'm sure he expects me to get started on the remodel and renovations. It's what Bren wanted, so it's what Max and I want, too."

"Of course," Janie Lyn said graciously, cutting off Maree, who'd opened her mouth to argue. "We'll get it all figured out."

"Exactly," M'Kenzee agreed, happy they'd gotten on the same page. "Let's go, Hankster. A winter wonderland awaits."

Standing on the front porch a few hours later, woman and dog both shook to scatter the snow off their coats. Then they stomped their paws — feet, in M'Kenzee's case — and opened the door in search of food.

The crisp, sunny weather had been just what M'Kenzee and Hank had needed, but now they were hungry.

"Well, hello," a deep masculine voice said to Hank when the large red cane corso charged into the room. M'Kenzee put the leash in the mudroom and turned the corner. She paused to take in the scene in front of her. The dog sprawled on his back, unabashedly providing his belly for Rhys to rub. Hank's big strong tail thumped the gray-stained hardwood floors with the force of an ax.

"Good grief. Have a little couth, Hank," M'Kenzee admonished him as she walked past, shaking her head at the scene.

"Hello to you, too, M'Kenzee," Rhys said, standing and walking to her, forcing her to face him.

"Hello, Rhys," she allowed, pretending annoyance. "Merry Christmas," she added with a genuine smile as she reached out to give him a hug. "I'm glad you made it."

"Me, too. And I know Bren will be here soon, just as

quickly as he can," he added quietly as he returned her embrace.

"Thanks," she said with a lump in her throat.

"Let's eat," Maree called from the dining room, where she'd set the table with reindeer-themed paper plates, red plastic cups, and a smorgasbord of leftovers and sandwich fixings. "I'm ready to get to the game. Y'all know… Max is undefeated on Christmas Day."

M'Kenzee looked at her in horror. Rhys slapped a palm against his forehead. Even Janie Lyn muttered a delicate, "Oh no." Then all three dashed to the wooden table to knock their fists three times against the grain.

"If they don't win today, it's all on you," M'Kenzee warned her as she piled cold cuts, cheese, lettuce, and tomato on slices of homemade bread. "Better you than me," she added, giving her little sister a doleful look and a half shake of her head, before taking a big bite of her lunch.

*L*uckily for Maree, there'd been nothing to fear. The dominance with which Max and his team had handled each week of the season held true for their Christmas game as well. After he'd scored three touchdowns, and with a thirty-one-point lead at the end of the third quarter, the coach pulled Max. The backups would finish the day, and the starters could rest for the final few weeks of the regular season to be healthy going into the playoffs.

Max had been quick to shower after the game, and then their group had enjoyed a light dinner at home before attending the candlelight service at Max and Janie Lyn's church in the city. As they sat amidst the large congregation, the singing — M'Kenzee's favorite part — had given her chills. The carols, the prayers, and the message filled her heart.

She said a prayer of thanksgiving for her blessings, and one of protection for Bren.

On the drive home from the church, M'Kenzee remembered to turn her phone back on.

Immediately, three texts pinged from three different senders. The three numbers were unique from one another, but they also showed up as strange patterns of numbers — several more than the usual ten digits.

"Max," she gasped in uncertainty. He was driving and talking to Janie Lyn in the front seat, so he didn't hear her. "Max," she repeated. The panic in her voice must've worried him. He pulled the truck to the curb and turned to look at her with concern.

She held her phone to him, fingers wobbly and shaking, tears flooding down her cheeks.

- *mo*
- *ghràidh*
- *b*

22

***The Lord is close
to the brokenhearted
and saves those
who are crushed in spirit.
Psalm 34:18***

"I don't understand," Max said, trying to remain level-headed.

"It means *my love*." M'Kenzee spoke slowly, softly. "In Scottish. And he signed every letter in those journals with a B."

"Bren's okay," Maree exclaimed, joy exploding across her face.

"Maybe," Max cautioned, not wanting to give any of them false hope, but particularly M'Kenzee, whose temper flared at his remark.

"He has to be," she countered in angry defense.

"I want that, too. Just as much as you do," Max reminded her. "But we need to call Agent Vela, let him run these numbers, see what they can find out. His card's at the house; I'll reach out to him as soon as we get there."

"Then go," M'Kenzee urged. "Now," she barked, prompting Max to pull the truck back into the flow of traffic. He drove home as quickly as possible.

"You can't leave tonight." Max ran a hand through his hair; talking sense into M'Kenzee felt at times akin to beating one's head against a brick wall. "It's Christmas, 'Kenz."

"What did Vela say?" She continued to half fold, half mangle clothes she'd yanked off hangers, stuffing them into her duffle bag.

"Stop," he commanded. "Take a breath." She looked at him with stabbing agony. "Come sit down so we can talk." He tugged a t-shirt out of her hand, tossed it onto the bed, and then wrapped his fingers around her wrist to pull her behind him, down the hall, and into the living room, where everyone else had gathered in front of the fireplace. The stockings hung on the mantel, the tree twinkled in the corner, and the gifts had been forgotten.

"I'm here," M'Kenzee huffed. "Now tell me what Agent Vela said. Please," she tacked on at the end.

"Promise you won't leave tonight," Maree begged.

"Fine. I won't leave tonight. But I'll be on the road first thing in the morning."

"Thank you," Max replied on the group's behalf. He joined Janie Lyn on the couch; M'Kenzee took a chair opposite the one Rhys and Maree were sharing. "It *is* Christmas. And this is where Bren would want you to be."

"*Wants*," M'Kenzee snapped, correcting him, and then pursed her lips. "This is where Bren *wants* me to be."

"That's what I meant." Max tried to reassure her, meanwhile maintaining his patience with her. He took a calming breath, thankful for the years of yoga that helped him channel stress. "Agent Vela reported back that the three phones you received texts from are African telephone numbers."

"I knew it," M'Kenzee declared.

Max continued without acknowledging her certainty. "He feels it's promising that you received them. Although, there's no way to know for sure that Bren sent them."

"What?" M'Kenzee sprang from her seat, arms thrown out wide. "Of course Bren sent them. Who else would send me a chain of texts that say *My love, B?* What an id—"

"M'Kenzee, calm down," Max instructed. "Please try to remember: we all want the same thing. Vela's doing his job… investigating the facts and *not* jumping to conclusions. Hopefully, Bren sent those messages. Vela said it would be a smart move to use different numbers, and Bren's a very smart agent. But he could also have begged, bargained with, or paid someone else to send them in his place — if something were to happen to him. It could just be a coincidence that you received them on Christmas." He trailed off.

M'Kenzee whipped her head up to shoot daggers at him through fuming eyes.

"Agent Vela's leading a special investigative task force to locate Bren. They're listening to chatter, gathering intelligence, looking for signs Bren is alive."

"I just gave him a sign that Bren is alive. Now they need to go get him." Her voice reflected anger, but her body language was pure desperation. "Please, Max." Her voice cracked. He'd have done anything to wipe away her imploring anguish.

But all Max knew to do was hold her, offer whatever support and sympathy he could.

He rose from the couch and walked over to her. He hugged her into his wide chest and refused to let go when she tried to pull away.

"They're trying, honey. I promise," he cajoled. "And we won't let them stop until Bren is home."

"So, now what?" Rhys asked.

"Now that there's the possibility of a lead, Vela's going to keep us updated daily," Max answered.

"And in the meantime," Janie Lyn added, "we pray — without ceasing."

23

When upon life's billows
You are tempest tossed,
When you are discouraged,
Thinking all is lost,
Count your many blessings,
Name them one by one,
And it will surprise you
What the Lord hath done.
Words by Johnson Oatman, Jr.,
in Songs for Young People (1897)

Thursday, December 26, 2019 — Somewhere along the Indian Nation Turnpike in southeast Oklahoma

M'Kenzee adjusted the tuner on the car radio. Then she did it again. Still not what she wanted to hear, so she tried a third station.

The snow had melted from the roadways so cruise control maintained the car's speed. That left M'Kenzee free to tap her foot against the floorboard, her body's attempt to expel nervous energy. Her knee bounced, doubling the tempo of the song…possibly jumping in triple-time.

Her hand tapped the armrest, fingers alternating up and down in constant movement.

When that didn't help, she gripped the steering wheel with both hands to force them still.

Ughhh! What is wrong with me?

The anxiety— Make that irritation— No, *agitation* fit better. The agitation had crept into her consciousness while she'd been enjoying a delayed Christmas celebration with her family in Kansas City before getting on the road to Green Hills.

First thing that morning, they'd gathered in the living room to open presents. Before they tore into the packages, Max had read the Christmas story from Luke 2:1–20. M'Kenzee's favorite part had always been verse fourteen: *Glory to God in the highest heaven, and on earth peace to those on whom his favor rests.*

That time she heard it, however, the next verse had resounded in her chest like a homing beacon calling out to her: *When the angels had left them and gone into heaven, the shepherds said to one another, "Let's go to Bethlehem and see this thing that has happened, which the Lord has told us about."*

Certainly, Green Hills wasn't Bethlehem, but with each second that passed, her need to be there grew. She had to get home.

Home? How could an empty, run-down house she'd never stepped foot in feel like home?

The sense that she needed to be there surfaced out of nowhere, but once it arrived, she couldn't shake it.

Yes, she needed to be there. And she *wanted* to be there. Had she ever felt such a call? To home?

No wonder she'd avoided love like the plague… Allowing it into one's life — into one's heart — made a person irrational, out of control, and completely insane.

Great. Now I'm arguing with myself about being crazy. Boy, how the mighty fall.

Regardless of her self-recrimination, M'Kenzee's heartbeat intensified when she saw the first sign for Green Hills: Exit 38, 2 miles.

Home. I'm almost there.

Bren wasn't even there.

Even so, his connection to the little house on Main Street made it feel like home.

Yes — *finally* — after a childhood of being passed from one temporary house to another, after college life in shared dorm rooms and campus housing, and after years spent traveling for work, M'Kenzee was heading *home.*

She couldn't get enough of the word, or the feeling. She'd found the place she belonged.

Easing on the brake to cancel the cruise control, M'Kenzee made a mental note to reset it once she'd turned onto the farm-to-market road leading into town. She could just imagine her conversation with a highway patrolman if she got caught speeding…

I'm speeding to get home. My husband is missing. In Africa. But I have to get home, to the house he bought us. Although I've never seen it. I've barely even seen him since I married him on a fake-drunken whim in Las Vegas, after the Super Bowl, three years ago. I just have to get there as quickly as possible. To simply be there. Because I can't get inside. I don't have the keys yet. No, I don't actually live there. Because it's a ramshackle wreck that has to be remodeled. I just need to get there. Now. For when he comes home.

They say truth is stranger than fiction, so the officer would have to believe her. Who in their right mind would make up such a wild story? No one.

Yep, M'Kenzee had just confirmed it: she had lost her mind to love.

Thankfully, no flashing lights appeared. No sirens sounded to halt her progress to 401 E. Main Street.

She pulled into the drive and stopped the car. Her heart fluttered in her throat.

She remained strapped into the driver's seat, looking at the property. The front yard had turned to dirt, the grass and flowers dead long before the plants would've gone dormant for the winter. The intricately designed iron handrail, originally intended to guide one up the steps to the substantial wrap-around front porch, leaned to a precarious degree. The third step had rotted completely out, leaving a gaping hole where one would need to step to actually use the steps. A large section of the ornate gingerbread-style trim dangled from a third-floor gable, ready to drop and decapitate unwanted guests.

And it wasn't so little. Indeed, the house was quite large. The gables might've been a fourth floor or attic, not the third as M'Kenzee first thought. Various shades of pink and green poked through the most recent coat of ivory paint, which had faded and begun peeling in large patches. Birds, gone south for the winter, had left behind sizable nests where missing gray slates created gaps in the roof.

It was awful. M'Kenzee loved it.

That morning, after Max had read from the Bible, and before they'd shared their gifts, they'd sang carols and hymns. One had been Momma's favorite: "Count Your Blessings." With Maree's voice high, M'Kenzee's midrange, and Max's low bass, they'd harmonized a lively rendition that had blown Janie Lyn away. It had been a little silly — trust Max and Maree to go dramatically overboard wherever possible. It had also been joyful and reverent. M'Kenzee had questioned it as one of Momma's favorites when she'd felt slighted in the bless-ings department. Being orphaned just before turning seven years old, growing up "in the system" and desperate to stay with her siblings, spending the bulk of her life wanting a man she'd believed could never be hers, therefore pushing away hope and happiness... Those life experiences had created doubt, a certainty that God had forgotten her along the way.

But in that moment, sitting in the driver's seat of her car, staring at a decrepit old house, with the love of her life missing in action, she felt it. Felt *them*: her blessings, rich and abundant.

A tear slipped down her face. M'Kenzee lifted a hand to wipe it away, only to realize the apple of her cheek had firmed, lifted. She was smiling.

M'Kenzee looked at herself in the rearview mirror. A new wisdom shone in the eyes looking back at her. A strength that could only come from peace radiated in the knowledge those eyes held. The irises practically glowed, sparkling a brighter, more vivid blue than she'd ever noticed them to be. It was a bit like seeing a stranger for the first time and finding the new acquaintance so intriguing it was impossible to look away.

M'Kenzee shifted her gaze back to the house. Oh yeah— She loved it!

Just as she put the car into gear and pulled further up the drive, a truck turned off Main Street and parked behind her. Large and imposing, the vehicle took up the width of her broken and busted concrete drive. With the truck's spotless cherry red paint glistening in the sun, a vision of Santa's sleigh as a transforming toy car skittered across M'Kenzee's mind.

"Ho ho ho," a masculine voice rang out, drawing M'Kenzee's attention from the beautiful vehicle to the gorgeous man driving it.

She stepped from her sport-sized SUV to greet her visitor.

"Are you Santa Claus?" M'Kenzee questioned, a hand to her forehead shielding her eyes from the beaming sun. Had the day become freakishly brilliant?

"I'm not at liberty to divulge," the man said sneakily. "But my day job is carpenter, job supervisor, and all-around handy-man. Jinx Malone," he added with a genuine smile, reaching a hand in her direction. "It's nice to meet you, M'Kenzee Stewart."

M'Kenzee tried to lift her hand to shake his, but she'd frozen in place.

There it was again: *M'Kenzee Stewart.*

"You are M'Kenzee, right?" Mr. Malone asked with an inquisitive slant to his chin.

"Oh, yes. Sorry," M'Kenzee stumbled through in response. "Yes, I am. I'm M'Kenzee Stewart." Pride might've made her handshake a little more aggressive than it needed to be. "It's nice to meet you, too," she managed, easing off her death grip. "Bren mentioned you. In his letter. One of his letters. Maybe more. I haven't finished them yet."

What a blathering idiot; where is this coming from?

Jinx Malone's eyes centered on her, a faint crinkling at the outer corners.

I amuse him.

The thought surprised M'Kenzee. And pleased her.

"Anyway," she said, trying again. "I understand you own the hardware store and lumberyard. It looks like we're destined to become fast friends. It seems I have quite a lot of work to do before Bren comes home."

Jinx sobered at the mention of Bren coming home. With a town the size of Green Hills, with this particular town's knack for taking care of fellow residents, with Miss Sadie being one of those residents, and with the fact that Maree and Janie Lyn had kept Miss Sadie in the loop and up to date over the past few days, everyone would know Bren had gone missing. They'd know M'Kenzee had married him and kept it a secret. They'd know he'd bought a heap of crumbling — yet glorious — bricks without her knowledge. They'd know of her desperation to have him back.

"I want to fix it up. I intend to make it beautiful again. And I have little time; Bren will be home soon." She dared the handyman — or a single soul in town — to say a thing to the contrary. Bren was very much alive. No one would convince her otherwise.

"Well, luckily, Blake called to say you needed the keys, and I offered to pick them up and meet you here. It's gonna be a project, all right. I knew we'd need to start sooner rather than later." This man — Jinx Malone — didn't back down from M'Kenzee's prickly exterior. He seemed entertained by it, but also appreciative of M'Kenzee's determination.

She liked him. His agreement — his affirmation — that Bren would be here *sooner rather than later* pleased her. The fact he'd volunteered to give up his day-after-Christmas spoke volumes to his character as well.

Green Hills never ceases to amaze.

Blake Fisher, the real estate agent, had been very polite, even kind, on the phone. M'Kenzee appreciated Blake's efforts to help her as efficiently as possible. Janie Lyn and Mary Beth were using the same agent to purchase the old warehouse and land for The Christmas Collection. Just like that, the fold of community connections enveloped M'Kenzee. She felt welcome rather than put off by the instant familiarity. She didn't mind that the townspeople had been talking about her — and about Bren — behind her back. They hadn't been gossiping with malice or spite. They'd been concerned and eager to help. Had the world always been this way? Had M'Kenzee judged too quickly, too harshly? Or was Green Hills truly the majestic gem Maree professed it to be?

"Why are you here? In Green Hills," she asked when curiosity took over her train of thought.

Easily six-foot-two, with a long, lean, athletic build, the man in front of her looked like he should be playing professional football with Max. A close-cropped beard drew one's eye to his chiseled jaw and cheekbones. A tight fade from the back of his neck to the line from his temple led to medium-length curls crowning the top of his head. Jet-black lashes and thick brows framed eyes the color of wheat fields, glistening in the sun and dancing in the wind. The richest velvet, his beautiful umber-brown skin appeared too exquisite to be real. "Shouldn't you be on a runway in New York? Maybe Milan?"

"No," he laughed. "Definitely not." Sliding his hands into the front pockets of loose, ringspun-washed duck canvas utility pants, he glanced down at his work boots while shaking his head. Apparently, her assumption that no human this aesthetically perfect would live in Tiny Town, America further amused him. After a moment, he looked up, turning his glossy pale brown eyes on her. "I grew up here, played some college basketball, got a degree, and happily came back home."

He leaned against the grill of his sleigh — truck, whatever — presumably content to chat in the frigid December cold as long as she wished.

"Where'd you play?"

"Texas Southern, down in Houston."

"I pegged you for a D-1 athlete," she boasted, prompting him to laugh at her again. "They've been pretty solid the past several years. When'd you graduate?"

"A year and a half ago," he answered with a challenging grin.

"And how far did you take the Tigers?"

"Never made it past the round of sixty-four, but had a blast trying," Jinx replied.

"Wow— March Madness. I bet it was incredible." M'Kenzee couldn't help being impressed. Big fans of college basketball, she and Max followed the championship, picked brackets, and paid attention to the teams turning heads each season. Texas Southern, one of the country's largest historically Black colleges and universities, had made quite a splash the past few years as a team to watch in the big dance.

"Unimaginable," he agreed. "I got to play five tournament

games in four years; that's more than most basketball players dream of. I loved every second."

"So you graduated in 2018? Why, you're just a baby," she teased. "You didn't want to see the world a bit before coming back to Oklahoma?"

"I thought about it; considered staying at TSU for law school." He paused with a reminiscing look of *what if* into the distance. "But I'm needed here."

M'Kenzee detected the subject was closed — for now, anyway — and reined in the hundred follow-up questions on the tip of her tongue.

"And you're sure you didn't do any modeling?"

"I might've posed for a picture or two, just to pay the bills while I was in Houston." He shrugged with chagrin.

"I knew it," M'Kenzee pounced in exclamation, making the big strong man blush. "You're way too pretty to have *not* attracted a photographer's lens."

"Do you want to see inside this castle or not?" Jinx teased right back, dangling the house key from his hand, waving it back and forth.

"I do," she confirmed. Then she set the joking aside. "I'm just a little scared, I guess."

"I understand," he empathized. "But you're not alone; I can promise you that."

M'Kenzee faced the once-beautiful house. Jinx followed, setting a hand under her elbow when she maneuvered around holes in the rickety porch steps.

He gently grasped her wrist, rolling her palm over to set the key in her hand, and then he curled her fingers closed around it.

"I need to grab a measuring tape and clipboard from the truck. You go on in," he encouraged with a nod.

M'Kenzee stood frozen, looking at Jinx but not really seeing him.

"Go on, you've got this," he nudged before walking away, leaving M'Kenzee to take this step on her own two feet.

You've got this.

With that bit of a pep talk, she turned the key, opened the door, and walked inside.

M'Kenzee was home.

24

***The dinner hour is a sacred, happy time
when everyone should be together and relaxed.
Julia Child***

"You lucked out with the foundation," Jinx said, writing a final note on his clipboard. It had shocked him not to find a single crack in the walls of the house. "I'll call Zeke Harris, see if he can send a roofing crew over tomorrow to measure and drop off a few samples. Once he gives us a schedule, we'll coordinate with the electricians and plumbers."

They'd spent the previous few hours touring the house, Jinx pointing out and jotting down every minute detail needing attention. He'd been thorough, taking copious notes and building a lengthy punch list for M'Kenzee to follow.

By the time they finished surveying the last room, her shoulders slumped and dark circles shadowed under her eyes. The remodel project must've felt like a lot, especially on top of everything else the world had tasked her to handle. Jinx didn't doubt her determination, but he worried… Everyone had a breaking point.

He intended to do all he could to keep M'Kenzee Stewart from reaching hers.

"Thank you, Jinx. Really — I can't tell you how much I appreciate your help." She set a hand on the doorknob to show him out, when a light knock sounded from the other side.

M'Kenzee squinted at Jinx in confusion, obviously not expecting anyone. He stepped in front of her and opened the door, but relaxed and moved aside when he saw M'Kenzee's guest.

"Miss Sadie!" M'Kenzee immediately brightened upon seeing Sadie Jones smiling on her doorstep.

"Well, come here," Miss Sadie ordered with open arms. M'Kenzee fell into the hug, burying her head in Miss Sadie's shoulder and holding on for dear life. After an afternoon spent witnessing her unyielding strength, Jinx guessed such vulnerability was out of character for M'Kenzee.

Miss Sadie gave him a wink, let M'Kenzee release the pent-up emotion she'd been carrying, and then patted her on the back. When M'Kenzee drew back from their embrace, Miss Sadie framed M'Kenzee's face with her hands, drying her tears, swiping a thumb across each cheek.

"You're home now, and everything is going to work out just as it should. You can be sure of that." Miss Sadie looked directly into M'Kenzee's eyes, brooking no argument.

"Thank you," M'Kenzee whispered back.

"Hey, 'Kenz," a stunning woman said from behind Miss Sadie.

"Hey, Landry," M'Kenzee answered. "Thanks for coming to see me." She stepped back to invite them inside.

"Jinx Malone, this is Landry Stark and Miss—"

"I've known Jinx since he was born — helped shower his momma with gifts before he'd even arrived," Miss Sadie announced with a voice that held so much familiarity and fondness, one couldn't help but feel cherished. "It's good of you to come help M'Kenzee," she added as he leaned down for a quick hug to say hello and placed a light kiss on her cheek. No one turned away a hug from Miss Sadie Jones.

"This is going to be a fun project. I'm hoping I can convince M'Kenzee to let me stick around to see it through. Can I take that?" He approached the stranger — Landry Stark, apparently — who carried a covered casserole dish with a bread basket balanced on top, a quilt folded under one arm, and a paper grocery sack hanging from her other wrist.

"Yes, please, Mr. Malone," she said. Her voice hinted at laughter, like it floated on a wave of boundless energy wherever it went…not flirtatious, but open and friendly.

"Just Jinx," he corrected without criticism. "Mr. Malone is my grandpa."

"How's Duke doing?" Miss Sadie asked as she followed M'Kenzee to the kitchen. "He was fighting a persistent cough when I was there a few days ago."

She'd been kind to word the question so innocently. If pneumonia had caused Grandad's cough, it would likely be his official cause of death. Since Duke's Alzheimer's diagnosis six years earlier, Jinx had done his homework. If his grandpa had begun aspirating food and liquids, then Duke's mind and body had reached the point where they could no longer work in tandem to swallow correctly. It was only a matter of time before an infection took hold of his lungs and the doctors would recommend end-of-life care.

Miss Sadie knew it just as Jinx did, yet she'd graciously tiptoed around that fact.

"Thanks for asking, Miss Sadie. He's not doing so well, actually." Jinx made a production of looking through empty kitchen cabinets in search of— *anything*. He needed a second to slow his racing heart. Jinx couldn't handle the thought of a world without Duke Malone in it.

He found nothing. No cleaning rags, no plates, no cups, no utensils. "Are y'all sure you want to eat here?"

"We'll be fine," Miss Sadie reassured him. "You were saying about Duke?"

"He's not showing other signs of a cold or allergies. The nurses at the memory care facility haven't said it, but I suspect he's choking almost every time he eats or drinks anything. It's happening so fast. When I moved home, he could still go to the shop with me, hang out behind the counter, even talk to our customers a little here and there. Less than two years later, he's wasting away right before my eyes." The strongest man he'd ever known could no longer speak, could barely move. And now he couldn't eat.

"The Lord is preparing his way." Miss Sadie set a gentle hand on his forearm, her words too certain to be preachy. Jinx couldn't handle preachy these days, either. He simply didn't understand a God who allowed such devastating suffering in good, servant-hearted people. Childhood cancer…senseless acts of violence…Alzheimer's disease… What kind of ruler, who had the power to do away with such pain, put His loved ones through it, anyway?

"I know Duke," Landry said, walking back into the kitchen with another box she'd retrieved from her vehicle. Jinx turned to look at her as she continued. "I'm surprised we've never met. I'm a doctor at Green Country Medical Center, and I do a weekly rotation at Memorial Care."

"She *volunteers* on a weekly basis," Miss Sadie corrected. "She filled in for Janie Lyn a few times last fall and never stopped going. She's a huge blessing to everyone there. We're living in the middle of a neurological desert, desperate for more specialists, yet little training for Alzheimer's care is included in medical school. On top of that, very few hours of dementia education, if any at all, are required for EMTs, fire-fighters, police, nurses, facility administrations, and assisted living staff. Everyone living or working in dementia care needs all the help they can find."

"Don't get yourself all worked up, Miss Sadie." Landry's voice soothed in the same melodic way she'd spoken earlier. "You'll be in a tizzy all night, and this pork chop roast is too good to *not* enjoy. It's true that dementia-care requirements are severely lacking." She unloaded the box as she talked, setting out paper plates, plastic silverware, napkins, and disposable salt and pepper shakers — all the items Jinx had hunted for in the cabinets. "But we're lucky to live in a state that has a legislative plan in place to address Alzheimer's disease, and it's one that requires at least a few hours of coursework. I'm not the only one determined to learn more; many of the medical and nursing students I've met are seeking additional information on their own, too."

Handing him a plate, napkin, and fork, she smiled at Jinx with empathy and care. "Duke's in excellent hands," Landry promised. "Doctor Sands is phenomenal, and the staff at Memorial Care are diligent and compassionate. They'll help you through." She gave him one last reassuring smile before turning to face M'Kenzee. "Now, tell us about this fabulous house while we eat — I'm champing at the bit to hear all about it."

Landry Stark guided their conversation from defeat to hope with the smooth ease of an ice-skater swishing across the rink. Quite impressive. And brilliant, it seemed. A bubbly bundle of energy, Landry balanced that constant motion with a talent for listening. Patience, Jinx realized; that was her secret super-power. She'd be an incredible doctor — attentive, calm, and caring.

M'Kenzee read from her punch list and notes, explaining the big picture of the remodeling effort, while the rest of the group fixed their plates. Jinx agreed with Landry, the casserole looked — and smelled — too good to not indulge in. A thick, buttery gravy covered round roasted potatoes, caramelized onions, tender carrots, and juicy pork chops at least an inch thick and browned to perfection. Jinx's mouth watered, although he would've sworn he wasn't hungry before Miss Sadie and Landry arrived.

A large wooden bowl held a green salad with fresh vegetables — bright red cherry tomatoes, slices of orange bell peppers, chunks of yellow squash, whole black olives, and quartered pieces of crisp pale cucumber — tossed in a vinaigrette giving off hints of garlic.

"This is awful nice to mess up," Jinx commented, looking down at the salad bowl. "What are these toppings?"

"A mixture of dried cranberries, walnut pieces, pine nuts, and sunflower seeds, lightly salted and toasted," Landry filled in. "That's my measly contribution to dinner and the extent of my cooking skills. Between Miss Sadie, Maree, and Janie Lyn, I'm surrounded by amazing chefs, and that" —she tilted her head toward the side dish— "is all I can bring to the table."

"We'll just say Landry has other skills," Miss Sadie confirmed with diplomacy. "Dig in, and Jinx, please grab that quilt for us to use as a tablecloth," she ordered.

Without a table or single chair in the house, they moved their dinner party to the back porch, where the early evening air felt crisp but not unbearably cold.

"Now this is a pleasant surprise." M'Kenzee blinked in shock when she stepped out the back door. She'd spoken the words they'd all been thinking. "Not a rotten board in sight."

To the contrary, the porch had been rebuilt, and somewhat recently. The wooden planks had aged or weathered to a beautiful, bronzed pecan and remained strong.

"What kind of wood is it?" M'Kenzee cascaded her hand

across a smooth bench seat that ran along one side of an extra-long picnic table that matched the boards of the decking.

"Western red cedar, with teak accents. Every single joint is dove-tailed, so there are no exposed nails or screws. Each board was sanded by hand. I watched the spindles being shaped on a lathe, one at a time."

"Matthias's work?" Miss Sadie asked in a soft voice. The reverence in her words caused both M'Kenzee and Landry to stop midstride. Like spectators at a tennis match, they looked at Miss Sadie, then at Jinx, back at Miss Sadie, and back at Jinx.

"Yes." Jinx cleared his throat, dispelling the thick emotion that had crept up on him in an instant. "It's beautiful, isn't it?"

Matthias Noble was a subject Jinx struggled to discuss, one he struggled to understand.

His best friend for eighteen years, roommate at Grandad's house, coworker at Grandad's lumberyard throughout adolescence, and Jinx's constant companion since they'd been old enough to walk, had left at dawn the day after they'd graduated high school. A note on the refrigerator explained Matty had enlisted in the Marines, said it was time to take responsibility for himself. He'd written that he appreciated Duke and Jinx, the life and home they'd provided for him. Matty had said he'd love them always. And that was it. Jinx hadn't heard from him since. Six years, and he'd not heard one word.

"Well, it certainly won't need replacing." M'Kenzee stated the obvious. "Hallelujah, I can check one thing off that list!"

Her dry wit provided the comedic relief they'd needed.

"You might have to sleep right here on the picnic table," Landry added with sass.

"True," M'Kenzee agreed. "After looking closely at the roof, the walls, the plumbing, and the electrical wiring, my safest bet might be living *outside* rather than in. At least I have a blanket to keep me warm." She grinned at Miss Sadie, appreciation shining in her eyes.

Miss Sadie covered M'Kenzee's hand with both of her own. "Every young woman should have a special quilt to decorate her marriage bed. This one is for you. May it warm and protect and bless your union."

M'Kenzee's eyes filled with moisture. Instead of saying anything, she nodded her thanks. M'Kenzee shifted the stack of their hands to hold Miss Sadie's. Then she lifted them to place a kiss on the back of Miss Sadie's fingers. M'Kenzee set their clasped grip on the table and rested her forehead on them.

Miss Sadie slid one hand out to pet M'Kenzee's short spiky hair. Such a nurturing, mothering gesture. It had to bring M'Kenzee great comfort.

After a moment, M'Kenzee sat up, wiped away a stray tear, and told Miss Sadie, "Thank you."

"It's beautiful, Miss Sadie," Landry said. "Did you make it?"

"No," she answered. "Momma's friends made it for Sam and me as a wedding present. It's a double wedding ring quilt. The interlocking rings are symbols of love and romance, joined in a way that is without beginning or end. The pattern became quite popular in the early 1900s, particularly during the Great Depression when fabric scraps had to be salvaged from any available materials, becoming smaller and smaller each time people reused them."

"Such lovely colors," Landry pointed out. "Were these fabrics scraps from other things?"

"Oh, yes." Miss Sadie set down her fork, settling in to share her story. "Green was my signature color. I wore all shades of it, with golds and yellows as a close second in my list of favorites. Several of these prints are from shirts and skirts I'd outgrown throughout my childhood." A wistful smile played at the corners of her mouth as her fingers traced the seams between small pieces of fabric. "Sam tended toward browns and tans. His mother sent Momma a few of his old things to add to the quilt, too." Her hand trembled as her touch smoothed over a deep burgundy, geometric pattern on a light khaki background. "She sent a note pinned to this one; it had been his prized pearl-snap shirt when he went to first grade. She said she'd have to peel it off him to put it through the wash every few days." Miss Sadie looked up at each of them, both sadness and joy clear in her glossy eyes, moist with emotion. "And then Momma and her friends added the peaches, reds, oranges…all the colors of the Oklahoma sunset. They said it was to remember home, where we'd come from and where we'd always belong."

"But y'all never left Green Hills, did you?" Jinx asked, pretty sure he knew the answer, but wondering if he had the history wrong.

"No, we never did," Miss Sadie acknowledged. "We talked about it, but Sam was brilliant with the land and the ranch. Daddy had started Marshall Cattle Company before the war, and Momma had done her best running it after his death, but she was more than happy to hand it over to Sam. In no time, he'd built the business up. Between boarders at the house, helping cook in town, and selling what canned fruits, jellies, and vegetables we couldn't use ourselves, Momma and I had more to do than we could keep up with. We had such full lives right here, we never felt a hankering to go anywhere else. We were meant to be in Green Hills." Miss Sadie fell silent, not with remorse or regret, but with certainty and peace.

"I have to know, Miss Sadie," Landry began, a gleam in her eye. "Are any of these scraps from drapes? Like in *The Sound of Music*? I always wanted a jumper made from thick brocade just like the von Trapp girls," she said with a giggle, her knack for soothing and guiding those around her evident once again.

"Well," Miss Sadie answered, a guilty giggle shaking her

shoulders. "You know those two brown armchairs by the entryway table? The ones with the burnout velvet flocking that matches the powder room wallpaper?"

"Yes," Landry and M'Kenzee said in unison and with wide eyes.

"Momma special ordered that fabric from France when she and Daddy designed the house. But by the time he'd finished building it, he'd put so many windows across the front parlor that they didn't have enough yardage to make draperies. Instead, she pasted the fabric to the walls of the water closet and reupholstered two rickety old chairs that Daddy basically had to rebuild. The story goes he saw the chairs on the side of the road coming back from a business trip to Tulsa. The moment he saw them, he knew Momma would love them, so he circled back to the house set off the road and drove up the long drive — half worried someone might shoot him for trespassing before he had time to offer for the chairs. Then he talked the woman who answered the door *up* to five dollars. Per chair! She'd asked for two-fifty total, but he'd noticed the house needed repairs and paint, figured she was widowed and alone. He wouldn't pay less than ten."

"Sounds like quite a man," Jinx said with respect.

"I barely knew him before he died in Sicily. But the stories Momma told made him bigger than life, bigger than death. They kept him alive in our hearts, so we always felt his presence and his guidance." Miss Sadie paused before grinning at the girls. "And that fabric has withstood the test of time. When I was in high school, Momma took out the remnants to make a table runner for the buffet. When I held it in my hands, I had to have it. I begged and begged until Momma relented, said I could have what I needed to make a skirt. Let me tell you, it was something…had to have weighed about thirty pounds, but I didn't care. I loved it, and I wore it every chance I could. Of course, wearing it was like being wrapped in the world's heaviest blanket, so it had to be freezing outside to tolerate it." She laughed out loud at the memory, shaking her head at her own adolescent stubbornness. "I'll tell you: I wore that drapery fabric with pride."

Jinx chuckled, more at the tears of laughter running down all three women's faces than at the tale. They were like teenagers; once they started giggling, they couldn't seem to stop. Then they had him laughing, too.

"Where is the skirt now, Miss Sadie?" Jinx asked.

"Oh, I outgrew that waist measurement a long, long time ago. I ended up cutting into it to make the throw pillows that live on the leather couches in the front room and coordinate with the chairs."

"And the walls of the half-bath," Landry reminded her, still laughing through her words.

"Yes," Miss Sadie agreed, beaming. "And the walls of the powder room."

"I want memories like that for this house." The sound of M'Kenzee's staunch determination drew their attention. "I want stories that live on and silly tales that get passed down. I want so much love and joy to fill this house that sadness wouldn't dare knock on the door or even try to seep in through the cracks."

"You will have all those things. And more, dear," Miss Sadie said as she squeezed M'Kenzee's hand. "You will."

25

It takes courage to grow up
and become who you really are.
E. E. Cummings

After her company left, M'Kenzee inflated an air mattress Jinx had loaned her with the plug-in air pump he'd also loaned her. She planned to go by Maree's shop, which happened to be just down the street from the house, to load up the boxes of random housewares she'd left boxed up in Maree's storeroom, but Miss Sadie and Landry's arrival and impromptu dinner party had derailed her intentions in the best of ways.

Plastic tubs of sheets and towels, a dish crate of mismatched plates and bowls, and a trunk full of books could wait; an evening with friends could not.

M'Kenzee had never believed relationships beyond the love she felt for her family were a necessity. She'd been wrong.

Lying on the borrowed air mattress, wrapped in Miss Sadie's incredible quilt, thinking back to Landry's buoying humor, M'Kenzee readily admitted to herself that without her friends and their kindness, she'd have truly struggled through the day. Especially through the night.

She rolled onto her stomach, propping her weight onto her elbows. Using the beam of a flashlight — also on loan from Jinx — she opened the next journal from Bren's box.

As she'd mentioned to Maree and Janie Lyn the morning before, the two books she'd scanned through had been school journals. They began in second grade and contained random schoolwork through intermediate school.

Bren's room in the Stewart house during that time appeared clearly in M'Kenzee's mind...

She remembered the way his blue and ivory striped comforter covered the pristinely made bed; the top turned back precisely and the corners tucked tightly under the mattress, foreshadowing the career he would choose. A patchwork quilt in blues, tans, and grays lived folded across the foot. A variety of sports equipment — a football, a baseball bat and glove, his bicycle helmet, or tennis rackets, depending on the season — tossed in the center was the only nod to typical boyhood sloppiness. The honey-brown oak headboard matched two bedside dressers, a tall wardrobe, and a desk. A hutch sat atop the bedside dresser on the far side of the room with books lined, stacked, and wedged to overflowing on the shelves. Bren loved to read, even then.

Apparently, he'd loved to write as well. M'Kenzee easily imagined Bren saving old spirals and binders, shuffling them into the drawers on either side of his sturdy desk when he cleaned out his backpack after another school year ended. Based on the journals she found in the love box, he'd continued to fill them with thoughts, wishes, and dreams for years to come.

Still waters run deep.

Her big brother's kind, confident, and cute best friend had been a thinker from a young age.

Reading his writings brought back so many moments M'Kenzee had forgotten, and several she'd remembered differently than how Bren described them. How uncanny that two people saw the same event in such a different light.

The entries from his elementary and intermediate grades revealed a sweet boy with an enormous heart.

> You're moving again this weekend. I prayed extra hard for it to be better than the last house. I'm not sure God is listening, though. I asked him to cure my mom's cancer, but he ignored me...

———

> I think I'd like these trips to Scotland if you and Max and Maree could come. Then we could explore the ruins of Kindrochit Castle and play tag through the Highland meadows...

———

> Da says we're getting a dog! Da wants to name her Sterling because he says she's going to cost a lot of money, and here in Scotland, dollars are sterlings, but I want to name her Alba, which I learned is Gaelic for Scotland... Granda and Nan said I could name her since she's officially my dog. Alba it is. She's the smartest Border Collie you've ever seen.

A crayon drawing of a green-eyed, peach-skinned, auburn-haired boy holding a leash connected to a black and white dog dominated the bottom half of that page. Thick dots of purple, lilac, and silver, sprinkled across the grass Bren had drawn around the happy pair, represented the dense heather flowers and created a beautiful background for his artwork.

We're not coming home.

A ghostly ache permeated through M'Kenzee's chest as she'd read those words. Those had been dark days, ones she remembered all too well, despite barely being eight years old at the time.

Mom's responding to a new treatment, which is wonderful. But she has to go to the hospital one weekend every month to take it. So we are staying in Scotland...

I start school here next week. Their idea of football is really soccer. I like soccer fine, but I want to play American football. With Max.

I don't know when I'll get to see you again. This really, really stinks.

Random notes and letters throughout that notebook had described schooling in Scotland, explaining that fifth grade was called "year 6" of primary school, but his entrance exam results had been exemplary, so the school administration required he go directly into year 7. With only twenty students in years five, six, and seven, the three grades worked together most all the time, anyway. Judging from his commentary, Bren didn't seem to mind the tiny group size; he thrived under the increased attention the low student-to-teacher ratio allowed. He particularly enjoyed their Friday afternoons volunteering at Braemar Castle and repeatedly hinted at his budding interest in military history.

His letters to M'Kenzee grew more infrequent, but the journal entries provided a glimpse into his life. He'd learned to love soccer, although he mentioned missing "real football" and tackling. The Highland moors acted as Bren's personal playground. With his mom fighting for her life and his dad juggling her care and the job he'd found, Bren had spent hour after hour hiking, exploring, tracking, and imagining those who'd come before him as he traipsed through the terrain of the Cairngorm Mountains.

Bren often asked her questions in his letters, questions about how she was doing, if she felt safe, and if their foster family was kind. He requested she pass along tidbits of information to Max — albeit mostly about sports — and share funny Alba anecdotes with Maree. He thanked M'Kenzee profusely for a photograph she'd mailed to him, one she'd taken of a border collie with a shiny coat and a regal presence that had reminded her of Bren's dog stories.

How odd that he never sent a single letter or tore out a single page from a notebook to give me at the time he wrote them.

His parents had checked on the Davenport kids here and there, and they'd sent care packages and holiday gifts. The kids talked on the phone a few times each year. They had stayed in touch, yet Bren had never mentioned the journals, never let on that M'Kenzee had consumed so many of his thoughts.

As Max had begun junior high, Brennigan started his second year of secondary school. The next couple of semesters, which he called *S2*, filled the next book.

Battered and bent, spiral binding barely held together the pages she read that night. The ratty and stained sheets of paper were proof that Bren had carried the notebook with him, into the elements, and on his adventures.

M'Kenzee smiled. Bren had treasured this notebook. She felt it in her bones.

> Monday, August 5, 2002
>
> I can't believe it! Granda's been teaching me how to track and stalk, and today I saw a huge red deer. It was crazy — they normally only come out in the colder months like December and January, but when I came over a rise along the moorlands, there he was, standing proud, chest bowed, and antlers held high. His rack had to be three feet wide.
>
> M'Kenzee, I wish you'd seen him. You could've taken a picture of him. Then we'd remember him together. So magnificent!
>
> Miss y'all,
>
> B.

> Thursday, August 15, 2002
>
> Dear M'Kenzee,
>
> Summer is almost over — I hope you've enjoyed it.
>
> I've spent most of the summer outdoors,

collecting heather and flowers for Nan and Mom, fishing for salmon along the River Dee with Granda, and hiking in the national park. The crisp air carries a tinge of history and peace, which is weird as there was little peace throughout man's history here. But something in the breeze is settling. I can't explain it right, but I feel it. Hundreds of years of life have happened here. I think I sense it because the world buzzes so quietly out here, with just the animal noises and the rush of water in the streams and the wind through the grasslands to fill the space. Maybe that makes it easier to pay attention.

At night, I've been reading about this part of Scotland so I can sit in the den with Da — it's about the only way we get to spend time together. He gets up really, really early every day to help Mom get dressed. He says it's their favorite way to start the day, but I know she's too weak to get in and out of the bathtub by herself and too tired to stand under the shower water long enough to bathe. The doctor told them it's important for Mom to feel refreshed and ready for a new day, and Da's the only one able to carry her from their bed to the bathroom and to her chair in the living room where she spends most of the day. I hate seeing her struggle so much.

With him driving over an hour each way to work

in Aberdeen and helping Mom get back to bed after dinner, the only hour left for us is when Da likes to read before calling it a night, too. It's kinda cool, just the two of us, each with a book in hand. And when one of us laughs or gasps, the other closes his book to ask what happened. It's like we're both reading two stories at once because we share the best parts of each novel with one another. He likes thrillers set around espionage and military plots. When he reads a section to me, his voice gets deep and dramatic. I know he's doing it to entertain me, but I think it's really cool, anyway. He's promised to tell me when I'm old enough to read his books — the whole novel, not just the paragraphs he shares.

I've been reading Treasure Island. Robert Louis Stevenson lived here in Braemar during the summer of 1881. The cottage where he stayed — and where he wrote it — is one of my favorite landmarks to walk through. I think after I finish it, I'll read Kidnapped. His books are kinda for babies, but I like them. Da says that kids' books are even more fun to read when you're an adult; he says grown-ups appreciate words in a different way. I don't know if he means I'm mature, and that's why I like Stevenson's books now, or if he means I'm too young to understand them now and will need to read them again later. Either way, you should tell Max that he'd like *Treasure Island*, too.

When school starts next week, I'm gonna make sure I'm done with all my homework before Da gets home, so I don't miss our book talks. They're my favorite part of each day.

Sorry this letter is so long. Sometimes I think I could talk to you all day and never run out of words.

B.

P.S: What do you like to read?

———

Wednesday, October 16, 2002

I thought skipping a grade last year would make school hard, but S2 isn't too bad. Mrs. James wrote a letter to Mom and Da asking if I could begin advanced math classes with the year four kids. Nan says I have a gift for strategy and logistics, and apparently that comes from the patterns I see in numbers. The way they talk about me is embarrassing — I just want to be a normal school kid, like every other thirteen-year-old.

If I was still in Oklahoma, this would be fall break. I'd be tackling Max in piles of red and orange and brown leaves. We'd go to the high school football game tomorrow night, and then we'd play

outside for three straight days. We might've even
gone to the county fair in Tulsa. I would've liked
to win a prize for someone special. I think you
know who that would be.
Man, I miss my friends,
B.

———

Thursday, November 28, 2002
It was great to talk to everyone on the phone
today — I had a lot more to say, but hearing your
voice made Thanksgiving special, M'KenZee.
Thank you!
I'm so glad the family y'all are with right
now is kind and loving.
You deserve to be loved,
B.

———

Friday, December 20, 2002
Tonight's the winter formal at school. We only
have thirty kids in the entire school this year, so
it's really a homecoming for every person who ever
attended Braemar School or simply lives in the
village. Seems pretty dumb to me, but the entire
town is flipping out over it.

I asked Isla Scott to go with me to the dance.

I don't like her, though. At least not like a girlfriend.

She also got moved into higher classes, and the other kids pick on her out of jealousy. Boys are stupid, and girls are mean. Isla's a sweet kid, just too shy to stand up for herself. And she'll be pretty when she grows up. I imagine everyone will be sorry for the way they treated her when that day comes.

The dance wasn't too bad.

Mom cried when Da took pictures of me in my suit. Isla looked nice in her dress, too, and she wasn't weird at the dance. I made sure to slow dance with her so she didn't feel left out. Once I did, some of the other boys asked her, too. I think she had fun.

I hope we get to say Merry Christmas over the phone. If not, well... Merry Christmas.

I miss you,

B.

As she read along, M'Kenzee thought Bren transitioned from writing *to her* to writing to himself, more like a diary. Had she become an imaginary friend, an idea of a person he remembered and clung to out of habit? Or had he continued to feel a unique connection to the person she actually was?

M'Kenzee would lean toward the former theory for a moment. But then, like in his retelling of the impressive deer or in his brief entry on Thanksgiving Day, her name would pop up, proving that he'd never stopped thinking of *her*.

If only she'd known he'd been sharing his life with her all along, she'd have answered every letter, every note, and every card he never sent. She'd have gladly shared her thoughts and hopes and dreams right back, so he would not have felt so alone or far away. Never one-sided, she had reciprocated his love; she only wished they'd have both known how the other felt. So many years wasted.

M'Kenzee couldn't remember if they'd spoken that particular Christmas. Their telephone conversations had been scattered randomly throughout the years. A few times, they'd gone several weeks — even months — without a phone call from the Stewarts; although looking back, M'Kenzee understood that the obstacle would've been the foster families they lived with more than Bren's family not trying.

Her back cramping as she leaned on her elbows to read, M'Kenzee flipped through the rest of that notebook quickly…

More vocabulary lists, lots of math problems, a mix of football and soccer plays diagramed throughout, but she found few journal entries.

He'd fought with the school bully when the boy had cornered two younger boys at the bus stop. M'Kenzee grinned at his irritation with The Dunce, as Bren called him. She figured there were "Terk-the-Jerk"s everywhere in the world.

He mentioned how silly the girls had become, constantly giggling when he walked by or, heaven forbid, sat at the lunch table next to theirs. M'Kenzee chuckled at how oblivious he must've been to the schoolgirls' crushes on him.

One line in all caps grabbed her attention:

I MADE UNDER-14 PREMIER LEAGUE.

Pride bloomed for the boy he'd been. Never one to toot his own horn, he'd needed to tell her when he'd accomplished such a lofty goal. For a new kid to prove himself on the pitch and earn a spot on the top team in an age group above his own would've been a big deal, indeed.

Shoulders aching and eyelids drooping, M'Kenzee closed the notebook and placed it face-down on the other two books she'd already looked through. She fully intended to revisit and reread every page once she'd made it through the stack.

After turning off the flashlight and re-fluffing her pillow, M'Kenzee nestled under the heavy wedding ring quilt and thought about her husband.

It's true what they say: at our core, we are who we are.

Bren's sense of right and wrong, his call to duty, and his love for the world and all its people formed the fibers of his being. They'd been part of his soul since boyhood. M'Kenzee loved the boy in those journals, just as she loved the man he'd become.

She looked out at the stars.

Doing so before closing her eyes helped M'Kenzee settle. The ritual served as a reminder that although the world was terribly large, she and Bren looked upon the same night sky, named the same constellations, and slept under the same glowing moon.

She slept soundly knowing they were together, even when apart.

26

Carpe diem...
because the early bird gets the worm.
Latin phrase and English proverb meaning,
"Seize the day...because success comes
to those who prepare well
and put in effort."

During the night, the air mattress lost its appeal, but with the house utterly freezing, M'Kenzee could not force herself out of her quilted cocoon. Despite the lack of air remaining in the inflated mattress, she remained burrowed until sunlight streamed through the grimy windows and a heavy knock jarred the front door.

Surely, whoever is banging down the door will have a heart and go away.

No such luck.

Giving up her attempt at hibernation, M'Kenzee shuffled, quilt and all, to the entryway and opened the door. Jinx Malone stood on the porch with an amiable-looking fellow whose cap logo read "Harris Roofing." She squinted up at them both, braving the intense sunshine and chilly air, hugging the quilt tighter with one hand while patting down her wild, spiky hair with the other.

"Mornin'," Jinx announced with a grin.

M'Kenzee merely grunted.

"Heard you're a tea-instead-of-coffee drinker," he added, extending a white paper cup her way, complete with a brown Kraft cup sleeve and steam curling out the lid.

"Mmm," she answered, inhaling the sweet and spicy scent of cinnamon, oranges, and black tea as she grasped the lifeline.

"And how about some donut holes?"

"You may enter," she grumbled, sliding her socked feet back just enough to open the door for her guests. "What time is it?"

"Five after seven," Jinx provided, his smile expanding at her groan. "Not a morning person?"

"Well, I can be," she said in her defense. "But it takes some doing."

"M'Kenzee Stewart—" There it was again, Jinx saying her married name in a way that both surprised her and made her chest fill with pride. "This is Zeke Harris, who is every bit a morning person and has been waiting to get started on your house — impatiently, I might add — at the coffee shop since it opened at 5:30."

"It's nice to meet you, Mr. Harris, and thank you." M'Kenzee reached out a hand to shake his.

"Just Zeke," he replied. "And I need to thank *you*." His bushy gray eyebrows lifted to frame eyes animated with joyful light. "Been wanting to reroof this beauty for years; I welcome the chance to be part of her restoration. I'll do a fine job for you, ma'am. And I've brought some samples to show you, ideas I've had for the best colors and materials for this property." Eagerness shone in his tone and posture, his enthusiasm contagious. M'Kenzee harbored no doubts she could trust Zeke Harris with her — their — new home.

"I'm excited to see them. Give me just a few minutes, and we'll take a look. Please, make yourselves at home, measure, do whatever you need. I'll be right back."

Fifteen minutes later, as freshened up as one could be with cold water, hand soap, and a few paper towels for a loofah, M'Kenzee popped one last donut hole into her mouth as she caught up with the two men in the backyard. Both stared up at the roof with scowls wrinkling their foreheads.

"What are we examining?"

"The roof," Jinx provided, completely serious in his answer.

"The *old* roof," Zeke added.

"Ya don't say," M'Kenzee pondered, looking with them, but not at all sure about what she was supposed to be seeing.

The two men turned their attention to her. She blinked twice and smiled at them.

"Well, you see… The problem is—" Zeke launched into a woeful explanation.

"Zeke," M'Kenzee interrupted. "There are no problems. Whatever needs to be done, we will do. If that means rebuilding every inch of foundation, framing, walls, and windows, so be it. But there are no problems." She tried to smile sweetly to soften her command. "Now, tell me your ideas for the roof." She waited patiently. "Please," she remembered to tack on as an afterthought.

To his credit, Zeke nodded his understanding before restarting his speech.

"The best way to reroof a Victorian is to copy the old roof line and use the same materials. But this roofline is particularly steep and, although what you see here is composition roofing, they originally built it with slate tiles."

"I follow. So, what is the challenge?"

"Slate is heavy and expensive. For this pitch, a thinner slate helps with weight, but it is even more expensive. I think a cupped corner pattern fits the split-elevation design of the house best. But that's going to cost you another premium." Zeke's pallor took on a green hue, confirming his pain at the admission.

"Are these examples of thin cupped corner tiles?" M'Kenzee gestured toward slate pieces stacked in a box on the deck. She kneeled on one knee to pick through and admire the samples. "These are exquisite."

"Yes, they certainly are," Zeke agreed with a doleful shake of his head. His concern amused M'Kenzee. She'd done very well for herself as a photojournalist, and she'd had no house to maintain, few bills, and little else on which to spend her earnings. She could come up with whatever budget the house project required. But Zeke and Jinx didn't know that; their concerns warmed her heart, kind and sweet.

"I'm noticing a grayish-purple-and-green theme. Which one do you recommend?"

"These are unfading stone, so the colors will remain consistent when exposed to the elements. The Deep Purple has an occasional green marking, while the Mottled Green and Purple has bits of green on every tile. The Unfading Purple has two distinct shades of deep purple and plum with no hints of green. Any of these will be striking and strong while melding perfectly with the landscape and mature trees."

"I can see it. Stunning!" Giddiness flooded M'Kenzee. "I'm leaning toward the Mottled Green and Purple. What do you think, Jinx?"

"I think you have wonderful vision. Zeke, are these available at the quarry, or would there be a delay?"

"I'll go call in our measurements and see what they have already cut and in stock."

. . .

"Thanks for being here," M'Kenzee said, leading Jinx to the picnic table on the back patio. "I'm sure you had other things to do this morning."

"Not one item on my to-do list," he said with an indulgent shrug. "And if you're up to looking through fan decks of paint colors, I arranged for one of my paint crews to stop by around 9:00 to measure rooms."

"I'm up to it. Is it better to redo everything in one room at a time, or should I get all of one repair done throughout the house before going to the next item on the list?"

"It's easier to schedule each contractor to do all of their work at once," Jinx explained, "like updating electrical wires and all the light fixtures over the course of a few days rather than having the electricians come out many times over several weeks. But if there is a certain room you want done immediately, we can focus on that while working our way down the punch list."

"I'd like to get our bedroom and bathroom finished," she admitted. "I want our personal space put together when Bren gets home."

"We can do that," Jinx promised. "Do you have furniture, bedding, lamps, stuff like that in storage somewhere that we need to ship here?"

"I have an apartment in Tulsa, and Bren has one in Virginia, but I'm not worried about using whatever we have there. I want this to be a fresh start and a new beginning for us. Maree's always talking about the antique stores she loves; I might check those out to find furnishings. And I can plan a trip to Dallas for the rest. I guess filling an entire house will take quite a bit of stuff."

"It'll come together in its own time; they always do," he reassured her. "The master suite is a perfect place to start. But wait until after Zeke gets that new roof on, so you don't take a chance on existing leaks ruining your new things."

As if his ears had been ringing from their conversation, Zeke returned to the backyard with good news.

"I've placed the order," he announced with gusto. "They're coming from Vermont on a truck; the pallets will arrive on Tuesday. Wednesday's New Year's Day, and I've already given my crew a few days off, so we'll begin Monday the sixth — bright and early," he said, an eyebrow raised as he pointed a teasing look at M'Kenzee. She laughed, enjoying his camaraderie, which made his eyes twinkle. "It'll take the better part of ten days to get her done. You'll have a weatherproofed house by mid-January."

"Only if we get the windows inspected, replaced where necessary, and recaulked where they're sound," Jinx chimed in.

"I'm guessing you've got a guy for that?" M'Kenzee asked. "Hoping, anyway."

"In a manner of speaking," he hedged. "I'll call Sammy." Jinx looked at Zeke when he said it.

"Only person for a job like this," Zeke agreed.

"Great," M'Kenzee said, clapping her hands and rubbing them for warmth. "Let's call Sammy. In the house." She picked up her clipboard of lists and notes and the now-empty cup of tea she'd been sipping while they talked. Ready to get out of the cold, she dashed for the back door.

*S*ammy turned out to be five foot five, no more than a hundred and twenty pounds, with luscious waves of dark brunette hair, and curves M'Kenzee dreamed of having. Definitely not a guy. Samantha Harris also turned out to be Zeke's daughter and a window expert, particularly with historic properties.

"Hey, Jinx. Hi, Daddy," she said, smiling brightly at the

first man and even brighter at the second as she set a canvas bag brimming with instruments on the kitchen counter. "M'Kenzee, it's nice to meet you; I'm Samantha, but only strangers call me that, so it's Sammy." She turned her megawatt smile on M'Kenzee before extracting tape measures, levels, metal squares that were actually triangular, and additional tools from her bottomless, Mary Poppins-style tote. "I've noticed a few broken panes and snapped grilles, but overall, I think we can salvage most of the original windows by replacing the casings, stools, and aprons — boy, are they beauties. I'll strip 'em down to the frame and sill to check for rot, so we'll know for sure what is worth saving. There's a company out of Washington that deals only in vintage hardware and lighting — sorry, Jinx, you're out of luck on this part of the job…we have to stay true to the time period — and I bet they'll have the sunken sash lifts that are missing. Of course, we can switch all of them out if you don't like the polished brass, but I sure do love how gold shines, don't you?"

"Oh, ye—" M'Kenzee tried to speak.

Sammy hadn't been looking for an answer and kept going, seemingly oblivious to anything in the room besides the windows she ran her hands over, as if she could diagnose their health by touch.

"What do you think about a stained-glass design for the transom above the sink? There's space for a larger one above the front door too. It would tie the spaces together and add a decorative touch of color. If you don't want color, you could go with a simple diamond design instead. Those are Tudor style and would sure look classy. We could add a few full-sized versions around the house; I'm thinking we'll want those on the library windows and the bathrooms, to distort the sun's intensity on the books and, of course, visibility into the baths. Have you decided what you'll do with the space between the foyer and the sitting room? Large side panels encased in ornate wood trim and set atop built-in bookcases would be ideal for the transition. You're doing wallpaper in that sitting room, aren't you?"

With that, Sammy walked out of the kitchen to explore the house. From the kitchen, M'Kenzee heard Sammy rambling, but to herself, as she commented on one feature of the house after another, pointing out ideas for every nook and cranny.

M'Kenzee liked the spitfire of a woman and found herself eager to shadow Sammy around the house like a puppy, picking up scraps of knowledge wherever possible along the way.

"Have you met my little sister?" M'Kenzee asked when she found Sammy in the attic scrutinizing the gabled windows that stood watch over Green Hills. "You remind me of her. A lot."

"Maree's the best! I helped her find the perfect windows for her studio. She wanted Main Street Design to showcase her fabrics on a grand scale, but we also had to consider security and the potential for bad weather. We went with an old-world bronze frame around double-pane, insulated glass. With containment-grade polycarbonate glazing, they're the most secure windows in town. And those floor-to-ceiling panels are absolutely gorgeous, aren't they? Yes, Maree and I got on like two peas in a pod."

M'Kenzee could see it: two Tasmanian devils working in tandem, leaving a whirlwind of jubilant dust in their wake. She had to giggle at the vision, and she understood why Maree had fallen in love with this town — the people who lived and worked there were adorable, just like her baby sister.

27

There is no work so rude
that man may not exalt it;
no work so impassive
that he may not breathe a soul into it;
no work so dull
that he may not enliven it.
Henry Giles

"M'Kenzee, where are you?" A sweet, yet strong, voice called out.

Speak of the Tasmanian devil.

"Up here, Maree. In the attic," M'Kenzee bellowed down the open stairwell.

"Is it safe?" Maree countered.

"Come on up," Sammy assured her.

"Oh, hey guys," Maree greeted, giving a quick hug to both M'Kenzee and Sammy. "Wow — look at this space. You should finish this out. It will make an ideal sewing room…"

Jinx also called up the stairs for M'Kenzee to go meet the paint supervisor, rescuing her from the "she should do this" and "she's got to do that" conversation that ensued in the attic. *Two peas in a pod to put it lightly*, M'Kenzee thought with a giggle as she dashed down to tackle the next job on her list.

The day continued in that same manner, discussing and deciding and scheduling with one contractor after another. Jinx proved to be both savior and taskmaster.

Maree had stayed, serving as sounding board, supporter, pep leader when M'Kenzee doubted her abilities, and finally meal provider when no one else noticed it was past time to eat. Spending the hours side-by-side with Maree illustrated to M'Kenzee what life close to loved ones could be.

By the time she re-inflated the air mattress and fell onto it that night, M'Kenzee had met a brick wall. She was exhausted.

Underneath the fatigue, a sense of accomplishment, a certainty she'd done good work, filled M'Kenzee. It warmed her heart, made her proud of what she would create for herself and Bren.

Too tired to read, M'Kenzee gazed up at the stars. She fell asleep thinking of Bren, who she hoped was thinking of her.

*S*he awoke to the smell of breakfast and the whirring sound of a power drill.

Someone had let themself into her home. How strange that it neither surprised nor startled her.

Taking her time, M'Kenzee brushed her teeth, washed her face and rubbed on some moisturizer, finger-combed her short spiky hair, and dressed in faded skinny jeans, her favorite and most comfortable pair of tennis shoes, and a thick, colorful flannel shirt over a soft, long-sleeved evergreen t-shirt.

"Good morning, intruders," she said, alerting the couple kissing in her kitchen that they were no longer alone.

Maree tried to jump out of Rhys's arms, but he held tight,

placing one last peck on her forehead before picking up the drill to detach another cabinet door from its hinges.

"I brought breakfast. And muscle," Maree beamed.

"So I see," M'Kenzee teased while sifting through the white paper sack next to the sink. "Breakfast burritos? These smell so good," she admitted.

"Triple T's," Rhys told her. "The best in town."

"Earl sent salt, pepper, salsa, ketchup, and hot sauce in that smaller bag, if you want anything to go on it," Maree added. She opened a small cooler to reveal bottles of water and orange juice.

"Mmm, I'll take some OJ." M'Kenzee traded Maree a burrito for a beverage. "Y'all thought of everything. Thank you; this is really delicious!"

Maree's smile grew wider under her sister's praise.

"But what about your yoga class, Maree? Why are y'all giving up your Saturday morning for me?"

"Maree mentioned you wanted to prep the cabinets for refinishing rather than lose the original woodwork for modern replacements. We figured three people could get it done in one-third the time it'll take you working by yourself," Rhys said matter-of-factly. M'Kenzee would never outright ask for help. They all knew it, so Rhys and Maree had taken the initiative, leaving her no choice.

"Okay. But only if I buy dinner for us tonight. We'll have earned it by then."

"It's a deal," Maree began. "On one condition."

"I'm scared," M'Kenzee muttered.

"You come to the apartment to shower and sleep in a proper bed tonight," Maree insisted.

"I'll take the shower— I *need* the shower," M'Kenzee agreed. "But I really love sleeping here. I won't be sad to get our bedroom furniture set up, but until then, the air mattress is fine."

Maree sighed, and M'Kenzee wanted to help her understand.

"It's silly, I know. But I belong here. I feel Bren's presence, knowing he wanted us to be here together someday. And I like looking out our bedroom window to watch the clouds move across the night sky, knowing he's doing the same thing. It's—" M'Kenzee paused, trying to find the right words.

"It's not silly," Rhys interjected. "From the first moment Maree stepped foot in my house, I knew it was meant to be hers as much as mine. She belonged there with me; that's all there was to it. She worked hard to create her apartment above the design studio, and it's great. But she belongs with me. So, I get it, M'Kenzee."

She nodded at him through the lump in her throat. She'd given Rhys such a hard time when he and Maree were falling in love. M'Kenzee had been critical and judgmental and accusing. She'd not taken the time to hear his story, to understand his journey. And it hadn't been an easy one. Like the Davenports, Rhys's family experienced the worst type of tragedy. He'd survived, but in the process, he learned to push away anyone who might matter, for fear of losing them. Rhys had developed thick walls around his heart. He'd believed anyone crazy enough to love him would pay through pain, as though loving him was a curse.

From the moment they first collided in the grocery store, Maree saw right through his barriers. She'd loved him through their challenges, through the rough spots. Much the way Bren had loved M'Kenzee through the years, despite the silent treatments and cold shoulders she'd given him.

M'Kenzee didn't think she deserved Bren. Or forgiveness. But thankfully, the Lord didn't give up on her as quickly as she'd given up on others.

How priceless is your unfailing love, O God! People take refuge in the shadow of your wings.

Psalm 36:7 — one of Dad's favorite verses. She was shocked to remember it from her childhood.

The memory instilled peace in her heart, difficult to explain, but no less present.

Keeping it to herself to savor and enjoy, she finished her breakfast and spent the next several hours tagging doors and shelves, removing hardware and knobs, and tidily stacking the pieces until she could help the painters sand, clean, paint, and seal each one.

Rhys played music on his phone, listening while he worked. Maree sang and whistled and chatted, a worker bee in constant motion. M'Kenzee dreamed.

She visualized the rooms as they'd look when the work was done…hardwood and parquet floors gleaming a deep, aged walnut brown…fanciful woodworking, delicate trims, and regal crown molding painted pristine white…vivid and bold large-scale prints that popped with color and depth, papering the walls. She'd choose different colors for each room, and she'd fill them with button-backed, rolled-arm leather sofas and chairs upholstered in heavy fabrics bursting with design. And books! Bren loved to read, loved to talk about books. She'd fill their home with everything he loved the most.

She stacked the last set of cabinet fronts from their bathroom and looked around their master suite and halted suddenly, stunned by the image in her head.

Her vision could only be described as whimsical. She was probably the least whimsical person she'd ever met. But she and Bren had known enough harsh reality. Between her assignments as a photojournalist and Bren's years serving on joint task forces, they'd seen plenty of minimalist spaces, bland colors, and harsh, real life.

This house — their home — would be light, airy, open, colorful, bright, happy, and full. Full to overflowing with love!

All the love M'Kenzee had withheld, all the love she had to give.

That evening, showered and scrubbed and worn out but happy, M'Kenzee dove into a big greasy hamburger with sweet potato fries and a tall glass of sweet tea at Three Bells. The sandwich shop and pub sat a few doors down from Maree's shop, facing the small-town courthouse square. M'Kenzee had grabbed sandwiches from Three Bells many times for a quick lunch at Maree's place, but she'd never eaten in the restaurant. She admired the atmosphere.

Teams from the Saturday night dart league laughed and joked throughout their games. M'Kenzee had worked at a dart bar during college in Stillwater, so she had fun listening to the familiar sound of camaraderie and fellowship between friends. Not half-bad at throwing, she considered asking to play a pick-up game, but decided to save that for another night.

A few families filled the front booths, opposite the wall-length bar. Children, still hyper from Christmas, appeared jubilant to have another week off school. What would that be like? Sitting at dinner, soaking up family time, sneaking glances at her hunky husband while the kids talked a million miles an hour about everything and nothing, all at the same time? Amazing… That's how it would be.

Will be, a voice whispered in her soul.

That same voice prompted M'Kenzee to join Miss Sadie, Landry, Maree, and Rhys at church the next morning.

The service began with announcements. A quaint and old-fashioned practice, M'Kenzee found solace in the reading of events, thank you cards, and prayer requests. It pleased her that some things rarely changed over time, particularly in small towns.

The remainder of the format followed exactly what she'd expected: songs, Lord's supper, songs again, sermon, and more songs before dismissal. They could have taken the agenda from any church bulletin from any decade from the past hundred years. Again, the consistency, the foundation of it all, reassured M'Kenzee in a way she'd not expected.

And the songs — they were phenomenal.

M'Kenzee felt sure the song leader had plucked them from her heart, as he'd chosen all her favorites for the day. He'd included classic hymns like "Blessed Assurance" and "It is Well with My Soul." They sang popular praise songs, including "10,000 Reasons" and "Ships in the Night."

"I have a solo today," Maree whispered, squeezing M'Kenzee's knee before standing to join the song leader on stage.

When her little sister belted out a stirring rendition of "You Say," M'Kenzee broke down; tears flowed down her face. Every word struck a chord. She questioned if she was enough — more than just the things that had happened to her, more than the tragedy she'd known. She'd survived, but not thrived. Could she really believe she was loved? Accepted? Wanted? Treasured? Had she looked in the wrong places for her identity and security all along?

Bless their hearts, Miss Sadie and Landry didn't bat an eye at her emotional response. Miss Sadie simply handed her a wad of tissues from her handbag, and Landry draped an arm over M'Kenzee's shoulder, lending strength without an ounce of judgment.

The sermon focused on faith, on believing, on trusting in the Lord in desert days. With scripture, the preacher explained how David used prudent communication through prayer to move forward during the worst of times. His lesson highlighted David's refusal to take on a victim's mentality and taught that David actually cried out in confession to take ownership of his situation and ask for help.

Have I acted like the wronged party? Have I accepted my fault and acknowledged my role in causing the hurt I've felt? Oh Lord, humble me.

"Wait for the Lord; be strong and take heart and wait for the Lord. Psalm 27:14," M'Kenzee read under her breath as the verse projected onto the overhead screen.

Maree entwined her fingers with M'Kenzee's, gripping her hand in encouragement.

Sunday morning worship sure had given M'Kenzee a lot to think about.

Just as Miss Sadie had ushered her charges into the pew before church, she led them out in reverse order…a momma duck, head held high, chest puffed out with pride, and her little ducklings following behind in perfect order.

"M'Kenzee, come along," Miss Sadie told her. "I want you to meet Mr. Mitchell, our pulpit minister. He's been praying for Bren, and praying for you, too."

A flush of embarrassment heated M'Kenzee's cheeks. Was there a living soul in Green Hills who did not know the intimate details of her life and shortcomings?

Doubtful.

Dutifully, though, she followed as Miss Sadie had instructed. Did anyone ever do otherwise?

Even more doubtful.

"M'Kenzee, it's wonderful to meet you," Mr. Mitchell said with such genuine authenticity that M'Kenzee couldn't help but believe him. "I've admired your work for a long time, even before Maree discovered our tiny slice of heaven here on earth. In fact, I've used several of your photographs in my lessons over the years."

"Really?" M'Kenzee froze in shock.

"Oh, yes! I first came across your series of international youth portraits, probably around 2014 or 2015. The photos captured the uniqueness of each region you visited, displaying both beauty and ugliness in each location. You proved that both extremes can be found everywhere around the world: glamorous first-world cities, heartbreaking third-world hovels, and everything between. You balanced those glimpses perfectly with the timelessness of teen concerns, stereotypes, and angsts. If you want to know the health and longevity of a nation — including God's kingdom — look no further than the young people in it. They're very wise." He paused, as if in reverence, displaying his respect for a population rarely lauded for their experience and knowledge.

"But young people often feel as though they have no voice to share their insight, no visibility or recognition," he continued. "Through portraits, you gave kids a voice, a light in which to be seen. And you must've gained their trust and confidence in the process; there's no other way they would've let you into their world so openly, otherwise. Anyone who instills such faith is someone I want to know. I've followed you ever since."

"Wow." M'Kenzee had no other words. A small-town, off-the-beaten-path preacher had seen her work. And not only seen it, he'd been impressed and impacted by it.

Those portraits included subjects with piercings, highlighted tattoos, depicted teen pregnancies, showed the ravages of eating disorders; the photographs presented the effects of physical, mental, and emotional abuse. Those pictures didn't hide the ugliest parts of adolescent struggles. They laid them bare. Still, Mr. Mitchell saw the beauty of the lives, the strength of the survivors she'd captured in the images.

"I'm glad you're here today. I hope you'll come back again," he said before turning to another parishioner who waited to say hello.

"Well, let's get home. Lunch is waiting." Miss Sadie called for Landry, who'd drifted off to visit with a group of kids, maybe in third or fourth grade. M'Kenzee fell into step behind her, mind still spinning.

She'd assumed she knew the world, the people in it. She'd

assumed she knew other people's opinions, Bren's heart. Just how much of life had she gotten wrong?

If only I could turn back time, she mused. *I'd do so many things differently.*

She sighed, exhaling a deep breath.

If only.

*A*fter lunch at Marshall Mansion, M'Kenzee returned home, changed into work clothes, and turned up a playlist on her phone as loud as it would go. Then she took to sanding the cabinet doors and shelves. Jinx had shown her how to use an electric sander and left it with her, making the work less strenuous, although her arms would still scream with soreness in the morning.

The work helped. It kept her busy, kept her from worrying quite so much about Bren.

Have faith.

Mr. Mitchell's sermon had implored her to grab hold of it and never let go.

Sitting in their bedroom, her back propped against the wall beside the fireplace, M'Kenzee opened the next notebook from Bren's box and said the word aloud: *faith.*

The empty room didn't mind, and she'd needed to test its feel, taste its flavor, hear its sound. Not too bad. *Faith.*

Yeah, she could hang on to that.

28

***

A kiss is the rosy dot over the "i" of loving.
Cyrano de Bergerac by Edmond Rostand

Friday, July 4, 2003

Dear M'Kenzee,

I'm sorry it's been so long since I've written.

I don't have a reasonable excuse — all I can say is that days turned to months too quickly.

But you're always in the back of my mind.

Happy Independence Day! I hope you are busy at a parade or festival, eating too much cotton candy (I know it's your favorite) and at least one funnel cake for me. As one might imagine, celebrating the USA's separation from British rule isn't much of a party over here.

He would've been close to turning fourteen when he

wrote that. M'Kenzee marveled at how his speech pattern had matured. He sounded like a proper English gentleman.

> I mostly fill my days with football (soccer, in America). My team is currently ranked in first place in the U-14 Premiere League. I'm still not part of the starting lineup, but I play quite a lot of minutes as the first substitute. I can be happy with that. For now. As my dribbling improves, I believe my contribution to the club will increase.

Quite level-headed, indeed.

> I'm also preparing for Braemar Gathering. It's the best of all the Highland games. I've submitted entries for the youth running events: the 100 yards, the 220 yards, and the 440 yards races. My age division is from twelve to sixteen years old, so I'm competing against boys who might be much faster than I am.
>
> I intend to smoke 'em so I cover them in the mud that my spikes spray as I fly by!

There was the young Bren M'Kenzee remembered.

> Please mark September 6 on your calendar. Say a prayer for me that morning, that I'll run well. The footraces here are the world's oldest, so they

are naturally very important. The royal family
attends the Braemar Gathering regularly, and the
track and field sports are said to be most intriguing
to Queen Elizabeth. I'd like to win in front of Her
Majesty.

I'm going to imagine you are here to watch, too.
That will make me run faster. I wish to make you
proud.

Always,

B.

———

Sunday, September 7, 2003

Your prayers worked!

I won two of the three races I entered (the 100
yards and the 220 yards - I guess I'm better at
the shorter races than the longer ones), and both
Queen Elizabeth and Prince Philip were there. They
even stood to clap for me when I received my
trophies.

Mom said Her Royal Highness looked very
smart in her yellow and white two-piece suit. She
also wore a boxy white hat with a yellow brim that
matched her dress. Mom went on to say the
Queen's pearls are stunning. Da says not to forget
that the Duke of Edinburgh looked rather dashing in
his formal kilt. I think they're making an awful

big deal about what everyone was wearing, but
Granda and Nan seemed to think I wasn't interested enough.

I was more impressed with Mom, and so glad
she saw me run. I couldn't believe it when she
came out to join us for the drive to the park. And
she stayed to watch all three of my events.

I've noticed she is up and about more these
days, even helping Nan in the kitchen a little when
it's a good day. Best of all, she's having more and
more good days. Her cheeks appear less sallow,
and her clothes no longer fall off her frail frame.
I don't want to get my hopes up, but I think the
treatments might be working. Perhaps she's getting
better.

I hope 5th grade is off to a good start,
B.

———

Monday, November 3, 2003
Happy Birthday, M'KenZee — I hope being
eleven is truly wonderful!

Enjoy your day, and when you make your wish,
please think of me.
B.

———

Thursday, November 27, 2003
Dear M'KenZee,
Remember when I told you that people in the
UK don't really celebrate July 4th? Well, they don't
care about Thanksgiving, either. (We did have the
Harvest Festival of Thanks back in September, but
it's not the same. At all.)
Luckily, Mom and Nan are cooking a traditional
feast with turkey, dressing, giblet gravy, and all
the sides so we can have our own party. They even
made pumpkin and chess pies, peanut candy, and
tea cakes with powdered sugar on top.
Da has arranged for us to call you tonight,
around three o'clock your time. I can't wait to hear
your voice, talk to Max, and say hello to Maree.
You haven't forgotten me, have you?
I pray not,
B.

———

Friday, December 26, 2003
Happy Boxing Day!
Here we have parties on Christmas Eve,
Christmas Day, and the day after.
Boxing Day began as a day to give a box of
needed items to the poor or to those in service — like
postal workers and police and firefighters — to

thank them for their work while giving them a day off. Now, it's really just a day to shop and give gifts of gratitude to the people you didn't see on Christmas Eve or Christmas Day. I don't care why we do it. I just think it's fun to pack the boxes and leave them on people's porches or in their mailbox.

I made boxes for you and Max and Maree. It might be a week or more before you get them, but don't worry, nothing in the boxes will spoil.

Fingers crossed you like it, and that your family had a nice Christmas,

B.

———

Thursday, January 1, 2004

Happy New Year!!

Did you do something fun for NYE? Here we call it Hogmanay, and it's crazy!

We attended a grand celebration at the Fife Arms, which is a fancy shmancy hotel that's been in Braemar since the 19th century. It became ultra-popular when Prince Albert bought Balmoral for Queen Victoria in 1852. That's the royal estate, which is only nine miles away.

They served a four-course dinner, and I had to wear a tuxedo. Mom looked amazing, glowing with radiance in her sparkling evening gown. She's gotten so strong. I asked her to dance while they passed around appetizers called canapés before dinner began, and she said yes. We'd only made it around the floor once, though, when I noticed Da wipe tears from his eyes, so I took her back to the table. I think he wanted to be the one to dance with her first.

At midnight, we went outside to cool off from dancing and watch fireworks that lit up the sky for over thirty minutes. Granda snuck me a glass of champagne, but it tasted awful, so I poured the rest in a flowerpot when he wasn't looking. Then we stayed another hour to eat a huge Scottish breakfast.

I'll never be hungry again.

If you didn't go to a party this year, promise me you will from now on. We should all take time to welcome in a new year of possibilities.

Bliadhna Mhath Ùr (that's "Happy New Year" in Gaelic),

B.

Saturday, February 14, 2004

Dear M'Kenzee,

It's Valentine's Day, and I swear this community is determined to throw a dance for every little reason they can find. Tonight, the community council is hosting one at the village hall, and Mom's forcing the whole family to go. She's even making me wear a suit. And a tie!

Da and Granda are no help at all — they're both downright yaldy about going (that means "excited"). Da said, "A noose is a small price to pay for a beautiful woman," and Granda said, "Och aye," (that means "oh yeah"). Then he waggled his thick, bushy eyebrows, and they both started laughing. Uproariously. It wiznae funny. I was so irritated, I stomped out of the room.

But then I felt bad. It's wonderful to see Mom so happy — and healthy. They haven't said the R-word yet, but I know the cancer's gone. It has to be. You should see her, back to her old self. But even better. She's lovely.

So, I wore the suit. And I let Mom fix my tie for me (even though we both know I tie one every morning for school and can do it in my sleep...and have on more than one occasion when I stayed out hunting too long before school). Fussing over me seems to bring her joy. And Da's right: it's a small price to pay to see her eyes light up.

Now Granda's reading the paper, Da's reading a book, and I'm writing to you while we all wait for Mom and Nan to finish getting dressed. Maybe the dance will be over by the time they're ready to go.

One can only hope.

———

Isla kissed me!

Hmmm — was that a happy exclamation point or a mad one?

She looked sad, standing by herself at the edge of the room, so I volunteered to dance with her. When the music ended, she tightened her arms around my neck, rose on her tiptoes, and pressed her lips to mine. Can you believe that? I'll tell you what: no good deed goes unpunished! That's what Granda likes to say, and he's right!!

M'Kenzee giggled. Out loud. Bren certainly seemed to protest a little too much.

His first kiss. She considered Isla a very lucky girl.

After she kissed me, Isla held onto my hand. ALL night. Then she tried to kiss me again —

AGAIN — when her little sister said it was time for them to leave. Luckily, I turned my head just enough so her lips landed on my cheek and not my mouth that time. I mean, really! She's always been so shy. And quiet. And timid. BASHFUL, even. Of all the ways to find one's confidence, did she have to discover hers by using me? I mean, REALLY!!

Bren had traced over the A, L, L so many times the letters were deeply indented in the paper, almost tearing through. He'd used more capital letters in one paragraph than she'd seen him use in full notebooks. The reserved, unassuming Isla had found her courage and went after what she wanted. In doing so, she'd made Bren mighty uncomfortable. M'Kenzee thought it was wonderful. Ah, yes, there was power in love.

I'm so mad I might not be able to sleep tonight. I told Mom that dance was a bad idea, that I didn't want to go. But no, we just had to. Now look. Isla's already called our house. Late at night! Everyone else had gone to bed. And the phone rang. Loudly! Talk about a disaster.

I answered just to make it stop ringing. Isla — introverted Isla — rushed into an explanation about why we should go together. What does that mean: "go" together?

Then she just sat there on the other end, waiting

for me to say something. What was I supposed
to say?

I don't want to be her boyfriend, but I also
don't want to hurt her feelings.

In a strange way, she showed a lot of courage
kissing me, holding my hand, and even calling on
the phone. That couldn't have been easy.

In the end, I told her that was fine. We could
date, but no more kissing.

We're already friends, anyway. And if she
wants to call us boyfriend and girlfriend, I don't
care. As long as she doesn't try anything else.
I've got football (soccer, ye ken) to focus on, and
she's a ballerina, so she needs to think about that.
There's no time for kissing and stuff.

Besides, I'm saving my kisses.

B.

———

Friday, March 5, 2004

Dear M'Kenzee,

We're headed your way.

I love flying during the night. It's dark and
quiet with everyone sleeping or watching movies in
their pods. The pods are the coolest, like being in a
one-man cockpit. I have my own controls for the
television channels and the volume and the lights.

I'm the only one in business class with my reading lamp on, but I wanted to write to you before I try to doze off.

I can't wait to see you. And hug you. And Maree, of course. And tackle Max!

I wonder who's taller between the two of us. I hope it's still me, but Da says I should be prepared for Max to look a lot like your dad, tall and strong. He said, "If it hasn't happened yet, son, it will." Then he ruffled my hair (I hate when he does that…like I'm still a little kid) and shrugged, as if he was sorry for stating the truth. Grown-ups are weird.

It's going to be a great week. Your foster family agreed that you and Max and Maree can come to Tulsa to stay with us for a couple of days. It's strange to think of you living in Oklahoma City — how has that been? Mom explained that agreeing to go to a family in OKC was the only way Max could keep the state from separating you into three homes, that no one wanted to take y'all together. I'm sorry. It's hard to switch schools, to find your place with a new group of classmates. I've been praying it hasn't been too bad.

Well, you can tell me about it soon. We arrive in New York in the morning. Then we're flying on to Minnesota for three days. Mom's oncologists at The Royal Marsden work closely with the cancer doctors at the London Mayo, and they asked her to visit the main Mayo Clinic in Rochester to meet with some of their specialists. I'm not sure what they want to do to her, but I know she's doing great. They better not mess anything up.

We get to Tulsa on Tuesday night. I'll see you Wednesday. Doesn't that sound good?

I'll see you in person in just five days,

B.

29

A faithful friend is a strong defense;
and he that hath found him
hath found a treasure.
Louisa May Alcott

Closing the cover with her hand wedged inside to save her place on the page, M'Kenzee rested her head against the wall and closed her eyes.

Fondly, she thought back on that spring break. Definitely one of the best.

The couple they'd been living with in Oklahoma City was kind, and although everyone understood going into the arrangement that it was temporary, as Mr. and Mrs. Clifton didn't have the energy or overall health to raise three active children long term, they'd made an effort to do right by the Davenport kids. Taking Max and M'Kenzee and Maree to see their family friends in Tulsa, allowing them to stay with the Stewarts for a few days, had been an act of kindness unlike anything M'Kenzee had known in a long time.

She'd been on her very best behavior.

Yes, ma'am and *No, sir* and *Please* and *Thank you* and *May I* and holding doors and letting Maree go first… She'd done it all to preserve those hours with Bren and his parents. She'd noticed Mrs. Stewart's new hairstyle, and that she looked thinner than M'Kenzee remembered, but otherwise, she'd had no indication that Bren's mom had been fighting for life for the past four years. She'd believed the Stewarts had chosen to live in Scotland simply to go. It would be years before she learned the truth of that time.

But M'Kenzee hadn't let that bitterness, the hurt she'd still felt about Mr. and Mrs. Stewart wanting to move away from them when her siblings needed family most, disrupt that week of spring break.

They'd stayed at a fancy hotel in downtown Tulsa. The indoor/outdoor pool was heated to counter the chilly spring air, so they'd splashed and played in it for hours and hours. Their room in the hotel had been the size of an apartment. The girls had been in one bedroom — with their own beds — while the boys slept on pull-out couches in the living room, and Mr. and Mrs. Stewart had a large bedroom and bathroom to themselves. Bren's dad had called it a "sweet," and M'Kenzee remembered agreeing at the time: it was super sweet.

Maree had helped Mrs. Stewart put together breakfast in the mornings, and they'd made sandwiches for lunch, which they ate together at the big table. Then they'd have dinner out — what a treat that had been.

The first night they'd watched a concert at the minor league baseball team's stadium. Max — who was indeed a hair taller than Bren (she remembered because Max had made a very big deal about it) — had challenged Bren to see who could eat the most foot-long hot dogs. M'Kenzee had hoped Bren would win, just so she could see Max puke. Boys were dumb. She much preferred the salted pretzels dipped in hot nacho cheese, soft and warm and delicious. Maree had ordered the chicken fingers and fries…her usual when they got to order for themselves.

The next night they'd gone to a movie theater where a tray to eat on was attached to each seat. Servers had brought pizza, breadsticks, salads, milkshakes, and desserts during the film — so awesome! They'd watched *Cheaper by the Dozen*, and they'd laughed and laughed. Except when Beans, Mark's pet frog, died. That part had made M'Kenzee sad until Bren quietly reached out to hold her hand, which had helped.

Their third night, Mr. and Mrs. Stewart had taken them to a huge trampoline park, where they'd bounced and ran and hopped and skipped and jumped until they dropped with exhaustion. Bren's dad had refused to leave Tulsa without indulging in Mexican food, so after the bouncing wore off, they'd spent almost three hours dining at his favorite restaurant, a hole-in-the-wall loved by locals. They'd started with *queso blanco*, then Mr. Stewart had requested a "fill your own taco" platter for the table and insisted that every person build the biggest, crunchiest, tastiest taco they could imagine. For their entrees, M'Kenzee and Maree had shared the chicken enchiladas doused in a thick, tangy sour cream sauce and a melted layer of grated Monterey Jack cheese, served with two bowls of refried beans and rice…one for each of the girls. M'Kenzee ate and ate until her stomach wanted — needed — to explode, but when the *sopapillas* Mrs. Stewart had ordered came to the table piping hot and covered in a blanket of dusted cinnamon and powdered sugar, M'Kenzee had trudged ahead like a trooper, forcing herself to eat not one, but two of the scrumptious pastries, drizzled in honey, of course.

That restaurant still held a special place in M'Kenzee's heart, and she ate there often when she found herself in Tulsa with free time for a treat.

Tears had flowed during hard goodbyes the next afternoon, but the wonderful week and memories forged had made the heartache bearable. M'Kenzee hadn't known when — or *if* — she'd see Bren and the Stewarts again. She'd decided then and there: the joy of those few days would tide her over; they'd have to be enough. They were all that remained of family, vacations, laughter, and being together.

*N*eeding a break, and a new place and position in which to sit, M'Kenzee laid the notebook down, open to the next letter from Bren. She padded to the kitchen in a huge sweater over long johns, leg warmers, cozy socks, and her fuzzy boots. After contemplating adding a scarf around her neck, she decided against it out of sheer principle... No one should be crazy enough — or hardheaded enough — to stay in a house that required a scarf when there were multiple offers to sleep in warm, soft, cozy beds just a few minutes away. She did, however, look forward to a visit from the chimney sweep scheduled for the next day. Once he'd cleaned and certified the fireplaces safe, she intended to keep the home fires burning around the clock.

In the kitchen, she used the plug-in burner to heat water in a small saucepan for tea but then opted for a cup of hot chocolate instead. Maree had brought a cute basket of cocoa supplies and left it on the kitchen counter. Rummaging through the basket, M'Kenzee found a variety of cocoa mixes in single-serve pouches, mini marshmallows, peppermint sticks, individual cups of creamer, a bottle of caramel drizzle, a shaker of sea salt, and a tin of glittery sugar for "salting" the rim of her mug.

Why not? Let's go for it.

Starting with plain milk chocolate powder, M'Kenzee added boiling water and stirred until the mix dissolved. She poured in three creamers, squeezed caramel over the top until it sank under the surface, and stirred some more. Finally, she gave half a shake of sea salt over the top and placed a pinch of the fancy sugar in the center.

Well, it looks incredible, no matter how it's going to taste.

She carried the indulgence back to her room, piled her pillows to make a cushion, and sat right on top of them beside the air mattress, upon which she flipped Bren's journal right side up so she could continue reading. With the mock desk arranged, she shone the flashlight on the page, promising to stop and sleep after the last few pages of that book.

Wednesday, March 17, 2004
Dear M'Kenzee,
I'm coming home.

M'Kenzee's heart stopped beating. She read the words again. And then once more.

I'm coming home.
Mom's meeting in Minnesota was a great one — they're willing to oversee her maintenance appointments now that she's in REMISSION. We can say it, the R-word!! I knew it. I just knew she was better.

I have to finish school here, but Da said the family renting our house in Oklahoma will move out when their lease is up at the end of May. We'll have to stay in a hotel for a couple of weeks until our stuff arrives from Scotland, and Mom wants to repaint and redo the carpets while we wait. But the timing is perfect. By Max's birthday, I'll be home.

They made me go ahead a grade when we moved here, but I have a plan to go back to ninth grade with Max in the fall. You'll be in sixth, and even though it's not the same building, we'll be right next door to one another on campus. It'll be just like before, Max and I walking you and Maree to school every morning.

Maybe you and Max and Maree can even move back in with us, now that Mom is okay.

I'm so happy! It's maist braw, M'Kenzee, so very good.

I'll see you soon,

B.

P.S. Happy Saint Patrick's Day — I hope you're wearing something green.

Bren and the Stewarts had moved back to Oklahoma, just the way Bren had said it would happen.

The Davenport kids had stayed with Mr. and Mrs. Clifton until the end of the summer. The sweet old man and his dainty wife had both cried when they delivered the kids to their next foster home, a group facility where Max had agreed with the social workers they would live until he turned eighteen. "Only three years to go," Max had said, determined he would obtain custody of the girls at that time.

Throughout those years, M'Kenzee had made it a point to

make the most of every moment she had with her brother, with Maree, and with Bren. She'd feared the future, but she couldn't have said specifically why. Something was coming, something that would take away her people, again. She was sure of it. All she'd known to do was enjoy the time they had and shore up her defenses to minimize the hurt certain to come.

With the benefit of hindsight, M'Kenzee could admit she'd done *too* good a job building those walls. She'd created an emotional distance that caused others to see her as standoffish, rude, and exacting.

Calling it a night, she closed the journal and placed it upside down on the stack of already-reads.

*T*he next morning, as she stood by the kitchen counter reviewing her list of house projects and appointments for the day, Maree called.

"Hi." For such a small human, Maree's voice could really boom. "What'cha doing?"

"Scribbling notes, circling meeting times, and jotting down selections," M'Kenzee said, distracted.

"Let's go to Dallas!"

"Come again?"

"Next week, let's take a few days to meander our way to the metroplex. I know the perfect places to hunt for hidden treasures along the way, and when we get there, you can buy whatever we don't find at antique and junk stores from the swanky upscale stores in Big D."

"How long do I have to be gone?"

Crickets sounded from Maree's end of the line. M'Kenzee's lack of an argument must've struck her dumb.

"And get your pitch for New Year's Eve out of the way while I'm feeling accommodating." M'Kenzee would finish her baby sister off completely with that one.

"Wha— Umm— Ye— Yes!" Maree finally spat out. "YES! Let's plan for three days. Maybe leave next Wednesday? And YES to New Year's! Rhys's friend, Daniel Davis— You remember him, don't you? Davis is having a party at his family's cabin on Daisy Lake. Please say you'll go with us. Landry'll be there, and a few other people you've met before."

"I'll go."

"Just like that? No begging, no bargaining, no bartering, and no arm-twisting? What have you done with my big sister?"

"Bren wants me to go."

Silence again from Maree.

"Rest easy. I'm not talking back and forth with figments of my imagination," M'Kenzee reassured her. "It was a letter he wrote when they were still living in Scotland. He talked about a fabulous New Year's Eve celebration at a fancy hotel, describing the food, the fireworks, and even his first sip of champagne in vivid detail. At the end, he asked me to always celebrate the new year and the new possibilities that come with a clean slate."

"I agree," Maree said in her glass-half-full, wholehearted fashion. "I love the feeling of doors opening, of rededicating ourselves to goals and seeing where that focused surge of determination takes us. Even when my resolutions fail within a few days or weeks, I have a blast focusing on them as long as they last."

"I'll let Jinx know what days I'll be gone next week; I'm sure he'll be thrilled to get me out of the house for some of the more involved projects. And count me in for Davis's party at the lake."

"Oh, M'Kenzee! I'm so excited," Maree shrieked. "Rhys and I will pick you up tomorrow evening. I'll text to let you know what time, okay?"

"Sounds good," M'Kenzee replied. "Hey, Maree? What *are* your New Year's resolutions?"

"I have a list that changes every hour. Right now it has three items: (1) Finish *Kitchen Quilts*, (2) Plan our wedding, and (3) Research inspiration elements for next fabric line."

"Those aren't resolutions," M'Kenzee argued. "That's just your to-do list."

"Well, that's why it keeps changing," Maree confessed. "I don't want to change anything about my life, except for Bren to be home safe and sound. But that's more of a prayer request than a task I can control."

"I'm glad," M'Kenzee confided. "You deserve every happiness, and I'm thrilled you found it, fought for it, and had the courage to embrace it."

"You deserve it, too, 'Kenz."

"I don't know. What if what's happened to Bren is my fault, my punishment for a lifetime of being difficult, hateful, and downright awful? Is he paying the price for my bad behavior?"

"You're not nearly as horrible as you make yourself out to be," Maree insisted with a good-natured laugh. "So you weren't all BFF-lovey-dovey with the fake girls in high school? So what if you put jerks like Terk Douglas in their place and told boys *NO* emphatically when you weren't interested? Those traits don't make you downright awful. They make you downright awesome. M'Kenzee, you are strong. And you are loved," Maree finished with emphasis.

Mr. Mitchell's face appeared in M'Kenzee's mind. She thought of the way Miss Sadie's minister accepted and found beauty in people who others deemed failures, miscreants, or difficult to love.

"You too, baby sis. I love you dearly; I hope you know that." M'Kenzee forced a smile to lend a lighthearted tone to her voice.

"Without a doubt," Maree promised. "I'll see you tomorrow night."

"I'll be ready."

. . .

*A*fter they hung up, M'Kenzee finished her punch list for the day, ordered a copper teakettle and a set of handmade green stoneware dishes off the internet, and finalized her paint and wallpaper choices for the master suite, the kitchen, and the living room — the three areas she wanted finished first.

Midmorning, electricians and plumbers showed up within thirty minutes of each other to diagnose and begin reconstructing out-of-date and out-of-code systems. Jinx wasn't far behind with a brick mason in tow. M'Kenzee offered to run to the Fish & Spoon to pick up boxes of fish and chips for everyone's lunch. When she returned, a man touted as the state's best framer and woodworking craftsman frowned, tsked, and muttered under his breath in conversation with the gingerbread trim lining the front porch eaves.

Good thing I bought a few extra boxes… Sounds like I need to stay in this one's good graces.

She needed to stay in everyone's good graces. She couldn't complete this project on her own. It required tons of help, something she had never been great at accepting.

But look what happens when you do.

"You okay?" Jinx asked from the doorway of her bedroom.

M'Kenzee had been staring into the fireplace; his deep voice startled her.

"Sorry," he apologized with a grimace. "Can I come in?"

"Of course. I don't know where my mind had drifted off to."

"How's that air mattress working out?" He looked down at the only piece of furniture in the room with disdain.

"Not as comfy as the commercials claim, but it's fine."

"Come on," he said with a flick of his head toward the door.

"Where to?"

"You'll see," was all Jinx said.

en minutes later, he pulled onto a long gravel drive that led to an old farmhouse set well off the road.

"Where are we?" M'Kenzee tried again.

"You'll see," he repeated, continuing to drive around the house and down to a dilapidated barn hidden under a canopy of overgrown trees.

"What is this?" M'Kenzee asked, then answered her own question, lifting a hand and shaking her head with a quick, "You'll see," before he could say it himself.

Jinx smiled over at M'Kenzee, a twinkle shining in those hypnotic eyes of his.

He swung the truck in a circle and backed it up to park by the massive double doors. Jinx punched a code into the padlock connecting a heavy chain to the door handles. M'Kenzee raised a questioning eyebrow in his direction — rather high-tech for a barn barely standing on its last leg.

"Don't let the outside fool you," he warned, before sliding each door along the metal rail above their heads to reveal a treasure trove of wood: beams, boards, mantels, and hearths stood a dozen deep, each one tucked in tight next to its neighbor to maximize space. Chairs — hundreds of them — hung from rafters, nails, and hooks, dangling from the ceiling. Dining tables, end tables, coffee tables, entry tables, poker tables, pool tables, and unique accent tables balanced in stacks, three and four tables high with drop cloths and blankets between them, all the way down the length of the barn. Antique desks, roll-top desks, secretaries, credenzas, dressers, and armoires filled every inch of floor space along the other long wall. When he pulled the handle on an industrial power switch, bright light flooded the room. The wood pieces included everything from raw lumber to weathered siding to antique shiplap to half-stained to fully painted to glossy finishes.

"Holy woodworking, Batman," M'Kenzee exclaimed.

Jinx laughed, wrapped an arm around M'Kenzee's shoulders, and led her into the magnificent den. "Let's find you some bedroom furniture."

She stopped midstride. "What?"

"Consider it my wedding-slash-housewarming-slash-welcome-to-Green-Hills gift. Grandad passed down his infatuation with wood. Between the two of us, we've collected way more than we can ever use. I want you and Bren to have something special."

"Jinx, this is unbelievable."

"Nah, it's just an old man's hobby and a young man's sentimental attachment to the old man. Come on; I think you'll find something over here."

He led her to an area of the barn filled with bed frames. A ray of sunshine from the open doors gleamed over a regal Queen Anne headboard connected to its footboard by detailed side rails. Simple designs carved into the wood lent an air of streamlined grace; the pad feet added pomp and nobility. The piece showcased a precise balance between sturdy and stunning.

"What's it made of?" M'Kenzee whispered, as though the piece demanded reverence.

"Walnut," Jinx answered on a chuckle, not whispering. "Good ol' Oklahoma black walnut. Grandad made this set after he returned home from the war. Carving and sanding worked like therapy to calm his nerves, reminded him that good things still existed in the world. This sat in his and Gran's bedroom for decades."

"It's exquisite, Jinx."

She moved to look at other options.

"Not the right look?" he asked kindly.

"No, it's absolutely perfect, but I can't take that one. You have to keep it; it's priceless."

"It won't fit in any room in my house. Besides, Grandad made a set for me before the dementia took away his skills. That's what I want to give my wife…when I find her. If you like this one, I'd love for you to have it, the whole suite. Let me show you the rest of the pieces."

For the better part of an hour, Jinx gathered furniture that matched the Queen Anne bed: two impressive bedside dressers, a footboard bench with a padded seat, an elegant lingerie chest, and a double wardrobe. He took his time explaining the unique characteristics of each piece, sharing stories about his grandparents, and reminiscing about the hours he and Matthias had spent playing in the barn while Duke worked.

"Jinx, that's six pieces of furniture." She stood looking at all he'd set out for her to see, astonished.

"All yours. They're going to be mighty impressive in that room, with the big windows letting in natural light, the tiled fireplace surround, and the raised ceilings. Quite a haven," he said on a whistle.

"Just the bed frame is worth thousands. You have to let me pay you something," she begged.

"Okay, whatever you think it's worth."

M'Kenzee's eyes bulged. She'd been quite successful and frugal with her money, but in no way could she afford what this furniture was worth.

"I'm teasing," Jinx laughed. "I want you to take the furniture as a gift. But if you feel like you have to pay something, how about a trade?"

"I have nothing to give." She slumped in defeat.

"You have a camera."

"You want my camera?" M'Kenzee squeaked, panic-stricken. Her camera might as well have been an appendage; giving it away equated to cutting off an arm. Or both of them.

"No," Jinx laughed. "You're an amazing, world-renowned photographer," he said, wonder in his voice. "I'd like a portrait of Grandad, before Alzheimer's makes him so frail he doesn't resemble the hero whose strength I've marveled at my whole life."

"Oh, Jinx, I'd love to do that for you. Not for the furniture," she added. "And not for all the help you're giving me. Just for you."

He nodded his agreement, exhaled to clear the emotion M'Kenzee recognized in his eyes, and tossed his arm back over her shoulder to guide her toward the door. "I thought you said you were difficult to love?"

"Just you wait!"

Jinx backed up the truck to attach a flatbed trailer. Together, he and M'Kenzee loaded the bed frame and the side dresser. He used blankets and come-alongs to cushion and secure the furniture without damaging the wood.

Jinx detoured toward the highway on their way to M'Kenzee's house. Again, her eyebrows rose in question when he stopped at the furniture warehouse on the outskirts of town.

"I believe we just left the furniture store," M'Kenzee stated.

"Ah, but here we can get you a new mattress, so you're not sleeping on the floor anymore."

"But what about the roofing and the flooring and the painting?"

"These two pieces won't be too hard to move out of the way when it's time to work on the master suite. And we'll wait to get the rest until the remodel of your room is done." He reached for his phone before getting out of the truck.

"Hi, Miss Sadie, it's Jinx," he said after dialing a number. "Yes, she picked out Gran's old set. Yes, ma'am, it's a pretty one, for sure. That's right, queen-sized. We're here now. Yes, ma'am," he repeated several more times before saying goodbye.

"Linens and dinner will be there when we get back to your house," Jinx informed M'Kenzee with a conspiratorial gleam in his eyes.

"Sneaky little angels, aren't y'all?" M'Kenzee teased as she stepped down from her seat.

That night, she climbed into crisp, lavender-scented sheets on a thick, soft mattress — not on the floor — and read the next journal in Bren's box by lamplight and with feathery pillows bunched under her head and shoulders. The wedding quilt Miss Sadie had given her lay atop a heavy down comforter. No more early mornings of frozen toes and chattering teeth.

M'Kenzee looked around the room, out the window, and up at the stars. She hugged Bren's book to her heart. So much work left to do, yet M'Kenzee smiled as peace washed over her.

Yes, this feels right.

30

———

And now let us believe in a long year
that is given to us, new, untouched,
full of things that have never been.
Rainer Maria Rilke

oo soft and relaxed in the luxurious new bed, M'Kenzee fell fast asleep just a few pages into Bren's next book.

Waking up warm and cozy did not inspire her to jump right out of bed and start the day. Plus, a holiday provided the perfect excuse for staying under the covers. Bren *had* asked her to enjoy the day.

Decision made… I'll read for just a little while.

When she'd left off, Bren and Max had just turned fifteen and couldn't wait to play high school football — the American kind, Bren was quick to point out at every possible moment.

M'Kenzee had been their biggest fan, cheering them on, correcting the referees, and advising the coaches (from the stands, and only when needed, of course). They'd been good — really good — that year, scoring lots of points on offense and shutting out opponents on defense, while the band marched through halftime in sharp, complex patterns. She'd relished the spirit of victory in the air. Their games had been a blast, and life had felt good.

Tuesday, August 3, 2004

Mom's ticked. I mean, really, really ticked.

I tanked the placement test on purpose. It was the only way they'd let me back in Max's grade. And it worked. We picked up schedules this morning, before football physicals, and I'm in almost every class with Max.

When Da saw that my schedule says ninth grade, he laughed. When Mom saw it, she went ballistic.

"How could they put you back a year?" She yelled it several times. "We're going up there right now to fix this. You were one of the top students in S3 last year, at an academically rigorous school, and taking advanced classes with the older students. Do Americans really think they're that superior, that an honors student a grade ahead in Scotland needs remediation in the United States? Well, I'll—"

I had to interrupt her before she hurt somebody.

Let's just say when I showed her the score from the placement test, she was even less happy.

"Brennigan Lance Stewart!" she bellowed. Have you ever heard my mom bellow? And she used my entire name. I hate it when she uses my entire name. "Why? Why would you do this?" Her look of agony was breaking my heart.

"Love, let's hear the boy out," Da said, coming to my rescue. Then I explained how I didn't want to be a grade ahead of Max, how I'd missed four years with him, and while I couldn't get that time back, I could have four more instead of just three.

I said it all wrong. A look of distress came into her eyes, like I'd struck her. I didn't mean that I blame her, but I'm afraid she took it that way. I tried to take it back, to make it right.

I told her it was fine, that I'd go on to sophomore year if that's what she wanted. I told her I'd had fun in Scotland — and I wasn't lying. I loved the Highlands, tracking animals, and fishing with Granda. Soccer was great, school was interesting, and I made friends there, too. I promised her with my whole heart that I was glad we had those years with Nan and Granda, and I wouldn't trade having Mom healthy again for anything.

It's all true. I just don't know if she believes me. I pray she does.

When we both stopped crying, Da came up with the perfect solution.

I get to stay in ninth grade with Max, but we're going to the school tomorrow morning before our first day of practice begins, and I have to change my schedule to take all the honors and advanced classes Mom can find. She's worried I'll be bored, but I convinced her there's always something to do and more to read.

She's still angry about me making a zero on the test. "You didn't just fail, Son; you determined the correct answer on each question to ensure you didn't pick it," she reiterated when I thought we were past it. I guess it's going to take her a little longer. That's okay, though. I'd rather she be mad at me than hurt. I'd do just about anything to keep her from ever feeling pain again.

I can't handle the thought of her hurting. Or you, M'Kenzee. I never want to cause you pain, either.

See you after practice,
B.

*A*mused by Bren's genius plan to go back a grade and Mrs. Stewart's livid reaction, M'Kenzee laughed at Bren's account of the story until tears rolled down her cheeks. Sympathy turned them to tears of sadness when she read the part where he thought he'd caused his mom pain. His desperation "to make it right" jumped off the page; Bren was forever a fixer, no matter the situation.

She could see Bren getting every test question correct just so he could pick another answer. And she could imagine how upset Mrs. Stewart had been when she figured out what he'd done. From page to page, M'Kenzee watched Bren maturing into the man he'd become. Just as she'd noticed before, strong hints at his noble character, his servant's heart, and his call to duty appeared in his writing, over and over again.

Without workers in the house, M'Kenzee skipped breakfast and lunch to remain huddled under the covers, indulging in a lazy morning and losing herself in Bren's books.

The boys' freshman year progressed. Bren wrote about every football game, drawing plays in the margins around class notes, X's and O's and squiggles representing routes he thought would work. M'Kenzee recognized Max's writing in a few places where they'd passed the notebook back and forth when the teachers turned their backs. He talked a lot about his history classes, particularly the military history he'd researched, and demonstrated a knack for STEM subjects, math being his favorite.

Just days after the school year ended, Bren had spent a week in Annapolis, Maryland, attending Summer STEM at the Naval Academy. Max had teased him — as brothers often did — about missing workouts for "nerd stuff," but without rancor as they'd all been so proud of Bren for getting into the program. M'Kenzee recalled Bren wearing his GO NAVY t-shirt *all the time* when he returned home. He'd gone on and on about the campus, the midshipmen he'd met, the classrooms and labs, and the projects they'd worked on. Bren must've had even more to say because he'd written several entries in a composition book he'd used for notes while at the camp. Most of what he'd written looked like thoughts one puts in a diary: lists of each day's activities, reminders to himself to look up this or that on the computer, and many notes to dig deeper on a topic when he got home. One particular entry, specifically addressed to M'Kenzee and rather longer than most of the others, stood out…

Thursday, June 16, 2005
Dear M'Kenzee,

I'll always belong where you are. But I think I belong here, too.

It's hard to explain — I just sense it, like there is something in the air, and when I take a breath here, the life inside me expands to be more.

Before lights out and room check, we had a shaved ice party. Snow cones might sound silly, but it's boiling hot in Maryland during the summer, and we were excited to have something cold. Most everyone here is rather confident, pretty sure of themselves and their ideas. A few people are annoyingly arrogant. But one kid, Jacob, is young for his grade, shy, you know? He doesn't say much. And he's small in stature (tiny - like Maree's size). Anyway, one of the cocky kids, Wayne, made it his mission this week to pick on Jacob. Tonight at the social, he took it too far.

After "accidentally" spilling his soda on Jacob, Wayne shoved Jacob hard enough to trip him. When he'd landed on the ground, Wayne poured his snow cone, full of sticky syrup, over Jacob. He grabbed another snow cone from a girl standing next to them, looking on in shock. I stepped between Wayne and Jacob before Wayne could dump more juice on Jacob. Wayne got in my face, and challenged me to "give it my best shot."

So, I did.

It only took one punch to drop him. But it only took that one punch for the midshipmen hanging out at the party to see what happened. Immediately, they took me to the camp director, Captain Gilley. I figured I was about to get kicked out for fighting. It was so embarrassing to be in trouble in front of the cadets, and Captain Gilley was one of the best instructors. I hated disappointing him - not to mention how mortified Mom was going to be.

But when I got to Captain Gilley's office, he asked me to take a seat and invited one midshipman to stay. Then they asked if I'd ever considered applying to the Naval Academy for college. They asked about what sports I play in high school, and when I told them about football and track, they said they'd like to introduce me to Coach K before camp ended. They also wanted to know which academic modules had been my favorite during camp, and the cadet — his name is Parker, and he's from St. Louis — offered to exchange numbers in case I have questions.

I already had two.

My first question: wasn't I in trouble for hitting Wayne?

And the second: would it matter that I'd lied to ensure I got to repeat ninth grade?

Captain Gilley laughed. Then he made a cryptic

remark that sounded like "duty, honor, country, son" as his huge hand landed on my shoulder. I think it was a pat of solidarity and support, but it still came down with a jarring thud. Captain Gilley is a very large man. I took that gesture as a sign that our meeting was over.

I never saw Wayne again to apologize. But I did spend the rest of the evening with Jacob, so he wouldn't be alone and he wouldn't hide out in his room after all that had happened.

Now, I can't sleep. I'm lying in bed, staring wide-eyed at the ceiling, wondering what it would be like to come here for college. Can I even get in? Maybe playing dumb wasn't so smart after all.

See you when I get home on Saturday,

B.

ad Captain Gilley known he'd planted a seed that day? Had he foreseen the incredible impact a single seed could have? Had he known the incredible man Bren would become?

A random verse of scripture popped into M'Kenzee's head. Something about the strength of a mustard seed. She opened an app on her phone to look it up.

He put another parable before them, saying, "The kingdom of heaven is like a grain of mustard seed that a man took and sowed in his field. It is the smallest of all seeds, but when it has grown, it is larger than all the garden plants and becomes a tree, so that the birds of the air come and make nests in its branches." Matthew 13:31–32

M'Kenzee clicked on the next result from her search.

He said to them, "Because of your little faith. For truly, I say to you, if you have faith like a grain of mustard seed, you will say to this mountain, 'Move from here to there,' and it will move, and nothing will be impossible for you." Matthew 17:20

There it was again: *faith.*

Bren's calling to serve had been set since the moment he was born. He'd been purposefully planted in a world where greedy nations and evil men created a desperate need for honorable and noble servants. He'd grown into a person who didn't have it in him to turn his back on those in need.

God, I love him.

And if I do, I have to have faith…faith in him, in our love…faith he'll come home to me again.

Please bring Bren home.

M'Kenzee continued reading, about two-a-day workouts in August, the boys' first JV football game in September, the homecoming football game in October when both Max and Bren had been moved up to the varsity team, and how his mom had "encouraged" him to invite Averie, who lived across the street, attended their church, and had been upset not to have a date, to accompany him to the Saturday night homecoming dance.

M'Kenzee thought of the photo of Bren and Averie and Max and Max's date. She had pasted it into an album years ago. When she got to college, M'Kenzee had been determined to preserve their family dynamic, even though she was in Stillwater, Maree was in Tulsa, and Max was in Kansas City. Taking their photos and memorabilia to school with her, and using colorful papers and stickers, she'd created several scrapbooks, beginning with pictures of their parents dating, then their engagement and wedding, going through the years when

Max, then M'Kenzee, and finally Maree were born, school portraits and class photos from when they began school, the obituary from their parents' deaths, the program from the joint funeral, a few photos from the years in foster care, and finally lots of clippings from the local newspaper of Maxwell Davenport, football star.

Maree probably had the scrapbooks. Maybe M'Kenzee could ask to keep them in her house for a while. Having them to flip through sounded comforting, a timely reminder that while rarely easy, their world remained good.

A chime on M'Kenzee's phone alerted her to a text from Maree.

- We'll be there to pick you up at 5:30. Wear layers. Rhys and Davis set up a bonfire on the beach between the cabin and the lake. Happy New Year's Eve!

M'Kenzee glanced at the time on her phone. Three o'clock? How had it gotten so late?

That explains why I'm starving.

She decided to finish Bren's high school journal the next night, threw back the mountain of warm covers, and sought food in the kitchen. Rhys had procured a dorm fridge from someone at the fire station, so she had milk for cereal — her go-to meal for the foreseeable future — as well as a variety of mini cereal boxes, and plastic spoons left unused from packs of disposable silverware tossed into takeout bags.

M'Kenzee showered, towel-dried her pixie hairdo, and stepped into a pair of skinny jeans to match her long-sleeved waffle tee. She laid out a huge cable-knit sweater, another pair of leg warmers, thick socks, and lace-up winter hiking boots to put on right before her ride arrived. Then she opened the box containing the Christmas gift she'd received from Maree: a wool beanie, hand-knitted in M'Kenzee's signature orchid pink with hand-embroidered flowers and vines and a fluffy pompom on top; a long, extra-wide scarf, also hand-knitted to match the beanie; and the most adorable convertible mittens, again in the same design and with the same hand-embroidered flowers and vines on the back of each glove. Finally, M'Kenzee dabbed on some makeup, stepping it up a notch from her usual routine of only mascara and lip gloss by adding tinted moisturizer, dusting on a light coat of powder, applying actual eye shadow — that glittered — and even brushing sparkly pale pink blush on her cheeks.

Maree will be so proud.

 nd she was.

"You look amazing!" Maree squealed when M'Kenzee walked out of the house.

"Yeah, yeah. I made an effort," M'Kenzee said, waving off Maree's compliment. "Now *you* look amazing. Wow!"

Maree twirled to show off her black leather pants, knee-high black snow boots, and formfitting ballet-pink cashmere turtleneck. Her strawberry-blond curls flowed from a perky ponytail, reminding M'Kenzee of a brand new Barbie doll, *before* they'd played with her hair. Round diamond stud earrings — Max's gift to both girls for Christmas — and Rhys's engagement ring sparkled as Maree's only jewelry. She shone like a star, a brilliant light bestowed upon the world.

"And she's got a nice big puffy ski jacket to wear over it," Rhys grumbled from the driver's seat of his truck.

"Ah, Rhys." M'Kenzee patted him on the shoulder, a gesture of sympathy as she climbed into the back seat. "You'll never be able to hide her beauty, so you might as well enjoy sharing her with the world." M'Kenzee thoroughly enjoyed ribbing the poor man.

Rhys grunted in reply, but he smiled and quirked an eyebrow at M'Kenzee in the rearview mirror.

"So, what did you do all day?" Maree asked as they backed

out of M'Kenzee's driveway and turned down Main Street to head for Daisy Lake.

"Absolutely nothing," M'Kenzee confessed. "I didn't even get out of bed until three."

"We heard you aren't sleeping on the floor anymore. Tell me all about Jinx's barn! It's legendary around here, but I've never been out there," Maree chirped, a ball of radiant energy.

M'Kenzee filled every second of the fifteen minute drive to Daisy Lake with detailed descriptions of the fantastic wood pieces she'd seen. Maree's eyes widened with amazement; she giggled with disbelief.

Her excitement must've been contagious because everyone at the party shared Maree's festive mood.

A buffet of potluck dishes ran the length of three worktables. Hot chocolate, pots of coffee, and kettles of apple cider with cinnamon candies kept partygoers warm, as did the bonfire and the s'mores station. M'Kenzee filled a plate of finger foods to munch upon as she wandered the party, visiting with people she'd met before and learning the names of those she was meeting for the first time.

She enjoyed the night very much. And when the group counted down the seconds to the new year, M'Kenzee strolled out to the dock, where she could look up at the stars in a moment of solitude.

But she wasn't alone. Bren was out there. She felt his presence, blew him a kiss, and wished him a Happy New Year.

The days following the girls' successful scavenger hunt to Dallas settled into a pattern that held throughout all of January and into February.

Each morning, M'Kenzee met with contractors to review

the day's projects at the house. The work progressed smoothly — all thanks to Jinx and the incredibly accommodating and skilled craftsmen — and women — he invited to work on the iconic Victorian home. Honored to be part of the remodel and beautification, everyone did their best work; or maybe that was just how things were always done in Green Hills. Either way, M'Kenzee fell more in love with the place every single day.

Afternoons usually involved photography work, taking the final shots needed for *Kitchen Quilts*, Maree and Janie Lyn's book incorporating Maree's fabric creations with Janie Lyn's food creations, and taking pictures of the Memorial Care residents whose families had agreed to their loved ones taking part in M'Kenzee's latest photojournalism project, *The Face of ALZ*, which had developed from Jinx's request for a portrait of Duke before he passed away from Alzheimer's disease.

M'Kenzee spent her nights with Bren, getting to know the teenager, the college athlete, the soldier, and the special agent through the notebooks he'd left for her to read.

Some pages she'd skim over, others she'd read multiple times. Most of the entries left her with a feeling of peace.

A few haunted her. Those were the ones that she'd revisit again and again before turning to the next page.

31

Fill your paper with the
breathings of your heart.
William Wordsworth

Friday, July 27, 2007
Dear M'Kenzee,

We arrived at Annapolis for football camp, and it is just as I remembered: special.

Mom and Da and I signed up for a campus tour through the admissions office. It was so cool - when we arrived, we weren't allowed to drive on the Yard (that's what they call it). And we could only walk around once we'd cleared security restrictions and received credentials to go through the gates.

The first thing we did was enter the Quarterdeck and stop in the Visitor Center and Gift Shop (Mom picked out t-shirts for Max and Maree, but

I got you a NAVY sweatshirt — I know how you hate to be cold). On the tour, we saw so many awesome things: the Athletic Hall of Fame, the Brigade of Midshipmen, the crypt of John Paul Jones, and lots of statues of important people. We had lunch at the Drydock restaurant and saw a model of a Wright B-1 Flyer. We toured Bancroft Hall, the largest dorm in the entire country, walked through the U.S. Naval Academy Museum, and got a drink and dessert at the 1845 Coffee Shop.

I think we'll see even more tomorrow. They invited me to come to football camp a little early to check out the weight room, locker room, and meeting rooms before check-in. Since the stadium is off campus, I'm sure camp is on the practice fields, so I'll get to work out on those, too.

This is the USNA Mission:

To develop Midshipmen morally, mentally and physically and to imbue them with the highest ideals of duty, honor and loyalty in order to graduate leaders who are dedicated to a career of naval service and have the potential for future development in mind and character to assume the highest responsibilities of command, citizenship and government.

Do you think that sounds like me?

I hope so — I really like it here, M'KenZee.

Love,

B.

Saturday, July 28, 2007

Dear M'KenZee,

Camp was awesome!

And I received an offer. To play here. For Navy.

Tears stung my eyes when Coach K extended it, sitting in his office, just him and me and my parents. I'm glad I was strong enough to keep the tears from falling. I don't think soldiers are supposed to show weaknesses.

I didn't commit yet. Mom and Da said I need to think it through, pray about such an enormous commitment. Not just a commitment to the football team, but to the country. Signing on here isn't like signing a letter of intent at other universities. They said I have to be sure. I am sure, but I don't want to make Mom cry, so I'm waiting to tell everyone.

I always said I wanted to make them proud. And you. This is how I'm meant to do it. I still have to secure a formal nomination to be accepted for admission, but Coach K says several congressmen have asked to sponsor me, so it's really just a formality. It's all going to fall into place; I know it.

See you Monday morning at school.

Love,
B.

———

Saturday, December 1, 2007

Holy cow, M'Kenzee - you should've seen it!
The Army-Navy game was crazy. I got chills
just standing in the stadium during pregame.

The processional, pledge, and national anthem
were so inspiring. Mom cried, and I saw Da
holding his breath. The flyover was unreal.

And we won, 38-3. We dominated the entire
game, all three phases: offense, defense, and
special teams.

All that's left of my official recruiting visit is
breakfast tomorrow morning and then a one-on-one
meeting with Coach K. That's when I'm gonna tell
them: I'm committing to NAVY.

It's so exciting. I'll tell you and Max all
about it during lunch on Monday.

Hope y'all have had a great weekend at Max's
official visit to West Virginia. Sorry they lost to Pitt.
Man, that was wild. Talk about this year's "Curse
of the #2" - Pittsburgh was only 3-7 on the
season, and they knocked the Mountaineers out of
the national championship.

I guess that's why we line up and play every

game... You never know who's going to come out on top.

Can't wait to see you at school.

Love,

B.

———

Saturday, December 22, 2007

WE WON!!

State Champions! We are the champions - it's incredible and surreal at the same time.

Did you see Max's block to set up that final play? There's no way Joel gets that throw off without Max taking out two d-linemen. When I saw it floating toward me, knowing they had left the end zone wide open, I said a prayer for dependable hands. Over the years, I've caught hundreds of passes in practice and games, but that was the most important one. I had to watch it in; I just knew I couldn't drop the ball.

You'll never know what it meant to me that you ran to me when the fans stormed the field.

Max didn't notice, too surrounded by kids and coaches and cheerleaders.

But you found me first, which was perfect, because I was looking for you.

I could've held you in that hug forever. Sorry I was so sweaty and stinky.

You didn't seem to mind, though. That smile you gave me when I set your feet back on the ground — Well, that smile is one I'll never forget.

Thanks, M'KenZee!

Love,

B.

———

Tuesday, August 7, 2008

It is not the critic who counts,
not the man who points out how the strong man
stumbles,
or where the doer of deeds could have done them
better.
The credit belongs to the man who is actually in the
arena,
whose face is marred by dust and sweat and blood;
who strives valiantly; who errs, who comes short
again and again,
because there is no effort without error and
shortcoming;
but who does actually strive to do the deeds;
who knows great enthusiasms, the great devotions;
who spends himself on a worthy cause;

who at the best knows in the end the triumph of
high achievement,
and who at the worst, if he fails, at least fails
while daring greatly,
so that his place shall never be with those cold and
timid souls
who know neither victory nor defeat.
Theodore Roosevelt

Dear M'Kenzee,

Plebe Parents' Weekend starts tomorrow. I sure wish you'd been able to come with Mom and Da. What I wouldn't give to see you, even for just a day. I have your picture here, but it's not the same.

Don't get me wrong, I'm thrilled to see my parents — Plebe Summer has been tough, really rough — but I miss you something fierce.

I tried to tell Max how I feel about you, but I chickened out. You're just going into sophomore year. You need to date guys there at the high school, have fun at the football games, and enjoy the dances and parties. I don't like thinking about that, but I know it's true. I want you to be happy. You wouldn't be happy dating me from so far away.

I told Max I can't come home for a long time, and I asked him to ask you and Maree both to write to me. I pray you will. Max is too busy with school and football, but I need to hear from you.

Take care, M'KenZee.

Love,

B.

P.S: That quote is from a speech President Roosevelt gave in 1910; that particular passage is called "The Man in the Arena." It means that in a tough situation, when others are standing back to stay safe, keeping to the sidelines to watch, those with tenacity, courage, and honor jump in. They're in the arena. We had to memorize it. I want to be that man, the man in the arena. I thought you might like to read it, too.

———

Wednesday, November 26, 2008

Dear M'KenZee,

Why am I so nervous to see you?

Maybe because I never wrote back when you sent care packages and photos and cards? Well, I did write back — obviously. But I never sent them, as you well know.

I think I've been talking to you so long, through these diaries (Lord, wouldn't Max have a heyday with that one!) that I don't know how to let them go. If I send them to you, I won't have this connection to you anymore.

Connections to the people we love are important. I've seen that firsthand this semester. The cadets who don't have a support network at home, they suffer. The photos you send, the letters from Mom and Da, the movies from Max, the cookies from Maree... Those are lifelines. Being away is something I can handle. I can handle the Academy. I think I can handle anything, as long as I know you're out there, a lifeline specifically for me.

I got lucky this is our bye week and Coach cut us loose since we all received holiday leave for Thanksgiving. It'll be fun to have us all together on Thursday, and I'm excited to see Max's game on Saturday. I'm hoping we can spend some time together on Friday, too.

There's so much I wish I could say. Someday, M'Kenzee. Someday, I'll say it all.

Love,

B.

———

Wednesday, December 24, 2008

Merry Christmas!

We're traveling to the bowl game — on the plane as I write. It's going to be a great trip. A week on the beach, practicing for an extra game, and playing on New Year's Eve. I only wish Max's bowl game wasn't the same day on the opposite side of the country. What were the odds of that?

It's not ideal that I'll use my entire leave on football. I wouldn't trade it for missing a bowl game, but it still stinks that I won't make it home for the holidays at all.

I miss you.

Have a great Christmas.

Love,

B.

———

Monday, May 4, 2009

Dear M'Kenzee,

I know you're mad. If not mad, definitely frustrated. I could hear it in your voice on the phone. And I don't blame you. Mom's not thrilled, either, that I'm not coming home for the summer.

Zero Block is my only chance to attend the MAGTF program cruise since we have classes and workouts for football when the regular summer blocks are going. MAGTF stands for Marine Air-Ground Task Force, and it's an area of training I'm really interested in. When you're done being irritated with me, I'll tell you more about it.

Luckily, you never stay too angry for too long.
Hope to hear from you soon.
Love,
B.

———

Tuesday, December 8, 2009
Dear M'KenZee,

Thanks for your text on Thanksgiving. It brightened my day. I really missed being with y'all.

And thanks for watching my game on TV. It's been a great season. Nothing like what Max is having — man, is his stock rising! But we beat Army, we beat Air Force, we beat Notre Dame, and when we beat Missouri in the Texas Bowl, it'll be a ten-win season. Those are hard to come by.

The game is on New Year's Eve again, so I won't make it home this year.

Just know I'm thinking about you. And Max and Maree and Mom and Da. I love y'all. Even when I can't be with you.

B.

———

Sunday, April 25, 2010

Dear M'Kenzee,

You were beautiful last night. I was the luckiest guy at the prom. And so glad to be there.

I never imagined saying that, especially two
years into college. But it's true. Max'll never know
the absolute gift he granted me when he asked me
to surprise you.

I'll be holding on to that night — that kiss —
for a very long time.

Love,

B.

Monday, June 7, 2010

Dear M'Kenzee,

I guess I got lucky that you were with Max
when I called to wish him a happy birthday...since
you're apparently rolling my calls. You couldn't say
no when Max handed you the phone, even though I
could tell by the venom in your voice that you
wanted to hang up on me.

If only you knew how much I think of you,
how these letters I write to you keep me grounded,
sane.

That last training cruise was a lot — forty days
underwater. The submarine was cool, but even after

studying and briefings and simulators before the
cruise, I didn't understand what it would be like.
If I am placed on a sub deployment after graduation, I'll get used to it, but I'm really hoping for
the Combined Joint Task Force. Not many of us
will be tagged for CJTF, but they invited me to
attempt some elite training modules to see if I'm a
good candidate.

Wish me luck, M. That's where I know I can
make the most difference.

And forgive me for not calling.

Love,

B.

PS: Congrats on graduation. I'm so proud of
you — can't believe you crammed two years into one
and graduated early. Sorry I missed it.

———

Wednesday, November 3, 2010

Happy Birthday, beautiful. I'll try to call you
tonight.

Love,

B.

'Kenzee remembered receiving a text that day — her eighteenth birthday — from him. One that said the same thing he'd written.

She'd been a freshman at Oklahoma State University. When Max had turned nineteen two years earlier, he'd petitioned the courts for custody of the girls. And won. Since then, they'd lived on campus with him in an apartment provided by his scholarship. With Mr. and Mrs. Stewart nearby to fill in with Maree when Max traveled with the football team, M'Kenzee had felt free to do whatever it took to get out of high school as quickly as possible.

She'd felt judged and disliked there, as if the world and everyone in it had teamed up against her. She thought college would be different, but instead, she'd found more of the same in Stillwater. School was fine, her job waiting tables at a local pub was fine, and she was fine. Never good or happy, but *fine* was fine enough.

Bren and Max had been in their junior years and third seasons of college football; everyone else had seemed great.

Bren hadn't called that day.

he pattern that evolved in his journals mirrored the one she'd lived, one of hopeful ups when he had time to call, text, or visit, followed by depressing, emotional downs when she'd go months without a word.

A thousand times she'd told herself to get over Brennigan Stewart. She'd find some determination, agree to a date with someone at school, spend the evening unfairly comparing the poor guy to Bren, and go home resolved to live a life alone, loving Bren from afar…her secret to bear.

As the months passed, she'd embraced her loneliness more and more, pushing friends away, refusing to participate in study groups, shunning anyone daring enough to attempt a conversation.

Why try if everyone goes away in the end, anyway?

Not surprising, Bren and Max had both been busy with football practices and bowl games over the holidays — third year in a row. Max's coach had invited all their players over for Christmas Day. Maree had joined in the fun; M'Kenzee had pretended to have a cold, so she could beg off and sit in her dorm room by herself. That had just seemed easier than faking joy she didn't feel.

Extricating herself from the world became a habit. Presenting an outer layer of pointy quills became the most efficient way to keep her distance. The sharper the needles, the better they protected her heart from the jarring effects of that roller-coaster ride that had left her so bumped and bruised in the past.

With a long-suffering sigh, M'Kenzee closed the book she'd just finished. Feeling heavy and ready to end the day, she turned to switch off the lamp. Her cell phone rang, stopping her midmotion.

"Hey, Max," she answered, trying to sound less "down in the dumps" than she felt. An obstetrician had confirmed Janie Lyn's pregnancy, and Max's team was dominating their way through the playoffs; Max had plenty on his plate without worrying over M'Kenzee.

"Whatcha doing?"

"About to turn in," M'Kenzee replied. "Everything okay?" Her nerves flipped to high alert. Max rarely called so late.

"Yeah, everything's good. The day got away from me. Sorry to call past bedtime."

"Well, not everyone goes to sleep as early as I do," she joked. "But Jinx is a taskmaster, and every single one of his subs likes to begin work — with hammers and drills and banging and clanking — at the crack of dawn."

"We can't wait to see the house. The photos you've sent are incredible. And as someone who's been working on his remodel for months—"

"*Years!*" M'Kenzee heard Janie Lyn add in the background.

"Yes, well, a long time… I'm impressed by how quickly you're getting everything done."

"Thanks. Sorry that working on the house has meant I've been watching your games on TV instead of in person."

"That's why I'm calling. I'm submitting ticket requests for the Super Bowl, in case we earn another shot at it. I want you there. You've been putting in long hours on that house, not to mention the portrait project Maree told me about. You deserve a few days off."

M'Kenzee hesitated. What if Bren came home while she was gone? Or would he expect her to be at Max's game and look for her there? What to do?

She panicked, which was completely out of character for her. Then she thought through the notes, the letters, and all of Bren's messages to her over the years.

"Of course I'll go," she agreed. Bren would want — *did* want — her to go. She felt sure of that.

"Great!" Max exclaimed. Then his voice took on a serious tone. "I'm proud of you, 'Kenz."

"Whatever for?" She'd done nothing to earn his admiration.

"For the way you're tackling life, the way you're moving forward — without the weight of anger you've carried around for so long. I hear a peace about you. Maree sees it. Miss Sadie says you've found your place and your stride. You're going to be okay. No matter what comes, you're going to be *better* than okay. That's all I ever prayed for you."

"Thanks, Maxwell," she said in return, while wiping away

a tear that had fallen down her cheek. M'Kenzee used Janie Lyn's pet name — his full name — to convey her love and appreciation while lightening the moment. If only he'd known how gloomy she'd been when he called.

But she did feel better. Not just as they said good night and she snuggled into bed, but overall.

Bitterness had been her constant companion since the night of her parents' fatal car accident. Finally, she'd released it. She'd let go of her irritation with the world, even found goodness in it. She'd learned how to choose joy.

With Miss Sadie, Landry, Davis, Jinx, and the work crews, she'd somehow become surrounded by friends. She'd gained a social set, people who liked her. M'Kenzee could admit she wasn't a great friend, often forgetting to check on others as she got immersed in her routines and projects. But for the first time in her life, she could confidently say that her friends knew she cared, that she'd be there for them at a moment's notice and without hesitation.

Life was looking up.

Now, come home to me, Bren.

32

"Working My Way Back to You"
Song written by Sandy Linzer
and Denny Randell;
Recorded and made popular by
The Four Seasons (1966)
and The Spinners (1980)

Monday, February 3, 2020 — Landstuhl Regional Medical Center, Germany

"**Y**ou've got to let her know."

"No." Bren flatly refused, cringing with pain at his attempt to sound forceful.

Mikey could hound him to death, but Bren wouldn't budge. And Bren's friend and co-worker, Special Agent Michael Vela, seemed determined to make it his personal mission to hound Bren relentlessly. He might not have to pester Bren much more… It was no secret throughout the hospital that Agent Brennigan Stewart did not look long for the world.

"It's not right. You don't understand what she's been

through," Vela urged. "She calls the bureau every afternoon — EVERY SINGLE DAY — desperate for crumbs of information."

"Not until it's good news." Bren struggled to get the words out.

"It *is* good news. You're essentially on American soil, *alive*."

"Promise, Mike—" Bren broke off in a fit of coughing. When he regained control of his breathing, Bren tried again. "Promise you won't call her." His words faded into nothingness as his eyes closed.

Same day — *Green Hills, Oklahoma*

"You up for a ride to Dallas again?"

"Where are you getting all this energy?" Maree countered M'Kenzee's question with a question.

They'd spent the past week in Florida, attending luncheons, style shows, shopping sprees, pep rallies, dinner outings, and fundraising events, their trip culminating in Max and the Kansas City Chiefs defeating the San Francisco 49ers Sunday night, 31–20. That morning, they'd flown from Miami to Tulsa, driven to Green Hills, dropped their luggage at their houses, and reconvened at Main Street Design. The whirlwind hadn't slowed M'Kenzee's pace one bit.

She snapped photo after photo of a fabric display and sample quilts. They'd use the images to create social media content and advertisements promoting Maree's latest design line. The bolts of quilting cotton boasted deep jewel-tone colors, perfect for the cold but sunny winter days, and traditional patterns of ticking stripes, small-scale florals, and layered geometrics, equally perfect for the quilt patterns and comfort-food recipes in *Kitchen Quilts*. Maree had mastered the current trend of product bundling with coordinating fabrics, threads, yarns, printed papers, decorative stickers, buttons, mini note-books, recipes, blog posts, and social media campaigns to go along with her pattern books. The collections provided fun projects for quilters, knitters, scrapbookers, journalers, cooks, bakers, readers, and online community members. Maree had constructed a brilliant business plan and created beautiful products to support it.

"Well, what do you think?" M'Kenzee asked.

"About the pictures you took or the invitation to Dallas?"

"Both," M'Kenzee said, shifting the laptop computer to reveal the pictures she'd uploaded from the camera.

"Wow! You make my designs gorgeous."

"YOU make your designs gorgeous. I just capture the beauty in two dimensions."

"No, M'Kenzee, these photos are incredible." Maree continued to flip from image to image, pointing out her favorites, the unique angles and interesting points of view, and how the lighting set the mood for each layout.

"I'm glad you like them," M'Kenzee allowed, her only acknowledgment of Maree's praise and gratitude. "If you go to Dallas with me, I'll turn a couple of them into prints you can hang here in the shop."

"When do we leave?"

Cruising down I-75 and recalling Maree's expression when she'd answered, *Tomorrow*, M'Kenzee laughed at her snoozing sister in the passenger's seat.

Thinking back over their conversation at the shop, M'Kenzee couldn't pinpoint the source of her energy. She simply couldn't sit still.

Remodeling construction on the house continued to roll

from sunup to sundown. And even though lots of work remained, the house truly felt like home already.

The elements M'Kenzee had worried about most had turned out immaculately — wallpaper with damask designs of deep hunter green flocking over a soft, medium green background hung above white wainscoting in their bedroom, a coordinating wallpaper with sleek stripe patterns in their master bath; multiple built-in bookcases with intricate lace woodwork trim in every room; modern, state-of-the-art appliances in the kitchen, right next to an exquisite nostalgic-style, seven-burner gas range and double oven, vintage white with brass trim; the original kitchen cabinetry repainted a luscious grass green and topped with charcoal soapstone, and wild upholstery prints on the windows, chairs, and throw pillows. The house had come alive. Verdant greens mimicked the Scottish terrain Bren had written about so passionately, pops of violet represented the purple heather he'd gathered in the Highlands, vivid whites and bright yellows brightened every inch of space, while bits of poppy orange, victory red, and fuchsia pink lent a whimsical, lyrical feel.

From the tip of the new roof to the back corner of the refinished basement, M'Kenzee loved it.

Bren would, too, as soon as he came home.

Come home to me.

M'Kenzee had teased with Max about going to sleep early, but in truth, she only climbed in bed early. She spent hours and hours reading through Bren's love box every night.

At one point, she'd been tempted to stay in bed around the clock, ignoring the world in lieu of devouring his words. Too afraid of a trap she'd never escape once ensnared, M'Kenzee set parameters and stuck to her guns when the timer went off, indicating she needed to close the book.

She'd finished the notebooks from his time at the Naval Academy. She'd cringed with nausea but made it through his descriptions of final tests and physical challenges, cried through his decision to accept a position on a joint task force rather than his invitation to BUD/S to become a Navy SEAL.

M'Kenzee felt bone-slicing humiliation at her memories of temper tantrums, crying jags born of frustration, and selfish demands she'd wanted to make of him as ultimatums.

Awful. She'd been completely awful, all the while rejecting the most incredible man's love, when she could've been — should've been — supporting him.

Then she'd started on the journals from his time in the Navy.

She'd only thought she'd known nausea. She had soon learned that she'd been completely ignorant...

> *Monday, August 20, 2012*
> *Talked to your brother today. He said you start classes next week. I hope you have a great year. I hope you'll let yourself enjoy it.*
> *Sorry I haven't called in a while.*
> *After the draft party, I figured you didn't want to hear from me. Then I was unable to call because of block training, which rolled right into summer workouts for football.*
> *I thought I'd make it home for weekend leave, that we could talk through things in person. But the game schedule didn't line up right with the extra responsibilities I had on the Yard. Somehow, fall turned into spring semester, and it had been a year since I'd seen you.*
> *In all that time, you've barely answered my*

texts. Maybe that's why I was hesitant to call — because what I have to say needs to be said face to face.

I appreciate the gift you sent with Mom for my graduation — the scrapbook is wonderful. So many great memories. I missed you being there, but I understood you needed to stay for your sister and what she had going on.

Just days after graduation, I was on a ship bound for ————

A thick, black line of permanent ink marked through whatever he'd written there.

After that, we were off to ———— and ————
We got back from a deployment in ——— five days ago, and now we're ———————

More black ink.

It's unreal how one spot on a map can be so beautiful and so ugly at once, how people can be both good and evil at once. Today I watched a woman calm a little boy who cried after falling on broken glass that cut his hands and elbows. Then I watched the same woman set a fuse to blow up an apartment building filled with families. What makes one life worth soothing but the others so insignificant that she didn't even hesitate to kill them?

I wish I could tell you more, but as you can tell from above, I have to learn what's not safe for you to know. Keeping things from you is hard. I've told you everything for so long. You're my rock, ————

I know you don't realize it, but you are.

Bren had even crossed out her name. What kind of hellhole had he been in?

Over the past sixteen months, I've relived that kiss in the elevator a million times. I should be sorry for manhandling you, pushing you against the wall. But good night, ———— you have an uncanny ability to drive me crazy. In ways no one else does. In ways I can't even describe. I—

I'm being called to a briefing.

I love you,

B.

PS: They didn't die. She had to, but the families are still alive.

Tuesday, December 25, 2012

I wrote you a letter — a real one — that I was going to send to you for Christmas.

When I saw everything the security officer redacted, I burned it. I'll just tell you Merry Christmas here.

I imagine you and Mom will have some things in common to say about me today. She tried to be upbeat on the phone, but I heard the sadness in her voice. I hate disappointing y'all during the holidays. Well, anytime, but especially during Christmas.

I won't be able to call tonight. Where I am, it's not safe to use a signal. In fact, I'm writing this in the pitch dark, underground. That's why the words are all over the page.

"Not a creature was stirring, not even a mouse" has a whole new meaning here.

Good luck to Max. I think he played yesterday, if I remember right. Hopefully, they won. I know it's been a tough rookie season for him, accustomed to winning and dominating as he is. But he's doing what he loves, and that's a blessing, for sure. No doubt they'll get things on track.

Out of space on this scratch of paper I found littered next to me.

I love you. And I miss you.

B.

That note topped a stack of scraps, napkins, cardboard torn from food containers, and an odd piece of actual writing paper, all tied together with a shoelace.

Mere snatches of Bren's thoughts. Few of the notes made any sense. Bren hadn't addressed any of them, much less mentioned M'Kenzee by name. All of them conveyed a darkness that had never been present in Bren's writing.

A chill ran through M'Kenzee after reading them.

What does service cost?

The next notebook, a small spiral, did nothing to help her answer the question.

Saturday, May 4, 2013

It's been a rough stretch these past few months. Since March 11, we've lost more than twenty service members, and that doesn't include covert operatives and civilian contractors. Those are the fatalities identified and reported publicly. There are more that no one knows about, deaths from teams that operate off the grid.

We lost one this week, and no one beyond his family will ever know his sacrifice.

There's no good answer to this war. If we leave the world to fend for itself, we're all dead the moment some insane faction takes control of nuclear weapons. And if we don't leave the world to implode upon itself, we sacrifice good lives, create widows, and leave orphans questioning why their *mom or dad had to die.*

The older guys say it never hurts less to lose a teammate, that we just learn to accept the pain as part of the price we are all willing to pay. I don't want to accept it.

Sorry I'm in such a foul mood.

B.

Assuming no one would ever read the notebooks, Bren had let loose several times after that entry.

He described injuries that turned M'Kenzee's stomach, detailed injustices that infuriated her, and depicted hopelessness that the world's general population couldn't fathom.

Agent Vela's explanation of the joint task force structure scared M'Kenzee. She tried to imagine the types of missions Bren's CJTF team was called to perform, but nothing she came up with seemed severe enough, intense enough — important enough.

Several times, she'd had to walk away from the journal… take a break outside, find something to clean in the house while listening to a light-hearted playlist, anything but envision the mental picture Bren's writing painted. Then she'd find herself reaching for the journal, needing to finish another page, and turning to the next.

If Bren lived through it, surely I can read through it.

So she continued, all the way to the last page of the small book.

Thursday, September 19, 2013

Leave granted. Coming home.

God, I need to see you. I only hope you're happy to see me, too.

I love you,

B.

M'Kenzee had been.

So happy!

Max had surprised his sisters with a flight to Philadelphia to watch his game that night against the Eagles. When she and Maree had found their seats, Bren had been there, waiting.

Maree had jumped in his arms with abandon, screaming and crying and causing quite a scene. By the time she'd hugged her fill, M'Kenzee had been a self-conscious jumble of nerves.

Bren had wrapped his arms around her, tucking her in for a hug that, while less exuberant than Maree's, had been much more meaningful. She'd sensed in that hug he found what he needed to heal wounds she couldn't see or understand, but ones that were one hundred percent real.

M'Kenzee had also noticed Bren's build. His arms had felt like vice grips around her frame, his muscles like steel.

She snuck glances at him throughout the game, inspecting the changes in him.

For as long as she'd known Brennigan Stewart, he'd been trying to grow taller and gain weight, mostly in an effort to catch up with Max. Not anymore. He'd filled out his six-foot, one-inch frame quite nicely. Boyish cuteness had matured into chiseled features, defined cheekbones, and a classically romantic square jaw. Still high and tight, his hair maintained its military style, yet somehow the short, auburn curls on the top of his head begged to have fingers feathered through them.

The thought prompted an itch in the tips of *her* fingers. M'Kenzee's eyes widened.

Bren was hot.

Not boy next door, brother's best friend, childhood crush hot.

Smokin' hot.

Bren must've felt her staring because he looked over at her. He smiled when he caught her eyes on him. And winked. And grinned a little more.

Oh, my. This is not what I need, she'd thought.

Try as she might to cheer for Max, pay attention to the game, and focus on the field, M'Kenzee's eyes continually drifted to Bren. And each time, he seemed to be looking right back at her.

She'd wanted to drum up the hurt feelings she'd nursed all alone after their kiss at her prom. She attempted to harness the anger she'd unleashed on him after their kiss in the elevator at Max's draft party. All to no avail.

Bren's good mood was catching. The stormy seas of their past seemed to be water under the bridge.

Could she let it all go? Simply forget it?

Perhaps she'd read too much into it all along. Maybe Bren saw M'Kenzee as a family friend, fun to be around and not too bad to kiss on rare occasion. Nothing more than Max's little sister.

Her mind whirled — not quite the speed of a hurricane, but possibly in line with a weak tropical storm.

Pulling up her hypothetical bootstraps, M'Kenzee decided if Bren wanted to move forward as if nothing had happened between them, then she could — and would — do the same.

That settled, M'Kenzee thoroughly enjoyed the rest of the weekend in Philly with her family and Bren.

Sunday night, after they'd landed in Tulsa, she gave equal hugs to Max, who had a connecting flight to Kansas City, and

Maree, who had homework to finish at home before her college classes Monday morning, and Bren, who'd promised to spend the rest of his leave with his parents. Then she hopped into her car, drove back to Stillwater, and cried herself to sleep.

Tuesday, February 4, 2020 — Dallas, Texas

"So, you're going to use their equipment to print your pictures on metal?" Maree's inquisitive mind needed to hear and see and touch every step of the process to fully understand it.

"Exactly," M'Kenzee confirmed as they crossed the street from the parking garage to the camera shop. One code violation away from being condemned, the building had seen better days. Even the bars on the windows had given up on the neighborhood and sported rusted-out holes that a strong wind would break through.

"And we're safe?"

"At least until dark."

"Nice," Maree muttered.

An hour later, Maree had apparently forgotten all her reservations. She wouldn't stop oohing and ahhing over M'Kenzee's photos.

Encouraged by her conversation with Bren back at Miss Sadie's house in December, M'Kenzee had uploaded the photos she'd taken at the school carnival the day her parents died. From a strictly technical perspective, they looked like a child's photography. She'd had skills, even then, but overall, the photos bore the unrefined composition and high vanishing point of a short, young, undeveloped artist. The shots also possessed a timeless innocence, possibly because M'Kenzee and Maree knew so intimately what had come next.

M'Kenzee had selected several to print and frame for a gallery wall in the house.

She'd also chosen one of herself, standing with Bren, getting married in the stock trailer. She didn't remember posing for the photo. Both children looked at one another rather than the camera, so her momma must've taken it without M'Kenzee and Bren knowing while Mrs. Stewart performed their mock ceremony.

If the definition of true love could be illustrated through the charm of two small children, that photo portrayed it.

In a box stored at Maree's shop, M'Kenzee had also located the snapshot taken of two silly newlyweds in a Las Vegas chapel. Again, both the bride and the groom had eyes only for each other. M'Kenzee had needed to work a little magic on the brightness and color temperature before she reproduced it, but the final image provided quite a wedding picture.

She'd brought digital files for both of those photos, as well as her favorite portrait of Duke Malone.

In exchange for autographing a series of her prints for the camera shop to sell, they'd invited M'Kenzee to enlarge her prints onto pre-cut aluminum sheets using their dye-sublimation process, resulting in a brilliantly vivid, lifelike piece of art.

She had plans in the house for their two wedding photos to go with their two wedding certificates, which she'd kept safe over the years. The portrait of Duke would be a gift for Jinx.

M'Kenzee smiled the entire drive back home to Green Hills. She'd asked a few leading questions, opening the door for Maree to share her wedding plans, and then settled in behind the wheel, listening to Maree's elaborate vision for the day she'd become Mrs. Rhys Larsen.

With her renewed energy, M'Kenzee spent the next few days putting the final touches on rooms the workers had finished throughout the house. Hanging photos, artwork, and framed posters brought her joy. Discovering a new hobby, she arranged fresh flowers from the florist in town, and adjusting decorative pillows and sofa snugglers, M'Kenzee got the idea that she might like to try sewing and quilting after all. Successfully using recipes from Miss Sadie, Maree, and Janie Lyn to experiment with her fancy new oven made her feel downright domestic and accomplished.

Eight days later, when she'd filled the freezer with casseroles, fidgeted with every trinket and doodad, leveled every wall hanging, and straightened the spines on every bookshelf to the point of perfection, she stood back and smiled, proud of the space, the staging, and the welcoming ambiance in each room.

That night, she read the last pages of Bren's notebook from his time in the Horn of Africa, specifically Uganda and Somalia, as well as Yemen and Libya. M'Kenzee hadn't realized that Bren had seen action in the very worst spots, the most politically dangerous regions, of the world. She wanted and needed to know the truth, but each book made it more challenging to keep reading.

33

The truth is rarely pure
and never simple.
The Importance of Being Earnest
by Oscar Wilde

"*D*id you know Bren was abducted when he was in the Navy?" M'Kenzee demanded, her voice thunderous with anger.

"Whoa, 'Kenz — what are you talking about?" Max's placating tone didn't help the situation.

"In the spring of 2016, Bren was captured. Did you know and never tell us?"

"His story was not — *is* not — mine to tell."

M'Kenzee considered reaching through the phone to strangle her big brother until he choked on his mollifying air.

"*Did you know?*" She emphasized each word, enunciating to control her rage.

"Nothing specific, I promise. I guessed something major went down," Max conceded. "But I never asked him for details. I just tried to listen when Bren wanted to talk, and I let whatever he said be enough."

"How?"

"M'Kenzee, whatever is in those journals you're so obsessed with, Bren got past. He faced his demons. Can't you let them lie, too?"

"How did you know something bad had happened to him?"

"Before being admitted to the Naval Academy, midshipmen sign a contract to serve for five years of active duty after graduation. Bren's tour finished in June 2016, eleven months shy of five years. I can only think of a few reasons why he would receive an honorable discharge early. None are good scenarios."

"Oh, Lord. No." Her useless prayer escaped on a broken breath. The past could not be undone.

M'Kenzee hadn't put two and two together at the time. A couple years into her career as a freelance photojournalist, she'd been accepting every assignment offered. She'd embraced the thrill of global travel…areas in conflict, dramatic subjects, intense deadlines, and endless obstacles to challenge her. With tunnel vision on her own work, she'd done a poor job keeping up with her family and loved ones. Bren had gone through so much. All the while, she'd been oblivious to his suffering.

"How did I not know?"

"You didn't know because Bren didn't want you to know. He was adamant about that. You and Maree and his mom— He refused to tell any of you the depth of the truth. Confronting his uphill battle with PTSD almost broke him. He couldn't share the gory details of what he'd seen and done to survive, not with any of us. M'Kenzee, there is nothing for you to feel guilty about. Please believe that," Max begged.

"That's when he went to Scotland? I remember. When he

left the Navy, he disappeared to Braemar for a few months." It clicked into place in her memory.

"Yes, he—"

"I have to go, Max. Thank you for telling me the truth."

M'Kenzee hung up the phone before Max had time to utter a response.

She looked for Jinx, found the construction foreman instead, and explained that the work crews were welcome to come and go as much as they needed, but she would be indisposed and unavailable for a bit.

Locking the bedroom door, M'Kenzee gave in to the ever-present urge to hide away and read Bren's journals, one after another, until she'd seen every word he'd written.

Monday, August 1, 2016

Dear M'Kenzee,

It's a new month, a fresh page on the calendar. I'm trying to take a breath of fresh air.

I'm so sorry I came home damaged.

My arrogance led me to believe myself untouchable – ridiculous, really, when I've watched so many soldiers fall. Warriors much stronger and faster and wiser than I've ever been.

I'll fix this; I'll learn to manage the nightmares and the terrors that visit in my sleep. I'll work my way back to you. I won't stop until I'm worthy, able to take care of you in the manner you deserve.

You're my why, have been all along. It's

crazy... I don't remember a day before I loved you.

B.

———

Thursday, August 4, 2016

I met with a counselor at the veteran's center today. He's a vet, too. And he overcame PTSD symptoms much more severe and dangerous than what I'm experiencing. Hearing his story gives me hope.

We're meeting again tomorrow. Just to hang out. I want to tell him about you, tell him how spunky and fierce you are, how nothing scares you.

I wish I knew where you are. I asked Max about you. And Maree. But he sort of brushed off my question, not out of meanness. He's so worried about me, he's having a hard time talk about anything else.

I don't want my loved ones to be scared for me. And definitely not scared OF me.

I'd never hurt you, my love. I'd kill myself before I let that happen.

B.

———

Friday, August 5, 2016

Dear M'Kenzee,

Pete wants to meet you someday. His real name is Peter; he grew up in London, says he's from a posh background (his words, not mine). His family didn't know what to do with his anger and hostility when he returned from combat in Afghanistan.

It's bad there, M'Kenzee. Worse than what you see on television — worse than you can comprehend.

Pete remembers everything. I think I'm glad I don't. But that bothers me, too. What did I do that was so atrocious my own mind refuses to acknowledge it?

Anyway, Pete came to Scotland to backpack through the Highlands, fell in love with the land, and decided to make it his home. He likes to act like an old wise man, but he's actually only thirty-five. I'm afraid to introduce you to him; what if you prefer someone less shattered, someone who's got it figured out instead of someone who feels so confused?

Time, my love. Please give me time.

B.

Three letters in, and M'Kenzee's heart lay in shreds.

Still, she read on.

Bren shared tidbits of his sessions and conversations with Pete. She wanted to meet him, to say thank you for being who

Bren needed at exactly the right time. Miss Sadie would say the Lord sent Pete; she didn't believe in coincidences.

Just in case Miss Sadie had a point, M'Kenzee spoke a prayer of thanks and praise for Pete being in Bren's life.

After two weeks of meeting with Bren, Pete had invited Bren to go backpacking in the mountains with him. Just a few days after they'd begun their hike, Bren had elected to take off on his own. Pete had understood, said that for some, solitude provided great healing. They'd agreed on a date and location to meet back up. Then they'd checked their emergency radios and gone their separate ways.

Over the next four weeks, Bren walked, wrote, slept, thought, remembered, wept, and worked his way through the effects of trauma. He admitted to M'Kenzee in his journal that he feared those effects would never go away — physical ailments like fevers, sweats, tremors, bouts of shaking, unprompted crying, insatiable hunger, nausea, vomiting, exhaustion, and insomnia. She couldn't imagine how he'd faced each symptom on his own.

After Maree's car accident and knee replacement, she'd developed a physical dependency on narcotic pain medications required to enable her physical therapy. The withdrawal symptoms that doctors had predicted would take ten to fourteen days for her to get over had clawed at her for months. She'd been a terrible mess. Watching her go through such an agonizing ordeal had been heart-wrenching. Maree swore she'd never have made it through without a strong support system encouraging her and checking on her every hour of every day.

Certainly not the same thing, Bren's challenges were unique to his own situation. But how in the world had he fought through that on his own?

Somehow, he'd made it to the other side, stronger for the road he'd traveled.

Maybe too strong.

Tuesday, September 27, 2016

Dear M'Kenzee,

I'm good. This time has been good for me.

There's so much to discover walking these hill-sides, shuffling through the grasslands, and wading through crystal clear rivers and streams. I pray I can show it to you someday.

I'm not convinced someone who's suffered PTSD is ever cured — I expect to experience moments of distress here and there in the months and years to come. I can never undo what I've done or unsee what I've witnessed.

But I'm better than I was. I feel strong again, ready to make a difference. I need to make a difference in this world.

I dread telling you, but I'm going back to my CJTF team. Not as a naval service member, but as a special agent through the FBI. It's where I'm supposed to be.

I see that now. The places they have deployed me challenge the notion of good in the world, but no matter how ugly humans become, the world itself is still beautiful, full of gifts and blessings. Me avoiding the ugly parts won't help the good guys create a better world, so I've got to go back.

I hope you'll forgive me, mo ghràidh.

B.

Sunday, October 23, 2016

Dear M'Kenzee,

Not much to report...really just wanted to write your name to see it with my own eyes.

Quantico is intense, but so interesting. I've been able to provide an up-close, first-hand account of what's going on out there. These agents need to know what the war really looks like, what to expect both domestically and abroad. I see the disgust in their eyes when I describe things. I'm not sure if they're disgusted for me or by me. Probably both.

Doesn't matter. It's who I am, and it's what they'll be up against.

Man, Max is having an unbelievable season. When I'm finished with Q-school, I'm hitting a game. It's funny... I remember one evening after flag football practice, I complained nonstop through dinner, frustrated because I'd missed a tackle, just to be shown up by Max tackling his guy and catching mine to force a fumble, recover the ball, and run it all the way back for a touchdown — ninety yards, pushing people out of his way the entire time. We were in the fourth grade, but the whole thing is as clear in my mind as if it happened yesterday. Later that night, Da told me, "Complaining won't change anything, Son. Your gifts differ from Max's. It just so happens Max's gifts are taking him to football's grandest stage." Then he ruffled my hair on his way out of my room, the way he always did, which I hated back then but wouldn't mind so much now.

We've had some fun times, mo ghràidh.

I love you, M'KenZee.

B.

———

Sunday, January 29, 2017

Dear M'KenZee,

We're headed for the Super Bowl — I'm so ready to see you.

The FBI life is good. It's actually really nice to be back with my team. My replacement on the naval side is an impressive kid. I guess you could say I've taken him under my wing. I can't help but watch out for him.

I picked up a copy of TIME from a street vendor last week. Something about the cover photo called my name. The sun slashing clean and fresh over the darkness of blood drying on an abandoned street sent cold chills down my spine. That's one incredible shot, M'KenZee. Breathtaking. Congrats on the cover, and sympathies that you were the one to see it in real time.

Take care, mo ghràidh.
B.

$\mathcal{B}$ ren had tucked a torn-off copy of her magazine cover, folded in half, into the composition book. M'Kenzee unfolded it, stared at the photograph, remembering how she'd thought nothing could be worse than the aftermath of violence she'd encountered that day. She'd been so naive.

$\mathcal{W}$ hen she and Maree had arrived in Las Vegas for Max's game, Bren had surprised them, waiting for them at baggage claim. He'd looked every inch a sexy secret agent. Tall, broad, confident air, easy smile, gleam in his deep green eyes… M'Kenzee had been smitten, impressed. She hadn't known what he'd been through to become that man. All she'd known in that moment was that her heart raced at the mere sight of Brennigan Stewart.

They'd filled the days leading up to the big game with preparty events, people-watching on the strip, and playing a few games on the casino floor. She, Maree, and Bren had paraded around like the three musketeers, indulging in carefree fun while Max sat through position meetings, watched hours and hours of game film, and practiced with the team.

By the time the game clock hit all zeroes and Max received the Super Bowl MVP award, she and Bren had cheered, teased, and flirted with one another for days. All dressed up, spinning in his arms on the dance floor, the disco lights over-head, she'd been completely lost in her love for him. When he'd said, "Come on… There's somewhere I want to take you," she would have followed him anywhere.

As she turned the page, a photo from their wedding, different from the one she'd been given that night and had enlarged for the house, fell onto her lap. The bride in the photo glowed with happiness, literally glowed. No wonder Bren had thought she was inebriated. With a photographer's eye, M'Kenzee had to admit it: she and Bren were gorgeous together. She stood the photo against the lamp on her bedside table, where it would be the first thing she saw in the morning and the last image in her mind at night.

Monday, February 6, 2017

You said yes.

That was the happiest moment of my life.

I'm sorry I got called away. But I'm taking that kiss we shared with me. That kiss, how you looked sleeping in the middle of that enormous bed, with your hair fanning out and a rosy glow to your lips, and the picture I snagged from the couple at the chapel will keep you with me until I see you again.

That's not entirely true. You are always with me, M'Kenzee Stewart. I've taken you with me — every second of every day — ever since you held your ground on the pitcher's mound when I was in the third grade. That's how long I've loved you, mo ghràidh.

And I'll never stop.

B.

PS: Just for the record, I wasn't drunk...

hadn't had a drop of alcohol. I married you completely on purpose!

After their wedding in Vegas, he'd been optimistic, excited even.

M'Kenzee had been furious.

Like always, Bren had taken off for places unknown, leaving her alone, just like everyone else had.

Her parents died, Max took off to be an all-star, Maree found a new home, Mr. and Mrs. Stewart went back to Scotland, and Bren chose duty over her. Same song, different verse.

M'Kenzee had been sick with grief and equally sick of being the one left behind.

Determined to live her own life on her own terms, she'd jumped into work with a frenzied determination that had her globe-trotting twenty-four seven, every day of the year.

If not for Maree's car accident, she'd likely still be saying *yes* to any and every assignment she could find to stay busy, stay engaged, and stay away.

And if not for Janie Lyn's family drama, M'Kenzee would've avoided Bren indefinitely.

Sunday, September 22, 2019

Nine hundred fifty-nine days. That's how long it's been since I saw you, since our wedding day.

You've avoided me for over thirty-one months.

Ridiculously, the way I feel for you hasn't changed a bit.

What is this hold you have over me?

And the more standoffish you pretend to be, the

more I want to shatter those impenetrable walls you've built around the pedestal you stand upon.

M'Kenzee Stewart, you are mine. And I'm going to make sure you don't forget it again.

Ah, mo ghràidh.

I hope you're ready.

B.

———

Sunday, November 3, 2019

Happy Birthday, mo ghràidh — I'll see you soon.

And when I do, we're going to talk. You can yell, I don't care. Raise the roof. Let all that anger you wear like a coat of armor off your chest. Because underneath the steel is the most passionate, warm, wonderful woman I've ever met.

I'm done letting you hide.

I hope it's a great day. I love you, birthday girl.

B.

———

Saturday, December 7, 2019

Dear M'Kenzee,

Walking away from you is the most physically

challenging task I tackle, time and again. Worse, it's getting near impossible to do.

I can't trust Axel Lyndale's arrest or Janie Lyn's safety to someone else; I need to see him behind bars with my own two eyes. Please try to understand.

I'll be home as soon as it's wrapped up, surely by Christmas. And when I get there, I've got a surprise for you. A big, multi-level surprise. I can't wait to show it to you.

I know you'll balk — you wouldn't be you, otherwise. I love that about you.

But I also love the way you look at me. That look tells me all I need to know. You love me. You always have.

We're going to build a life together, M'KenZee. We'll travel anywhere you want to go, chase the perfect photograph to the ends of the earth if you wish. I don't care as long as I'm with you.

We've spent enough time apart. I've done what I could for this war on evil. I don't doubt I've made a difference, but the truth is, it'll never end. I'm prepared to let someone else do the dirtiest work for a while, ready to wake up next to beauty instead of the ravages of greed and hatred.

You, mo ghràidh, are the beauty I see in this world.

You are everything.

I love you,
B.

———

Wednesday, December 11, 2019

We got him, babe!

Axel Lyndale is done, and we took down a branch of the Atlanta mob along with him. It was a big day for the good guys.

I just turned in my report, and my plane takes off in less than three hours. I'm walking out the door, headed to the airport.

I'm coming ho—

Hang on a sec… Mikey's hollering at me.

34

I'm selfish, impatient,
and a little insecure.
I make mistakes,
I'm out of control,
and at times hard to handle.
But if you can't handle me at my worst,
then you sure as hell
don't deserve me
at my best.
Often attributed to Marilyn Monroe

Friday, February 14, 2020

"M'Kenzee, honey? Open the door, 'Kenz. Please," Maree pleaded.

"Sorry," M'Kenzee apologized as she held the bedroom door open for her sister. "I must've fallen asleep early this morning."

Maree's stomach clenched at the dark gray circles under M'Kenzee's bloodshot eyes. Her pallor had taken on a pale vacancy; her cheekbones stood out, too stark. M'Kenzee looked terrible.

"Are you okay? We've all been trying to call for two days. I finally talked to Jinx, who said you've been locked in here since Tuesday."

"What day is it now?"

"It's Friday, February 14," Maree supplied.

"Hmm. Valentine's Day." Maree did not like M'Kenzee's flat tone.

"What have you been doing in here?" Maree walked around the room, searching for clues. Everything appeared to be perfectly in its place, except for Bren's love box, open in the middle of the mattress with notebooks flowing out of it and stacked haphazardly around the bed. "Did you read them all?"

"Ha, yeah," M'Kenzee said with a note of sarcastic humor. "He wasn't drunk."

"He wasn't drunk?" Maree didn't understand.

"Nope. Married me — and I quote — *completely on purpose.*"

"Okay." Maree didn't know how to respond.

"Well, I wasn't, either. He needs to know that!" M'Kenzee's shrill cry worried Maree. "He just stood there, watching me sleep until he left. Again. He's there, and then he's— just— not!" Her voice turned hysterical while her arms flailed at the journals to make her point. "He says I've always been with him. Wherever he went. But I wasn't," she cried. "I couldn't be there because he didn't give me a choice." M'Kenzee's shoulders stopped shuddering, but venom spewed with every sentence. "He made all the decisions. He decided for both of us. But he doesn't get to do that. I have a say. I get to have a say in my own life! I wanted his love. All the time he says he felt it, I didn't know. And I wanted it. I wanted to share my heart with him. But, oh no! He was called to duty." She spat *duty* as if it were the worst kind of four-letter word.

"Hun, Bren is a hero. He's—"

"Yeah, yeah, yeah. Bren's a hero. Max is a hero. Rhys is a hero. They're all heroes. If they're all so wonderfully heroic, why do they always leave? Why am I all alone?"

Maree didn't take M'Kenzee's anger personally. Her strong, brave sister was hurting, so deeply.

"Oh, sweetie. You're not. You've never been alone."

That did it. The dam broke.

M'Kenzee crawled onto her bed, curled in the fetal position, and wept uncontrollably. Maree sat on the edge, rubbed M'Kenzee's back, and let her release all the pain, all the anger, and all the fears she'd been juggling so beautifully. When M'Kenzee's body ceased heaving, Maree walked to the bathroom to run cold water over a washcloth and brought it back to her sister.

Maree's kind gesture prompted M'Kenzee to sit up, hugging her knees to her chin.

"I'm sorry."

"No way are you taking credit for this episode," Maree said with an arm wrapped around M'Kenzee's shoulders. "No, ma'am. This emotional overload is one hundred percent at the feet of one handsome, noble, loving, and heroic Brennigan Stewart."

M'Kenzee tried to smile, but Maree saw right through it.

"And missing," M'Kenzee added, a stray tear sliding down her cheek until it fell on her sweatshirt.

"I know, sweetie. And I wish I had words to make that part better. But all I can offer is prayers and encouragement. I truly believe Bren is alive. I have faith he's doing everything in his power to come home to you."

M'Kenzee nodded through another stream of tears. "Thank you."

"I have something for you," Maree told her, walking to where she'd dropped her purse when M'Kenzee had opened the door. She picked it up, retrieved a flat brown paper bag from the inside pocket, and returned to M'Kenzee's side. "Bren's notebooks have been such a gift — not always an easy one…more like a puppy or a baby…wonderful, yet difficult at times." M'Kenzee smiled for real at Maree's humor. "Reading his most meaningful thoughts has brought you close to Bren when he couldn't be present. Writing can be a cathartic release; I imagine creating those notes and letters with you in mind helped Bren through many tough times." She extended the present to M'Kenzee. "Maybe you could give it a try."

M'Kenzee pulled a small notebook from the bag.

"It's so cute," M'Kenzee commented. "I love the pink-and-green camo print — the perfect combination of my pink obsession and Bren's military obsession." M'Kenzee rolled her eyes playfully, and Maree nudged M'Kenzee's shoulder in solidarity. Loving heroes was tough work… The girls had to stick together to make the most of it.

M'Kenzee flipped through the lined pages, running her fingertips over the smooth surface.

"Thank you, Maree. I'll fill it with my truth, as Bren has given me his. And I'll pray that someday he gets to read it."

"I have a favor to ask, too," Maree mentioned, trying to sound nonchalant, as if it were no big deal. "Think of it as a way to thank me for the journal."

"Of course, what is it?" M'Kenzee answered.

"Let me exhibit your portraits of the patients living at Memorial Care."

"What?" M'Kenzee croaked.

Maree felt a tiny bit guilty for blindsiding her sister, but this opportunity outweighed her conscience.

"I'm lost here. What do you mean by exhibit my portraits? Like in a gallery show?"

"Yes, although Green Hills doesn't have an art gallery in town, so I'm planning to set it up at the Conrad."

The oldest, most exclusive venue in town — possibly in all

of southeast Oklahoma — the Conrad Hotel made ritzy look dull. Maree could see the entire event in her mind, and the vision redefined magnificent.

"You're *planning*?"

"Once you hear my ideas, and Janie Lyn's suggestions, there's no way you'll be able to say no." Maree shook her head as she explained the futility of trying to hedge. "You might as well agree, save yourself some time and effort." Then Maree smiled her most engaging, sorry-you-have-to-love-me-because-you're-stuck-with-me smile.

"Good grief," M'Kenzee bemoaned. "You are piling it on thick."

Maree had her; they both knew it. She jumped up from her perch on the edge of the mattress, clapping her hands and bouncing with delight. "Thank you, thank you, thank you! It's going to be exquisite. Extraordinary. Ex—"

"*When* is it going to be?" M'Kenzee interrupted her.

"Oh, Tuesday, March 3."

"That's two and a half weeks away," M'Kenzee exploded. "I can't put a full show together in eighteen days. And absolutely no one will show up on a Tuesday night!"

"Yep, before schools let out and the world goes crazy over spring break. You select the photos, blow them up extra big, and I'll do the rest."

"You'll do the rest? That's it. You'll do *the rest*."

M'Kenzee's air quotes around *the rest* felt a little overdramatic. But at least she wasn't mad at poor Bren anymore.

"You said it. Now, why don't you get dressed and come to Scooter's for V-Day Karaoke?"

"No way, no how," M'Kenzee said, digging in her heels in a way Maree recognized, so there was no reason to argue. "I have no desire to watch every couple in Green Hills and the surrounding counties fawn over each other on the dance floor, embarrass themselves on the microphone, and make goo-goo eyes at one another across the cocktail tables. Besides, a ton of photo editing just popped up on my calendar. Magically." M'Kenzee's right eyebrow lifted in accusation at the end.

It was the perfect time for Maree to make her escape.

"Your loss." She shrugged before giving M'Kenzee a quick hug. "I love you."

"I love you," M'Kenzee promised back.

Maree headed for the front door. "Thank you for the journal," M'Kenzee yelled just as she closed the door behind her.

Maree worried about M'Kenzee — as did Max and Janie Lyn and Miss Sadie and all their friends. Maree couldn't fathom the fear that would cripple her if Rhys didn't come home one day.

M'Kenzee had handled it all with such grace; she was entitled to a few breakdowns and angry outbursts. Maree felt blessed that M'Kenzee had let hers be the shoulder she cried on.

And she'd agreed to the photography exhibit. Janie Lyn was going to flip. Well, maybe not in her mother-to-be condition, but she'd be thrilled.

The visit had been a successful mission, if Maree did say so herself.

———

02/14/2020

I'm afraid to write your name, to put "Dear Bren" on the page.

What if I write to you, but you never get to read my words? What will I do if you don't come back? I've refused to consider it, but as the days pass, the likelihood of your returning seems to diminish. Please, please come home to me.

I finished reading your journals. Why didn't you send me a single one of them?

You called, texted, sent birthday cards and Christmas gifts. But these books— These are your heart, and you never shared it with me. Don't you know that you've had mine all along?

I want to be so mad at you, mad that you unilaterally put our relationship on hold until you deemed it time to let me in on it. But I want to hold you and kiss you and love you even more.

And if I'm being honest, I did the same thing. I pushed you away. In my attempt to keep you from abandoning me, I abandoned you. I'm so sorry.

You, Bren, are my love.

Mo ghràidh ~ M'Kenzee

———

02/22/2020

I can't believe my sister got me into this.

I've been editing photos to get the angles just right, taking more pictures to have enough to fill this ridiculously large hotel foyer, and begging frame shops to finish each portrait on time.

Janie Lyn asked to oversee the guest list and invitations. I'm reasonably certain she's arranged for guests to attend from all over the country. Last I heard, the Conrad had sold out of rooms. That's how many people she's invited.

I would've enjoyed helping with the decorations and centerpieces, but my hands are too full with the actual exhibit. Luckily, the hotel is taking care of the hors d'oeuvres, beverage service, and seated meal. That leaves Maree, Landry, Miss Sadie, and all their recruits to sort through the rest.

Who in their right mind throws together a gallery show in eighteen days?

Even with so much to think about, you are constantly on my mind and in my dreams.

I wish you'd come home to me, mo ghràidh.

I love you ~ M'Kenzee

———

03/03/2020

Tonight's the night.

It's not my first exhibit, but for some reason, I'm a nervous wreck.

There are so many people coming. I'm tempted to call in sick, climb into bed, and let them look at the portraits without having to hear and see their reactions.

But that's the coward's way. How can I, in good conscience, choose the coward's way when every step you've ever made has been an act of bravery? Thanks a lot.

Let's just say a prayer that I make it through the evening.

I love you, mo ghràidh ~ M'Kenzee

35

"At Last"
Song lyrics written by
Mack Gordon and Harry Warren
for Glenn Miller to preform
in Sun Valley Serenade (1941);
Recorded and made iconic by Etta James (1960),
whose version was inducted into the
Grammy Hall of Fame (1999)
and the Library of Congress
National Recording Registry (2009)

M'Kenzee should never have doubted Maree and her army of assistants.

An air of reverent admiration assaulted M'Kenzee's senses the moment she walked through the heavy aged doors leading into the Conrad Hotel. A sensual jazz quartet played on a raised stage in the center of the foyer. Skinny cocktail tables draped in black cloth were swathed in iridescent gold and silver tulle. Bows tied from ribbon threaded with gold and silver, at least twelve inches wide, secured the fabric around each table's pedestal.

Above every tall table floated an elegant hot-air balloon, made of a rustic wicker basket with gold and silver papers printed in gorgeous patterns of plaids, chintz flowers, paisleys, dots, stripes, and large blooms, suspended in place as if by magic.

With the foyer looking like that, M'Kenzee couldn't wait to see the dining room.

But first, she wanted to see her friends, the beautiful men and women she'd photographed.

Alzheimer's disease steals so much from its victims; memories were just the tip of the iceberg. M'Kenzee had given herself one goal in creating the series of portraits: to highlight the dignity and depth of character in those facing their sentence of death.

Please Lord, let others see the beauty I see in these patients.

She began walking to the left, stopped in front of the first easel, and stood, stunned at her own work.

She'd printed each photo in black and white, adding sepia tones to create a stark image with warm highlights. The effect illustrated life stories through the sharp definition of facial features: a brilliant, childlike grin fringed with creases in aged skin; smile lines formed from decades of happy moments; eyes dancing with wisdom long after the mind lost the ability to communicate the knowledge trapped inside; sunken cheeks depicting the process of starvation when the body could no longer chew and swallow; a serene glance into the distance, watching a scene no one else saw; a still-glamorous face framed in a thick, stylish bob of snow-white hair.

Each portrait, so clean in artistic simplicity, placed in a specifically-chosen 36-inch by 48-inch wooden frame. Each unique frame, ornate with carvings and opulent designs, added stately decadence. A spotlight hidden in the rafters radiated light onto each picture. The room was exquisite. Perfect.

M'Kenzee took her time moving from one easel to the

next, giving each person photographed the respect they deserved. She heard the surrounding conversations, but intentionally tuned out their critiques. The guests pointed at this, commented on that. M'Kenzee didn't need to know their opinions.

She'd made it to the far side of the gallery when the natural buzz of the room silenced unnaturally.

M'Kenzee turned to the center of the foyer to see what had caused the shift.

A man, standing apart from the crowd.

Bren.

At the sight of him, both her hands flew to cover her mouth, stifling the cry emerging from her constricted throat. Her pulse raced; her breaths quickened. Blood hummed in her ears; her body froze. The edges of her peripheral vision darkened, fuzzy, until nothing existed except Bren.

With each step he took toward her, M'Kenzee found it harder and harder to fill her lungs.

"He's here," someone exclaimed.

"That's Agent Stewart, her husband," someone else whispered loudly.

"I think she's hyperventilating," their friend Davis, a fireman and EMT, said with concern.

"M'Kenzee's okay," Landry, the doctor in the house, assured him.

"Open the doors to dinner," Maree ordered. "Ring the chime. Now."

"Where's Max? Go find him," Miss Sadie instructed.

M'Kenzee ravished Bren with her eyes. She tried to see every bit of him at once, but her eyes couldn't focus through the tears flowing from them.

He walked slowly across the tile floor, using a cane for support. His eyes never left M'Kenzee's face.

Haggard, that was the word she'd use to describe him. Thin, far too thin. But there, in front of her.

When he was three strides away, she bolted into motion, falling into his chest as she wrapped her arms around his neck. Bren leaned down, pulling her closer with one hand as he buried his face in her shoulder and neck. She clenched her eyes shut, desperate to hold on for dear life.

His cane clanked on the hard floor when his second arm wrapped around her back.

M'Kenzee couldn't tell if it was her body trembling with emotion or his. Perhaps both.

She wanted to look at him, drink in the sight of him, but she couldn't let go.

They might've stayed that way for minutes. Or had it only been seconds?

M'Kenzee could not have guessed how long it had been when her family surrounded the couple.

Max spoke first, setting a hand on each of their backs.

"Thank God. You're home." Max's rough voice conveyed devout gratitude and drew attention to the tears falling down his face. He stepped in to hug them both, and the rest of the family did the same.

M'Kenzee and Bren, at the core of an unbreakable element, clung to one another while Max and Janie Lyn, Maree and Rhys, Miss Sadie, Landry, and even Davis embraced them, covering them in comfort and prayer.

"Let's get you two home," Maree offered.

"No." Bren finally spoke. "Just give me a few minutes with M'Kenzee. Then we'll be in for dinner." He smiled down at her, a broken smile, yet beautiful beyond compare. Then he turned to hug Max, who embraced him with restrained vigor and wiped more tears from his eyes when they stepped back.

Max bent to pick up the cane. "You okay?" He asked it

quietly as he handed the cane to Bren. Bren nodded in reply, but he didn't take the cane just yet. Instead, he turned to Maree.

"Oh, Bren. I'm so glad you're okay," Maree said through her own tears, wrapping her arms around his ribs. He smoothed her hair with one hand, the other still holding on to M'Kenzee.

Rhys placed his hands on Maree's shoulders, easing her back from Bren in case her weight threw him off-center. Shifting Maree under his left arm to support her, he reached his right hand out to Bren. "It's sure good to see you," Rhys said as they shook hands.

Then Janie Lyn stepped up to Bren, her hands pressed to her cheeks.

"Hey there, *màthair*," he said as she stepped into his hug. He held her until her shoulders stopped shaking. The moment she stepped back, Bren pulled M'Kenzee closer to his side.

"What did you call me?" Janie Lyn asked through a watery haze.

"*Màthair*. Mother."

She gawked in shock. "How did you know?"

He merely winked in answer.

"Come on, guys. Let's give them some time." Maree gathered their family, one arm entwined with Janie Lyn, the other hand holding Rhys's, with Miss Sadie, Landry, and Davis close behind. As they reached the doors to the dining room, Maree glanced back to shine a brilliant smile on M'Kenzee and Bren.

Bren turned to face M'Kenzee; her nerves began skittering again.

He leaned on the cane he'd taken from Max and shifted his weight to close the small gap between them.

His free hand lifted to cup her cheek, his thumb stroking her skin as his eyes skimmed her features. His gaze flowed like a wave, studying her eyes, then her lips, and jumping back to her eyes. He said so much without uttering a word.

When M'Kenzee thought she'd faint from holding her breath throughout his examination, Bren finally lowered his lips to hers.

Her hands gripped the lapels of his sports coat. Bren deepened the kiss. M'Kenzee smoothed her hands across his chest, ran them up to his neck, and held him in place.

They kissed.

And they kissed.

Then, with one hand cupping the side of her face, Bren lightened his kiss until he nibbled her lips with small nips before lifting his mouth from hers.

Instead of releasing her, he rested his forehead against hers, which allowed her a moment to regain composure.

Eventually, her chest had stopped heaving, and Bren pulled M'Kenzee under his arm. He placed a kiss on her head and gripped the cane more steadily to step toward the nearest portrait.

"These are incredible," Bren said, admiring her photograph by looking deep into the face it captured. "Who is this?"

M'Kenzee told him about each portrait. Bren listened with rapt attention. She'd never known someone who listened as Bren did, with his entire self, as though what she said was more important than anything else, so *she* was more important than *anyone* else.

*T*he last picture they came to stood in a place of honor as the inspiration for the project: Duke Malone.

M'Kenzee had captured the candid photo of him looking at Jinx one day when she and Jinx had taken lunch to his grandad.

Jinx had explained to her on their way to the memory care facility that the greasy cheeseburger and curly fries from The Three-Toed Turtle — fondly referred to as Triple T's by the locals — had been Mr. Malone's staple lunch for the better part of forty years. He liked it with onions grilled into the patty, mustard on the top bun and mayo on the bottom, with two slices of cheese under one leaf of lettuce, a flat layer of pickles, and a thick tomato slice on top so that it pressed into the inside of the bun to hold it all in place. So, that was what they'd brought for lunch.

During her time at Memorial Care, M'Kenzee had learned that no two minds riddled with dementia behaved the same. Where one person might retain their ability to walk but not speak, another might be verbal but not mobile. One person might never forget their loved ones, while another person lost the names of their family members early in their diagnosis. There was no rhyme or reason as to what one held on to and what one did not.

Mr. Duke Malone had not yet lost his love of a Triple T's cheeseburger.

Jinx had laid out the lunch just so, making a production of opening the paper bag, flattening it on the table in front of his grandfather. Then he'd entertained Duke by ever so slowly unwrapping the burger and shaking the fries out of their thin paper envelope. Once everything sat in its proper place, Jinx had taken a tiny portable fan out of his backpack and turned it on to push the scent of the burger and fries directly into Duke's face. A look of pure bliss had descended over the elder man's features, as if he'd tasted ambrosia.

That was when M'Kenzee had clicked the shutter, preserving his expression of utter love and appreciation for eternity.

A heavenly feast, indeed.

And best of all, an out of focus image of Jinx smiling back at Duke filled one side of the foreground.

No other portrait in the show had a second subject in the photo, but the one of Duke and Jinx held a special place in M'Kenzee's heart. It served as the show's title image, the *pièce de résistance* of the exhibit.

"That's a great story," Bren agreed. "You've done something very special here, M'Kenzee."

She melted a little at hearing her name on his lips. Her gaze fell upon them. Her heart raced. Without thinking, she licked her own lips.

"Ah, *mo ghràidh*," he groaned. "You *cannae* look at me that way. We still have a dinner to get through."

He took her hand and began walking toward the dining room.

"We can go home," she said, a sound so raw she didn't recognize her own voice.

Bren gulped.

"You've put a lot into this show. I've waited three months to make my way home to you. I can wait three more hours."

M'Kenzee stopped him before he could open the door between the foyer and the dining hall.

"I promised myself that if you made it back, I'd never again waste an opportunity to tell you— I love you, Bren. I love you with all my heart. And I know I'm hard to lo—"

He silenced her with a kiss.

"I love you, too. I've loved you every moment of my life," he said.

"I know," she admitted through another round of tears. "I read all about it."

Bren laughed. It sounded so good to M'Kenzee's ears. Then he leaned down to kiss her once more before they joined the others.

. . .

*A*s they drove home after the fundraiser ended, M'Kenzee's nervousness reappeared.

She had so many questions.

Who had helped him get home? What had caused him to miss the extraction point when the missionaries were rescued? When had he arrived back in the United States? Where had he been the past three months? Why hadn't he been able to contact them for help? How had he been injured? Was he okay? The litany continued.

But something Max had said about Bren's recovery after he'd been captured in Syria kept replaying in M'Kenzee's mind: *I just tried to listen when Bren wanted to talk, and I let whatever he said be enough.* She would give Bren the space to heal. She wanted to be part of that process, but it had to be on his timetable.

M'Kenzee often described herself as a know-it-all because she liked to know it all. In this, however, she was content with whatever Bren wanted or needed to share.

A fresh wave of anxiety washed over her; Bren would soon see their home for the first time since he'd submitted a contract to purchase it. After the remodel and her decorating, it looked very different than it had then.

Her mind began ricocheting questions again.

What would he think? Would he like it? Was it too whimsical? Too over the top?

Stop! We can change anything he doesn't like. It's pitch dark outside. Too dark to see much of anything. And almost midnight. He's bound to have had a long day traveling home. The house can wait until morning.

"I can't wait to see the house," Bren said.

M'Kenzee's head snapped up to look at Bren as he drove down Main Street.

"Surely that can wait until morning," she croaked. "When it's light outside."

"True, we have all the time in the world," he promised as he pulled into the drive.

36

My heart is, and always will be, yours.
Hugh Grant as Edward Ferrars
in Emma Thompson's 1995
screenplay adaptation
of Sense and Sensibility by Jane Austen

*B*ren parked his black SUV behind the detached garage, which had once been a carriage house, so M'Kenzee took him through the side door into the kitchen rather than walking around to the front porch. She'd barely flipped the lights on when he stopped in his tracks.

"M'Kenzee—" Bren's voice held a note of wonder. She swallowed hard. "I love it!"

"You do?"

"It's perfect," he marveled. He released her hand to cup her cheek — he had yet to completely break contact with her since she'd fallen into his embrace earlier that night. It was as if he couldn't *not* be touching her in some small way at all times. "Really, it's amazing. I can't wait to see every detail." Bren paused, his eyes darting once more around the room. His gaze came to rest on M'Kenzee. "For now, will you show me our room?"

She managed a quick nod, but nothing more. She forced another hard swallow.

Since when have basic skills like walking and talking become so difficult?

M'Kenzee lifted the long strap of his duffle bag over her shoulder and took hold of his hand to lead him to the master suite.

Does he hear my heartbeat, or is it only in my ears?

Out of habit, M'Kenzee walked to the bedside chest to switch on the lamp. Once she had, she moved to face Bren. He stood mere inches away.

"Dreams of you kept me alive," he admitted. "And yet, you're so much more than I dreamed."

M'Kenzee let the canvas bag slide to the floor. She stepped out of her high heels and turned her back to Bren so he could unzip her dress, which he did without hesitation.

"I've dreamed of you, too," she said, facing him again. "Since long before we were married. Well…married the second time," she added with a grin.

Careful with the delicate fabric of the pouf sleeves and tight cuffs on her evening gown, she eased the dress off her shoulders and arms, revealing she had not lost her habit of indulging in lovely lingerie.

Bren inhaled sharply.

M'Kenzee smiled. Her nerves had disappeared. At last, she was truly home.

*W*aking to bright sunshine streaming into their room, M'Kenzee luxuriated in a full-body stretch under the covers. Unable to stop herself from smiling, she looked over to Bren's side of the bed.

Panic seized her — it was empty.

Then the splash of water running in the shower eased her fears, and she released the breath that had caught in her throat.

M'Kenzee dressed in baggy sweats, the worn, well-loved Navy sweatshirt Bren had given her years before, and her winter house-boots with warm sheepskin inside. She'd just finished scrambling eggs and frying bacon when Bren appeared.

"You cook now?"

"Don't sound so surprised," she teased. "Chefs and bakers and restaurant makers surround me at every turn these days… Something was bound to rub off. And I'm not guaranteeing anything tastes like their kitchen creations," she said in fair warning as she set their plates on the breakfast table. Bren pulled out her chair, ever the gentleman, and they both sat down.

"Bren?" He'd just taken a bite when she said his name, so he raised his eyebrows in response. "I want to go to Scotland. I want to see the Highlands, and the grasslands, and fish for salmon in the rivers and streams."

His hand covered hers, which rested on the table. He finished his bite and took a drink of coffee.

"I'm glad," he said, his tone heavy with appreciation. "I've wanted to take you to Braemar for a long time, wanted to show you God's creations in their most beautiful state. And I need to go see Mom and Da and Granda and Nan. Unless you or Max have spoken with them, they don't know about these past few months. I've had so many covert deployments that they don't ask when I'm off the grid for weeks, even months, at a time. I need to touch base with them, more for me than for them."

"All our communication went through Agent Vela. He gave me the impression that he'd call them when the time was right. I'm embarrassed to admit it never occurred to me to call them directly. How thoughtless and self-absorbed. I'm so sor—"

"M'Kenzee, you're the farthest thing from selfish. Look at what you did for those families last night. Think about the impact your show will have, the care and support the funds raised will provide. Please stop thinking you are hard to love or lacking in empathy. I've loved you for a very long time, and it's never once been a chore. It's been a gift, *mo ghràidh*. I've tried to tell you over and over: *you* are a gift — one I'll never let go or give back again."

Three days later, M'Kenzee and Bren stepped off a plane in Edinburgh, Scotland.

They rented a car there, spent a date night in the city, and made the drive north to Braemar.

Thrilled to see her, Mr. and Mrs. Stewart gushed over M'Kenzee. If they'd any idea of Bren's last few months, they'd have given him all their attention, but M'Kenzee happily accepted their affection. She thought it strange, however, that none of Bren's family seemed upset, or even surprised, to find out that she and Bren were married.

After church on Sunday, another unexpected guest arrived at the Stewarts' house: Peter Bennett.

M'Kenzee could've guessed Bren would want — possibly need — to talk to Pete after whatever he'd been through in Africa. He'd only been back with her a few days, but Bren seemed to be doing well. His leg continued to heal; he relied less heavily on the cane than he had just days before. And Bren was putting on much-needed weight with every meal they ate; he already looked less haggard and worn out than he had the night of the exhibit. But the experiences that caused PTSD could not be discounted or pushed aside; she wouldn't assume anything when it came to Bren's health, be it physical or mental.

When Pete arrived, Bren led him to the field behind the

house, where M'Kenzee was taking photos. Then Bren surreptitiously disappeared.

"So, you're the legendary M'Kenzee," Pete said with an inquisitive smile and a delightful British accent.

"And you must be the magical healer," she dished right back with a knowing grin.

"Perhaps our Brennigan over-builds his loved ones?"

"Perhaps," she allowed, loving the way he called Bren *our Brennigan*.

"Well, what do you think of our fair country?"

"I thought you were British?"

Pete covered the center of his chest with both hands as if she'd plunged a dagger into his heart.

"You wound me, fair lady." Pete sat on a rock close to where M'Kenzee stood shooting photos of Highland cows.

"Will they hurt me?" she asked, wondering how close she could get to the iconic *hairy coo* that kept eyeing her across the pasture of snow.

"Never on purpose," he answered. "Are you of a mind to harm them?"

"Of course not," she answered, indignant that he'd think her capable of such a thing.

"We never mean to…hurt others, *ye ken*."

M'Kenzee suspected they were no longer speaking about cattle.

"Yes, I know," she replied.

"He has a long road ahead of him. There will be bumps along the way."

"Bren seems to think I kept him alive at different times over the years, simply by being the unwitting recipient of his love. Imagine how I can support him when I'm actually in his life, reciprocating that love, measure by measure."

"And, if by duty or necessity, Brennigan must leave you again?" Pete asked.

"Bren's been part of my life since before my memories begin. He's never left. Just as my parents have never left. They are present in my brother, and my sister, and our family traditions, and our decisions, and—" M'Kenzee stopped herself before she got too upset. "Bren does not abandon the people he loves."

"And he loves you. Why, do you suppose?"

"Huh," she scoffed. "Now that is a question I've asked myself over and over the last three months, at least once a day since I opened his first journal." She stopped pacing, sitting on a boulder to face Pete. "I truly don't know. Bren's the most honorable, dependable, noble man I've ever heard of…not just met, but heard of. He's a listener, and he doesn't just listen to be polite. He hears. His sense of right and wrong is black and white. Bren is good through and through. Everyone loves and respects him for precisely who he is.

"I, on the other hand, am deeply flawed. I'm bossy and impatient; I overreact with emotion instead of reason. I get bored easily, so I flit from this to that. And then I get overwhelmed when all the projects I've collected become more than I can handle. Until Bren bought me a house in the smallest town in Oklahoma, I had no friends beyond my two siblings. They were *literally* the only people who liked me. I—"

"And Brennigan," Pete interjected, rolling the *R* quite dramatically.

"What?" Pete's interruption derailed M'Kenzee, who'd been on a roll listing everything wrong with her character.

"You said only your siblings liked you. That's incorrect. Brennigan liked you. But please, continue."

M'Kenzee frowned at Bren's friend.

"I think you get the point," she grumbled.

"Ah, yes. Where Brennigan is structured, you are fluid.

Where he sees black and white, you see color. Where one listens, the other speaks. So, in other words, you balance one another. Quite perfectly, it seems."

M'Kenzee had nothing to say in response to that.

"If Brennigan had not been— had not gone through this recent ordeal, would you be here with him now, professing your love, playing house?"

"I suppose the answer to that would've depended upon Bren." She heard the sauciness in her tone, but good grief — Pete knew how to push buttons. "Until I received that box of notes and letters, our relationship was only on his terms. He withheld his feelings, stealing a kiss once or twice, but never telling me how he felt. I guess whenever he deemed the time right to let me in on it, that's when I would've started — as you so eloquently put it — *playing house*."

"So, like your parents and your siblings, Bren has controlled when he comes and when he goes in your life?"

"Yes."

What is he getting at? Whatever it is, I wish he'd get there already, and then go on.

"And how," she added. Tears started building behind her eyes.

"You've been at the mercy of others' whims for a long time, M'Kenzee. Giving your love to people who drive through your life is difficult. Maybe you weren't the challenging one after all?"

"But the people you're talking about are wonderful. They are kind and giving and thoughtful. If people leave me, it's my fault. Not theirs." Fury built in M'Kenzee's gut.

"Or no one's fault." He sounded so matter-of-fact. "Would you like to take control, M'Kenzee? Put a few of your own terms on this relationship with Brennigan?"

"What do you mean?" She couldn't follow Pete; one minute he attacked, and the next minute he nurtured.

"If I'm not mistaken, Brennigan dragged you to a horse trailer the first time you married. Then he dragged you to a casino chapel the second time you married. After that, he dragged you against a wall to ravish you in an elevator. And most recently, he dragged you through twenty years' worth of emotional baggage. The boy is like a caveman, dragging his toy around wherever he wants, with no idea of the wear and tear he causes the toy."

"Bren's not like that. He'd sooner cut off a limb than hurt me." M'Kenzee wouldn't stand for Pete, or anyone else, speaking poorly about Bren.

"You must really love him," Pete said, shaking his head.

"Yes, I do." M'Kenzee stomped her foot to hammer home the point.

"Well, then," he challenged with a twinkle in his eye, "what are you going to do about it?"

That night's dinner turned into a rowdy event. Pete must've helped many soldiers and veterans through rough patches, because word spread of his being in town like wildfire, prompting random people to "drop in" at the Stewarts' house until the wee hours. M'Kenzee had called it a night around two thirty in the morning, and she didn't know what time Bren joined her.

He hadn't batted an eyelash or moved a limb when M'Kenzee left their room dressed for the day and hungry for some breakfast.

She fixed a cup of tea, heaped clotted cream and fresh jam on two raisin scones, slid her arms into her heavy coat, grabbed her journal, and headed for the table where the sun shone bright warmth on the back patio.

She'd just finished writing in her journal when Bren pulled out the chair next to her.

"What's this?" He picked up the pink-and-green camouflage notebook.

"A gift from Maree. She encouraged me to write to you for a change."

"May I read it?" If anyone knew the difference between writing *to* someone and writing *for* someone, Bren was that person.

"I hoped and prayed that you would someday," she admitted. "I'm going to refill my tea. Help yourself while I'm gone." She kissed his lips, already chilly from a few minutes out in the March morning, and darted inside the house.

03/09/2020

Dear Bren,

You were right about Pete: he's a magician.

We spoke yesterday, and I realized something. (Or maybe he secretly planted it in my head. I can't be sure!)

I've never had any say in the relationships in my life. My parents left without my permission; albeit without theirs, either, but I still had no control over the situation. And when your family left to move here to Scotland when we were young, no one asked my opinion. No one told me what was really going on at the time. I was simply forced to accept that y'all were gone. When Max chose to enter the football draft a year early, he didn't consult me. I understand why he did it, and I'm truly grateful he could use the sport he loves to take care of our family. But again, I had no control over what was being done in my life.

And you. Not only did I not have a say in our relationship, I never even knew there was an option for one. How could I have known? You kept your love a secret.

But so did I.

If I'd spoken up, if I'd stood up for what I wanted, perhaps you would have told me that you felt the same way. Maybe we would've gone to Max together to tell him we were in love. Of course, there's a chance Max would have killed us both... But we'll never know, because we hid our love not only from the world, but from each other.

I don't want to do that anymore.

I want to shout it from the highest cliffs: I love you!

And I want to play house with you, travel with you, and build a world with you.

I want to have babies with you...a little boy, strong and happy and kindhearted with thick, wavy reddish brown curls and brilliant emerald eyes like his da, and a little girl with sass and opinions, who will drive you mad while simultaneously wrapping you around her little finger.

I want to marry you. Again.

Brennigan Lance Stewart, will you marry me?

~ M'Kenzee

When M'Kenzee stepped out the back door, the patio was empty.

A small bundle of winter blooms tied with a long piece of grass lay next to her pen. It was holding the journal open to a new page.

Monday, March 9, 2020
Dear M'Kenzee,

Yes! Yes, I will marry you. Three times to make sure.

You have my heart.
You are mo ghràidh.
B.

———

The End

But not for long. Please enjoy this sneak peek into Book 4…

TAKE A CHANCE ON LOVE

"Landry, go home," the attending physician on duty commanded as he passed the young woman in the hallway.

"Almost there," she promised, glancing at her watch. Monday morning. She'd been at the hospital since Saturday afternoon and felt *more* than ready to leave.

Doctor Landry Stark had relinquished the care of her patients to a new shift of doctors and nurses; they were in excellent hands. And yet, the tug to complete her rounds prevented her from leaving without putting eyes on each person she'd treated just one more time.

Quiet as a mouse, Landry slipped into each room, consulted the monitors, glanced over charts, adjusted lines, and smoothed blankets. Seeing her patients resting peacefully helped lift the weight of the last thirty-eight hours.

Reminding herself to put one foot in front of the other, Landry entered the doctors' locker room, swapped her lab coat for her raincoat, grabbed her purse, and closed her locker. Finally, she walked toward the doors leading out of the hospital, ready to head home.

She turned down the last corridor on her way to the staff entrance and parking lot and immediately spotted a fireman sitting in a hard plastic chair along the wall. Alone. His knees supported his elbows, which kept his hands in place to hold up his head. Landry didn't need to see his face. She didn't have to look past the grime and soot covering every inch of his clothing. She knew exactly who sat there.

"Davis?" She kneeled in front of him, slow to put a hand on his arm so she wouldn't startle him awake. "Davis, do you need to see a doctor?"

When he barely lifted his eyes to hers, Landry had the impression that picking up his head might be too heavy a task for him. Davis's expression, along with the pain and vacancy in his eyes, scared Landry. The broken shell before her bore no resemblance to her friend, so well-known for his boisterous personality, his coquettish demeanor, and his endless charm. The fun-loving facets of the man her friends adoringly dubbed "The Flirtbird" had vacated the premises.

No, he'd not been asleep, but perhaps in a trance. They'd both seen such horrific things that day. It didn't stretch the mind to imagine Davis fighting *not* to close his eyes.

"Davis, are you hurt?" Landry persisted.

"No," his voice was raw. He took a deep breath, probably shoring up whatever strength he had left. He straightened and then stood, helping her stand up with a hand under her elbow. "No, I'm fine."

He sounded more like himself. He looked more like himself — steady and solid. But he was not fine.

"Are *you* okay?" Davis searched deep into her eyes, ferreting out the truth.

"That was my first large-scale catastrophe. I hope it's my last."

"I've never seen anything like it," Davis said, his voice hollow again.

They stood in silence for a moment, neither one having the right words to help process the tragedy.

"Someone said Earl opened Triple T's early to serve breakfast to first responders. Come with me?" Sensing they both would benefit from more human contact, Landry's request came out as a plea. Besides, they needed food. Neither of them would've eaten since they were at Daisy Lake on Saturday afternoon. Almost two days ago. The distance between the peace she'd experienced at the lake and the exhaustion she felt in that moment had to be greater than a mere two days.

She hadn't planned on going to the diner before coming upon Davis in the hallway, but her gut told her to take the detour. They both needed it.

"No, but thank you. I'm waiting for word on the Cadells. Eddie Cadell and his boy, Zane. Zane would've been on one of the earlier ambulance runs, but Eddie—" His voice hitched. He cleared his throat before trying again. "Eddie stayed in the building a lot longer. He was in bad shape."

"Yes, I know—" she started to say.

"Is he dead?"

BOOK 3 PLAYLIST

One good thing about music,
When it hits you, you feel no pain.
"Trench Town" song lyrics
written by Bob Marley (1982)

Enjoy the music that helped inspire the story…

1. We Found Love - Rihanna and Calvin Harris
2. Crazy in Love - Beyoncé and JAY-Z
3. Dancing in the Moonlight - Jubël and NEIMY
4. Marry You - Bruno Mars
5. Stay - Rihanna and Mikky Ekko
6. I Lied - Lord Huron and Allison Ponthier
7. Want U Back - Cher Lloyd
8. Can't Help Falling in Love - Elvis Presley
9. The Way I Am - Ingrid Michaelson
10. Every Shade of Blue - The Head and the Heart
11. A Dream is a Wish Your Heart Makes - Ilene Woods and the Mice Chorus

12. You're Still the One - Shania Twain
13. White Christmas (1947 Version) - Bing Crosby and Ken Darby Singers with John Scott Trotter & His Orchestra
14. Santa Baby - Eartha Kitt
15. Christmas (Baby Please Come Home) - Darlene Love
16. Nothing Breaks Like a Heart - Mark Ronson and Miley Cyrus
17. Always on My Mind - Willie Nelson
18. Blessed Assurance (Acapella) - Jones Sisters
19. It is Well with My Soul (Acapella) - Mallary Hope
20. 10,000 Reasons - Matt Redman
21. Ships in the Night - Mat Kearney
22. You Say - Lauren Daigle
23. If I Could Turn Back Time - Cher
24. I Want You Back - The Jackson 5
25. Our House - The Head and the Heart
26. Our House - Madness
27. The Arena - Lindsey Stirling
28. Come Home to Me - LÉON
29. Come Home to Me - Ernie Halter
30. Bring it on Home to Me - Sam Cooke
31. Come Home - OneRepublic
32. Right Here Waiting - Richard Marx
33. Come Back Home - Sophia Carson
34. Faces - Hayd
35. Remember - Lauren Daigle
36. Working My Way Back to You - The Spinners
37. At Last - Etta James
38. Big Jet Plane - Angus & Julia Stone
39. My House - Flo Rida
40. Three Little Birds - Bob Marley & The Wailers

Available on Spotify as
"Book 3: Three Times to Make Sure
by Virginia'dele Smith"

ABOUT THE AUTHOR

Ashli Montgomery is a wife, a momma, and an author whose passion is sharing love stories, books, quilts, yoga, recipes, and all of her favorite things in life. She is quilting to mend the mind by spearheading a community of quilters through Quilt 2 End ALZ, Inc., a 501(c)(3) nonprofit she launched to use her quilting hobby as a platform to advocate for an end to Alzheimer's disease.

Ashli writes wholesome and heartfelt, small-town romance under the pen name Virginia'dele Smith to honor Syble Virginia Tidwell, Adele Gertrude Baylin, and Etta Jean Smith. These three cherished grandmothers were beautiful role models, teaching Ashli to love without judgment and always put family first. Through Grandma Syble's journals and appetite for books, through Momadele's priceless cards and handwritten letters, and through many, many hours of visiting over fabric at Mema's kitchen island, Ashli also learned to treasure words.

Get to know Ashli by subscribing to her newsletter, *The Gazette*, at AshliMontgomery.com

Titles by Virginia'dele Smith

Sadie & Sam: PART 1 - Introductory Short Story (FREE)
Book 0: My Manifesto - Short Memoir (FREE)

The Davenports
Book 1: Grocery Girl
Book 2: In the Trenches
Book 3: Three Times to Make Sure
Book 4: Take a Chance on Love (coming soon)